Penny Perrick is the author of three works of non-fiction and two novels, *Malina* and *Impossible Things*. She has spent much of her life in London, working as a fashion editor for *Vogue*, a columnist on the *Sun* and *The Times*, and a fiction editor and reviewer for *The Sunday Times* Books Section. She now lives in the west of Ireland.

EVERMORE

Penny Perrick

BLACK SWAN

EVERMORE
A BLACK SWAN BOOK : 0 552 99701 3

Originally published in Great Britain by Bantam Press,
a division of Transworld Publishers Ltd

PRINTING HISTORY
Bantam Press edition published 1997
Black Swan edition published 1997

Set in by Hewer Text Compositions Services, Edinburgh

Black Swan Books are published by Transworld Publishers Ltd,
61–63 Uxbridge Road, London W5 5SA,
in Australia by Transworld Publishers (Australia) Pty Ltd,
15–25 Helles Avenue, Moorebank, NSW 2170
and in New Zealand by Transworld Publishers (NZ) Ltd,
3 William Pickering Drive, Albany, Auckland.

Reproduced, printed and bound in Great Britain by
Cox & Wyman Ltd, Reading, Berks.

For Astrid and Freddy

ACKNOWLEDGEMENTS

I should like to thank Rosemary Carr and Máireád Robinson for letting me pester them with questions about gardening. I am also grateful to Ursula Mackenzie, Francesca Liversidge and Shauna Newman at Transworld and, as always, to my agent Caradoc King, who cossets and encourages beyond the call of duty.

Effort, and expectation, and desire,
And something evermore about to be.
The Prelude, Book VI, William Wordsworth.

PART ONE

CHAPTER ONE

'THANK HEAVENS YOU'RE HERE,' Angela said. 'You can't imagine how much I've missed you. You're like a very special kind of girlfriend to me.'

Jared kissed her on both cheeks with his beautiful plump lips, and brought his suitcases further into the hallway. Angela gripped the heaviest one in her strong hand and led the way upstairs. She flipped back the duvet (how Jared hated them; he would go straight to Harrods and buy three blankets with satin edges) and said, 'You see, I've ironed the sheet.'

'Don't you always?' Jared asked, knowing that she didn't.

'Davy doesn't notice things like that,' Angela said.

'Oh, Davy,' Jared sighed. He thought that Angela had thrown herself away on Davy Stearns. Angela was a beautiful woman; tall and luscious with thick fair hair and amiable blue eyes under straight brows which were darker than her hair. Her long smooth neck was the kind that displayed diamond necklaces to perfection. She could have married a rich landowner or a promising politician, someone who mattered. In Jared's opinion, Davy Stearns didn't matter at all.

Davy ran a small company that thought up novelty promotions: frilly knickers packed into a tin for a tabloid newspaper; royal-blue umbrellas printed with gold stars representing the member states, for the European Commission. All terribly lower crust, Jared thought. Really, Davy wasn't much of a prize.

Angela sat on the bed watching Jared unpack suits and shirts from his expensive leather cases. Three suits, the pearl tie-pin and four pairs of shoes with initialled wooden shoe-trees. That meant he would be staying for some time, and that meant that Ellis Peregory must be in London.

Jared had been in love with Ellis since he was twenty, a handsome boy with full lips, black eyes and blacker hair that, in those days, had reached his shoulders. His head was slightly too big for his body, an imperfection less noticeable now, in his late thirties, since his shoulders had thickened and his hair was cropped short at the sides, falling in a glittering black wing over his forehead. Jared's powerful build and well-made clothes made him look as if he had been put together with no expense spared, able to withstand any onslaught.

Jared is thirty-seven, Angela thought. It's time he got over Ellis. But nothing has happened between them. That's the problem. Jared will never be able to move on until something has.

She stood up and her blue silk shirt arranged itself gorgeously over her bosom. 'I have to collect Elsie and Maud from school,' she said. 'Then we'll have tea. Jared, just one thing, please don't rearrange the furniture while I'm out. Davy gets so cross when you do that.'

Once Davy and Angela had gone on holiday, leaving Jared in their house in Fulham. They had come back to find that everything had been put somewhere else, even Davy's Apple Mac, which Jared had hidden under an antique Paisley shawl, fringed with gilded braid.

'It looked so much better my way,' Jared said.

'I know, but it's Davy's house. He pays the bills.'

Jared was nettled. He was sensitive about the fact that Davy worked for a living and he didn't. There was no need to, since he had inherited a large fortune from his father, who had built up mining interests in Central America.

Seeing Jared press his lips together, Angela put her hand on his arm. 'Jared, I don't want you to live like Davy; he works so hard that sometimes I feel I'm married to a walking dead man. I have lots more fun with you; anyone would. You remind me that life can be full of perils and possibilities.'

'Drivel, my sweet,' Jared said, but he was pleased.

Davy Stearns returned to his office at four o'clock, after an extended lunch hour. He was carrying a shop-bought sandwich in a triangular plastic carton, and his eyes were gleaming. His secretary, Joyce Arledge, typing in the outer office, lowered her eyes as he passed by. She felt outraged on Angela's behalf, as she always did when one of Davy's lunchtime liaisons was in full swing. All Davy's mistresses seemed to blur into one desperate woman: single, successful and lonely. Joyce was horribly familiar with the pattern. First there would be long lunches at the Savoy; then even longer lunches at the current lover's home, where not much food was eaten, if the sandwiches Davy bought on his way back to work were anything to go by. The final stage was the most unsettling for Joyce. It was she who had to cope with the telephone calls, increasingly shrill and unhappy, which Davy refused to return, until a brisk, despising tone in her voice caused the calls to falter and eventually cease.

This pointless philandering aside, Joyce was very fond of Davy. There was a snagging sadness about him, even when he was shaking with laughter at some preposterous proposal for a new product:

initialled condoms, matchboxes that played 'Smoke Gets In Your Eyes' whenever a match was struck against them. Joyce found this combination of sadness and jollity very attractive. She also liked Davy's crisp curly hair and the way that, when he was working late at night, his languorous grey eyes became pink-rimmed, like a calf's. She liked his easy athletic lope and his soft furry voice. She could understand why women made fools of themselves over Davy Stearns – he was such a pleasurably sensual man. What she couldn't understand was why Davy bothered with all his unnecessary seductions when he was married to Angela. Joyce looked through the glass panel that divided her office from Davy's and caught him in the act of lobbing the sandwich wrapper into the waste-paper basket. He blushed before whipping a file out of a drawer.

Davy Stearns was the only child of parents who didn't get on. Having no affection for each other, they gave a smothering amount of it to their son. However tentative and fleeting his childhood interests – model railways, bird-watching, skateboarding – they immediately and enthusiastically bought him so much equipment that he felt overwhelmed and daunted. The hobby that had begun to absorb him would become something he became reluctant to pursue. In time, he learned to keep his enthusiasms a secret from his father and mother. He felt guilty when they accused him of being furtive, but no guiltier than he felt about the expensive presents lying unused in cupboards, evidence, Davy thought, of his fickle unsatisfied nature.

He grew up, having acquired the two worst faults of a spoiled only child: an unwillingness to share what he had and a habit of not wanting things once they were his. His passionless affairs with lonely jaunty women were the consolations he awarded himself for being married to Angela, the most loving caring woman in the world. Angela loved people helplessly in a way that wasn't quite grown up. She almost bruised Maud and Elsie by the fierceness of her hugs and kisses, and was hardly less restrained with every member of her large messy family and the wide circle of friends who yearned clamorously for her attention – attention which was always unstintingly given since Angela couldn't resist shepherding people through their lives. She drew people towards her like a fire, and Davy felt left out in the cold, abandoned. His sense of exclusion was blackest when he came home after work. From the kitchen doorway, he watched his wife and daughters as they cut out dolls' clothes or scored home-made fudge into wonky squares, their pale heads shining in the brightly lit room, their voices warm and gurgling, each a part of the other. In that split second before Maud and Elsie threw themselves at him, bumping into his knees and tugging his hands, and Angela walked gracefully towards him, tilting her face for a kiss, Davy felt completely superfluous. Angela's almost suicidal generosity distracted her from Davy's crushing need to be at the very centre of her life.

Tonight, Jared Dauman would be there, a major distraction; the way he wore his heart on his Savile-Row sleeve. Jared lusted after Ellis Peregory who, for all Davy knew or cared, returned his lust; Jared was a handsome cove, after all. But Ellis wasn't stupid. He was set to inherit Hayden Castle and its estate, which included some of the most productive farmland in Wales. Ellis's father, General Peregory, demanded of others no more than the standard of rectitude he demanded of himself. He had married an admirable woman who had given him four excellent children; he expected Ellis, his only son, to do the same. Any hint of Ellis's deviation from this plan and Simon Peregory would leave his land to Eliza, the elder of his two daughters, who had taken the sensible step of marrying Warner Jones, a local farmer.

Anyone other than Jared would have cleared off years ago, but in Jared, persistence and constancy were a sickness; that was Davy's view. Jared was crazily convinced that, one day, Ellis would sacrifice the ownership of Hayden and become his lover. To bolster this conviction, Jared took samples of Ellis's handwriting to be analysed by graphologists; he consulted mediums and every kind of quack.

To learn what? That there would be a happy ending? Even the most fraudulent of the dodgy psychics whom Jared had beseeched over the years, baulked at confirming such an unlikely scenario.

Before leaving the office, Davy inspected his lapels for the glint of an auburn hair. He was careful about things like that. He never wanted to be in a position where he would have to lie to Angela. Betraying her was bad enough.

None of them heard Davy's key turn in the lock. Jared was helping Angela prepare supper. He had bought a side of smoked salmon on his shopping trip to Harrods and was arranging it on a platter with halves of lemon which he had put inside special muslin bags to retain the pips; he had brought these with him in one of his hand-stitched suitcases. Maud and Elsie sat close to him, freshly bathed and in their dressing-gowns, breathing the heavy breaths of absorbed children. Angela was bashing a clove of garlic onto a wooden board with a flat-bladed knife. The smell of garlic mingled with those of roast chicken and Johnson's baby shampoo. Davy, standing in the kitchen doorway, felt that he stood on the outside edge of the world. He let his briefcase thump onto the floor, which made them all turn their faces towards him.

'Good evening, Jared,' he said. 'How's life among the leisured classes?'

Simon and Lavender Peregory were delighted when Ellis told them he was going to give a house party at Hayden. They worried that Ellis was too solitary. He spent most evenings in the estate office reading *Farmer's Weekly* and picking over the accounts. Usually, when Lavender, who loved company, asked Ellis if he would like to invite some people over for dinner to try the first new potatoes or to admire the Japanese water garden she had designed, Ellis would say he was too tired. And he did work very hard: up all night during the lambing, giving the men a hand rebuilding stone walls, driving cattle to livestock sales. About two or three times a year he went down to London for a week or so, staying in a rented flat in Holland Park, and it was after one of these visits that he organized a house party at the castle.

'So who have you invited?' Lavender asked brightly. For years she had been trying to marry him off. She hadn't thought it would be so difficult. Ellis was a good-looking man, like his father. Ellis was tall and long-limbed with an intelligent narrow head and large ears that flared out magnificently from it. In the last few years his cheeks had started to droop and there was a defensive hunch to his shoulders. Such an elusive private man, Lavender found Ellis difficult to talk to; he seemed to resent having to part with every word he spoke. She persevered.

'So who have you invited?' she repeated.

'Davy and Angela Stearns,' Ellis muttered.

'Oh good,' Lavender said. 'Angela is so killingly gorgeous and quite an authority on composting. Should she ask you whether she should bring anything, you might drop some heavy hints about some cuttings from her Huntercombe Purple, that lovely dark pansy she has in Fulham. I've tried growing it from seed and failed miserably. Who else?'

'Ben and Ellie Cantalupo.'

'Always a pleasure,' Lavender murmured. 'Perhaps they could be persuaded to leave their children behind with Nanny. The last time they were here little Stella put stones in the lock of the greenhouse door so that I broke the key. And?'

'Jared Dauman. An extra man is always useful,' Ellis added quickly.

'Hardly, when there are no extra women.' Lavender had taken a dislike to Jared Dauman since the day, some years ago now, when she had taken him to see the garden and he had told her that it had great potential. She found it odd that he didn't seem to live anywhere, something to do with tax, it seemed, which made it essential for him to flit about from country to country. Lavender found Jared's way of life irresponsibly rootless, really quite bizarre. She frowned.

'Ah, there is,' Ellis said in a terse wary voice, hunching his shoulders; 'an extra woman, that is. Georgie Welliver. Sister of a chap I met in South Africa. She does something quite important in publishing. Quite a go-getter.'

'Unlike Jared then,' Lavender said unkindly. 'He seems to do absolutely nothing at all.'

'Ah, well, he doesn't really need to do anything, you see.'

'Sometimes, money can be too kind,' Lavender said. Later, it occurred to her that, even with the addition of the go-getting Georgie Welliver, there would still be one man too many at the house party.

'Phew, I'll be pleased to get to Hayden,' Angela said. 'You're quite impossible in London, Jared, when Ellis is around. He brings out the worst in you.'

The night before, Ellis Peregory had taken Angela, Davy, Jared and a girl called Georgie Welliver to have dinner at Nico at Ninety in Park Lane. Angela, who had always thought Ellis rather manipulative in a quiet, rather sinister way – beneath that narrow gentlemanly mouth, his chin was brutal – suspected that he had invited Georgie just to make Jared suffer; a cruel thing to do when Jared's suffering was already boundless.

Whenever Ellis turned towards Georgie, the expression in Jared's black eyes became soft, fretful and greedy; it made Angela feel quite hopeless about him.

The effect of Jared's sulkiness was to make Ellis determinedly hearty. 'Splendid, splendid,' he boomed, as the food was brought to the table. 'I think you'll find this is stunningly good.'

Before they had raised the first forkful to their lips, it was clear that Ellis wanted them to say that they had never, in all their lives, tasted anything so delicious. While the rest of them had murmured appreciation – the food was delicious, after all – Jared, with feigned unobtrusiveness, for they were all watching him, lifted his plate and sniffed suspiciously at his Dover sole. He then glared at his fork, and polished it on his napkin. Davy, glancing at Georgie Welliver, saw her smile, her mouth curling sharply upwards. He wondered why, at first, he had thought her rather plain. Perhaps it was because she was so drably dressed in some draggly grey outfit that hung loosely from her slight frame. Her mousy hair was a bit of a mess too, falling limply on either side of her high creamy brow. She looked as though nobody had told her that the usual thing with women was that they lived to be looked at. But that curved smile and the gleam it put in her severe grey eyes; that tiny nose, which was as flat as a kitten's; those delicate tapering wrists.

'I'm very pleased that you're going to be at Hayden this weekend,' Davy said.

'I'm not. I hate the country. I don't know why I'm going.'

Davy held her gaze. 'I know why I am,' he said.

Angela watched him fondly. How sweet Davy is being, she thought. He's really making an effort to be nice to that poor girl, who can't be having an easy time of it. I wonder if she knows what's really going on. How can she, when nobody else does? Ellis is the most extraordinary man. He hides his real self in deep dark folds and Jared keeps on trying to tug those folds and straighten them out.

When dinner was over, Ellis, a distant embarrassed smile on his face, had said that he would drive Georgie home.

Jared had been determinedly inconsolable. He stormed through the door of the Stearns's house and made a dramatic clatter of going upstairs. In bed, Davy said to Angela, 'Heaven give me patience. How much longer is Jared staying? I feel like I'm living on the set of a grand opera.'

'The opera could be called Abelard and Abelard,' Angela said and caught sight of Davy's dirty grin before he switched off the bedside lamps. He waited, as he waited every night, for Angela to fall asleep, before sleeping himself.

*   *   *

The next morning, having scolded Jared for ruining Ellis's dinner party, Angela at once tried to make amends. 'I'm not saying that Ellis doesn't care for you,' she told Jared gently. 'He spends his life hanging around for your next visit. One day Lavender is going to notice that he only ever invites his friends to Hayden when you happen to be in England.'

'I doubt it,' Jared said. 'Lavender's so stupid that she's almost wicked, but not quite.'

'That's unfair. Being good-natured is not the same as being stupid.'

'Hah. It's screamingly obvious that she doesn't understand Ellis.' Jared gave Angela a glistening stare, full of reproach. He was looking Hamlet-like in a black shirt and jeans, his recently showered hair splatted down with water, so that it glittered like coal.

'Darling Jared. None of us understands Ellis. He makes certain that we don't. He has a deep defensive vanity which won't let him reveal himself.' Privately she thought that Ellis had a treacherous heart, unequipped to love anyone. He was as self-sufficient as an animal.

'I love him so,' Jared said wretchedly.

Angela took him in her arms. 'I know,' she said. 'Love is necessary even when it's clearly impossible. It's useful to get that learned.'

When Jared had recovered himself a bit, she said, 'I'm thinking of growing my hair for a more interesting look. What do you think?'

'That you're changing the subject.'

'It was worth a try. Oh Jared, your life is only like this for you because you are rich enough to construct it this way. If you had something else to do, you'd see that the world doesn't revolve around Ellis Peregory.'

'You're on at me to get a job again, like Georgie Welliver, my current rival.'

Angela said, 'You know very well that Georgie was produced just to make you upset. Ellis will go to no end of trouble to pay you back for loving him.'

Jared looked at her out of hot black eyes. 'Don't you see that's because he's suffering so much himself? It's hellish not to be able to admit to your own desires. Shall we go to the Man Ray exhibition at the Serpentine? It might be amusing.'

Pleased that the subject had been changed at last, Angela went to fetch her coat. A walk through Kensington Gardens was just what she needed. Whenever she had to listen to Jared hold forth on the subject of Ellis Peregory, she felt the air around her become as slack and heavy as glue. Sometimes during these suffocating conversations, she thought she would have to find a new way to breathe.

She came downstairs wearing her new spring coat, which was a swirl of creamy white cashmere. Jared looked at her admiringly, thinking what an asset she would be to a man who wanted his wife to be an asset. 'OK, onwards,' he said.

CHAPTER TWO

When Ted Dimont, Angela's father, walked out on his wife, Nora, the day after their thirty-second wedding anniversary, Angela had behaved with her usual understanding. 'I love you both,' she had assured Ted and Nora in that reaching-out way of hers, so tenderly considerate that each felt betrayed.

Their younger daughter, Orly, didn't even try to hide her anger. Orly was a nervous, spiky woman, a professional counsellor on sexual problems – a lucrative profession, her Harley Street consulting rooms had been decorated by Colefax & Fowler. 'Think of the penis as your friend,' Orly would advise, sitting on the edge of her desk and jiggling her shoe on and off, while her clients, married couples whose relationships had reached their last gasp, shifted in the chintzy button-backed chairs, giggling in dismay. But although, professionally, Orly advocated the exciting possibilities of sex, when

Ted ran off with an auburn-haired florist who was younger than his own daughters, Orly was disgusted. 'All that genital thrashing about at his age,' she said crossly. 'What an idiot. I'm not sure I'm going to be able to forgive him.'

Angela blew into a pair of rubber gloves – she and Orly were helping Nora move into the house she had bought in Rottingdean – and Orly frowned at the way the pink rubber fingers suddenly stiffened.

'It's Daddy's life,' Angela said, looking at her sister out of her clear amiable eyes, and starting to wipe down the skirting-board. 'And mother will pull through, as long as we're always there for her.'

'Oh, you're so drearily angelic,' Orly snapped. 'You really live up to your name. I expect you even find it in your heart to forgive Evelyn.'

Angela wrung out her cleaning cloth with some force. 'No. I draw the line at Evelyn. Whoever it was who said you can never be too obvious for a man must have had Evelyn in mind.'

Evelyn Coote wore her dyed red hair in a collapsing mountain of curls. Her clothes looked as though they might drift away from her body at any moment: her blouses, carelessly unbuttoned, revealed the mounds of her breasts; her wrap-around skirts fell back from her beautiful legs whenever she crossed them. She was, Orly claimed bitterly, the last woman alive still to wear gold ankle chains.

Ted Dimont adored his young wife. He leaned forward in his chair to hear her purr, smiled fondly as Evelyn's yapping Yorkshire terrier hopped on and off her lap. He did not mind that Evelyn reeked of chaos, always arriving late, her hair wild, shrieking happily about handbags left in taxis and baths overflowing.

Ted's and Nora's divorce had been four years ago and Nora, as even Orly grudgingly admitted, had never seemed happier. She claimed that she loved living alone in her house by the sea, loved the feeling of being on a ship that its curved windows gave her.

Naturally, there had been a change of status. Without a husband, Nora found that she was demoted from dinner parties to scrambled-egg lunches in the kitchens of her women friends. She never saw their husbands any more, but insisted that this was not much of a loss. Abandoned by Ted, it seemed that anyone had the right to treat her with impertinence. On the other hand, for the first time in her life, she was able to enjoy the novelty of leisure. 'Time for darling self, at last,' she assured her daughters, and started to live in a pampered way, reading the newspapers in bed until late in the morning, going to poetry readings at Sussex University and hanging around the bar afterwards, buying glasses of white wine for the students, who were far easier to get on with than her own contemporaries, of whom she saw less and less.

At first Orly had nagged her mother to entertain, get a dog, perhaps do some kind of voluntary social work.

'Well no, dear, I don't think so,' Nora said. 'I don't really want to have to take anyone else's feelings into consideration ever again, you see. Not even a dog's.'

'Don't you miss Daddy at all?' Orly persisted.

'Not as a person,' Nora said oddly. 'There are times when I miss hearing his key in the door, or sitting in a room made ready to welcome him home. But then I remember that there's something rather good on television, and that I don't have to cook anyone's supper for them first. That cheers me up like billy-oh.'

Nora called Ted 'the ex-hub' and Evelyn 'the child bride'. At family parties, she wore a civilized smile. She would tell Evelyn how wonderful she was to take on 'all this', flicking her fingers vaguely in Ted's direction. Her smile swept over Ted as well, although the look in her eyes suggested that he had made a big mistake in walking out on her, and knew that he had.

The people Nora loved most were her granddaughters, Elsie and Maud Stearns, so she was pleased when Angela asked her if they could stay with her during the weekend of Ellis Peregory's house party. Angela thought they would have more fun with Nora than at Hayden with its stiff formalities.

'What a treat. Of course they can come,' Nora said. 'I'll take them into Brighton to see the ex-hub and the child bride. Ted will love it.'

Angela wasn't sure about that. Nora lost no opportunity to remind Ted that he was a grandfather. He wanted Maud and Elsie to call him Ted, but Nora had taught them to say 'grandpapa' almost as soon as they could speak. Ted didn't feel like a grandfather. Evelyn had made the world young again for him and he felt boyish and hopeful. He wore blue denim shirts over white T-shirts, and cotton trousers with pleated fronts; snappy, comfortable clothes that Evelyn had chosen. Wearing them, his body felt lighter and tenderly ardent. Looking in the mirror Ted didn't notice the slack folds on his neck or the liver spots that bruised the backs of his hands. He saw only that his eyes had lost their film of boredom and shone with expectation. He was devoted to Angela's little girls but wanted to be their playmate, prove that he was young at heart. But when he pretended to eat Evelyn's face cream with a spoon (he had filled the empty Lancôme jar with Greek yoghurt), rolling his eyes and saying 'Yummy, scrummy', Maud and Elsie had given him a disapproving look and gone off to find Evelyn, to report that grandpapa was eating her *best* face cream, as though he were an ancient lunatic.

Angela brought the children to Rottingdean on the Thursday of their half-term holiday. Elsie and Maud had shadows under their eyes from an excess of treats; they had been taken to see *The Sleeping Beauty* at Covent Garden, to Thorpe Park and the Museum of the Moving Image. All this activity had made them listless. Elsie sucked the two middle fingers of her right hand and twiddled a strand of her pale hair, always a sign of exhaustion with her. Maud, a sturdier child in every way, said in a rather whiny voice that she wanted to go to the beach.

'Lunch first,' said Nora firmly. Maud brightened. It was only at Nora's house that they were allowed what they called television food: fish fingers (while fishermen caught fresh soles beneath Nora's wide windows), shaped and crumbed pieces of chicken, bright pink puddings in plastic tubs; food made familiar through television commercials, but never served at home because Angela, unlike Nora, loved cooking.

'So who else will be at Hayden?' Nora asked, thumping the side of a bottle of tomato ketchup so that it would pour out in thick glops, and giving it to Maud.

'The usual crowd. We are all diversions, particular favourites of Lavender's. I think Ellis's idea is that she will be so pleased to see us, she'll forget about the other thing,' Angela said delicately, even though the children weren't listening.

'That's still going on then?'

'No. It's never gone on. That's the trouble.'

'And who is the obligatory decoy female?'

'A girl called Georgie Welliver. I'm not sure that Lavender will take her to her heart. She's something successful in publishing and doesn't know how to dress.. Very dry and offish. Even Davy found her hard going and you know how easily he gets on with people.'

Nora beamed agreement. She was very fond of Davy. When Ted walked out on her, Davy's first reaction had been an astonished, 'He left *you*?' as though he'd been expecting Nora to leave home for years, and would have understood if she had. His response had raised Nora's self-esteem immeasurably. 'How is Davy?' she asked.

'Got a contract to supply the merchandise for the House of Commons gift shop. Everything from brandy to china boxes, all tastefully stamped with a portcullis.'

'He's a clever lad,' Nora murmured.

Angela's face clouded. Whenever Davy was praised, she felt diminished. She had had nothing to do with Davy's success and he never pretended otherwise. He didn't like to share things and hardly ever talked about his job. Angela didn't blame him for that. She found it hard to take an interest in the junk that Davy produced, except to marvel that people were willing to buy it. All the same, it shamed her that Davy had prospered entirely by his own efforts, without ever asking for or needing her help.

She got up with a rather deliberately self-important rustle, and her daughters flew into her burnished arms and, almost immediately, wriggled out of them. Nora had produced the star of a hundred commercial breaks: an ice-cream gâteau, chocolate-striped and edged with stiff whorls of imitation cream.

'Bye, darling. Big kiss,' Nora said, preoccupied with cutting the unyielding ice-cream into slices of exactly the same size, while Elsie and Maud stared at the rock-hard rosettes of cream with unblinking fascination.

Davy drove with his fingertips, like a racing driver. The Audi purred through the country roads, between the shadings of grey and silver on the hills.

Night plummeted suddenly from the sky, a sudden curtain of black.

'We'll be there in good time for dinner,' Angela said contentedly. She slapped the dashboard gently, in time with Barbara Cook singing 'On The Sunny Side Of The Street' on the CD player, and leaned against Davy's shoulder. He had the right sort of shoulder for leaning against, firm and relaxed.

Angela was looking forward to roast lamb and some serious gardening. Davy was looking forward to seeing Georgie Welliver again. He thought of her wolf-grey eyes in their curved eyelids, fringed with thick fuzzy lashes. He thought of her small nostrils and the quick upward swoop of her mouth when she smiled. He wondered when and where he would kiss her, feeling sure that he would before the weekend was over. He knew that he wouldn't survive if he ever had to wonder where the next kiss was coming from, and drove carefully over the cattle grid that marked the beginning of Hayden's wooded drive.

Davy thought there was a touch of the pantomime aristocrat about the Peregorys. This evening, Simon was wearing a velvet smoking jacket with a quilted satin collar and matching velvet slippers with some kind of heraldic animal, worked in shiny gold thread, on the toe; clothes which, on any other man, would have suggested that he'd been kitted out by a theatrical costumier, but looked magnificent on Simon. General Peregory, as even Jared admitted, had presence. He was tall and angular with thick glinting grey hair and dark hooded eyes. When he spoke, he had a way of tossing his head, as though he were shaking the words out of his brain, having given them very careful thought. It was easy to imagine soldiers in wartime responding to Simon's commands, hypnotized by that handsome tossing head into performing tasks of stupefying bravery.

Simon bore down on Davy and Angela carrying silver goblets of champagne – another bit of absurdity Davy thought; those goblets look like stage props. '*There* you are,' Simon said, in a rather relieved voice. Lavender swooshed up to them, high-coloured and dressed in a long dark-blue cashmere robe. Long ropes of pearls lay tangled against her bosom. In spite of her red cheeks, Angela thought that Lavender looked rather wan. She was breathing heavily too, as though she were pushing upstream.

'It's so wonderful to see you,' Lavender said, pressing Angela against her pearls, and then, lowering her voice, 'you're such an angel of ease, you're bound to calm things down.'

Only then did they notice Georgie. She had been hidden by the high curving side of the huge fireside chair. Getting to her feet, she was scarcely taller than the chair's studded leather back. Shaking hands with her, Davy touched icy cold fingers, their bones thin as a bird's in the warm room where the fire made voluptuous swallowing sounds. Beside it, Ellis's collie nibbled delicately at its flanks.

'You're cold,' he accused.

'I was born cold,' Georgie said. 'In my parents' house, the water froze in the lavatory bowls, draughts sucked the carpets clean off the floors. None of us can get warm, even though we went to South Africa when my father died. The sunshine came too late. We'd been chilled right through to our blood and bones, you see.' She gave Davy a tilted smile. It was all he could do not to trace her mouth with his finger. She was wearing something silky and mouse-coloured, like her hair, with a sash that wound itself round her hard little hips.

'I'm afraid Lavender is cross about the faxes,' Georgie said. 'The New York office kept on sending them right through the night. I didn't know that her bedroom is right over Ellis's office. She was kept awake by that horrid shuffling noise the fax machine makes. Ee-um, ee-um,' Georgie imitated, inching her hands forward to suggest reams of shiny paper pushing through the machine and streaming onto the floor.

'Anything important?' Davy asked.

Georgie shrugged. 'Oh, you know, high-level stuff. It will end with someone having to clear his desk in twenty minutes and leave by the back stairs.' Her wolf-grey eyes glinted. Davy thought it likely that she herself had engineered this savage sacking.

Ellie and Ben Cantalupo arrived in a flurry of apologies, followed by Ellis and Jared, both looking rather sheepish.

Dinner was served by the Peregorys' butler, Tom Ward, whose wife, Lolly, had cooked it. Lolly nearly always served overdone roast joints and root vegetables of some kind which she had cubed and then boiled to a pulp. She had a repertoire of three desserts: rice pudding, trifle and a rather unpleasantly brownish fruit salad. The first course was usually a tinned soup to which either sherry or cream had been added.

Once, Angela, knowing how grudgingly Lolly cooked, had bought a tarte tatin at a Knightsbridge pâtisserie and had given it to Lavender, suggesting that it might be the pudding for Sunday lunch. Lavender had almost shrieked as she took the gold berib-boned box and neither Lolly nor Tom spoke to Angela during the entire weekend. The tart was never seen again. Jared had gone even further. The previous year, discovering that Lolly intended to bake a ham, he had sauntered into the kitchen and asked Lolly to find him the greens of six radishes, Madeira, a shallot and some thick cream so that he could show her how to make a sauce that he and Ellis had eaten in Saulieu, famous for its ham. Lolly had handed in her notice, retracting it when Lavender allowed her to boil the ham until it fell apart in stringy shreds, and she had the general's assurance that Jared was permanently barred from the kitchen.

But the war between Lolly and Jared wasn't over. Tonight, as he helped himself to a meagre portion of diced parsnips from the Spode dish that Tom Ward held out to him, Jared spoke loudly and yearningly of the superior vegetables that he and Ellis had eaten elsewhere: spinach lightly sautéd in butter and garlic, shelled peas cooked with lettuce, sugar and spring onions. Tom stalked the table with the dish of parsnips, his dark face impassive, while Lavender became fidgety and Simon tossed his head more than usual.

Ben Cantalupo broke into Jared's culinary recollections. He was an architect who, in a blaze of publicity, had demolished an old farmhouse and built on its site a house made entirely of glass with sloping walls where he and Ellie now lived. 'The reason why we were late', Ben announced – he was the kind of man who turned sentences into announcements – 'was that some damned conservation group came and demonstrated outside our gates. Blasted beard and sandal types. Must have heard the rumours that the house is up for more than one award.' With a flamboyant show of modesty, he took off his glasses, which had red plastic frames, and began to wipe them on his handkerchief.

A spirited debate on the subject of modern architecture flared around the table. Georgie said nothing. Davy watched her attentively, even as he sided with Lavender, who had tried to get a preservation order slapped on the farmhouse, although it was derelict and would have cost thousands to restore. He supported his hostess out of gallantry; he found Ben Cantalupo's opinion that every age should have its own buildings equally acceptable. It wasn't a topic that interested him. Far more fascinating was the sight of Georgie Welliver eating her dinner.

She ate like a starveling, wolfishly licking the corners of her lips with her sharp, pink tongue. Davy asked, 'What do you think about modern architecture?' jerking his head towards Ben, who was denouncing English Heritage as a load of pot-pourri obsessives.

'They can ruin you, houses,' Georgie said; 'ancient *and* modern. That's if you think about them too much, the way Ellis does.' She flicked her eyes around Hayden's beautiful dining-room, at the gilded plasterwork and painted ceiling, and the almond-coloured silk curtains that puddled onto the floor. 'Ellis would be better off with a life,' she said, turning her scrutinizing eyes on Tom Ward, who was approaching her with the rice pudding.

The next morning Davy made love to his wife while she was still sleepy and soft and not properly awake. Then he got up, showered quickly and went in search of Georgie. He was too late. Georgie had gone riding with Eliza Jones, the Peregorys' eldest daughter. They had left at first light and would be back soon for a proper breakfast, according to Lolly who was bad-temperedly tipping a saucepan of sloppy scrambled eggs into a silver dish that stood on the hotplate. Davy helped himself to very hard bacon and very soft tomatoes, and was presently joined by Lavender wearing her gardening corduroys.

'Well, what do you think of her?' she hissed, lowering her voice, although there was nobody else in the breakfast room. 'Can you see her settling down here? The thing is would Ellis and Hayden be enough? At least she was brought up in the country; that's some-thing.' Lavender looked miserable and anxious as she sipped her coffee. Davy noticed that she was beginning to get chins. 'If only Ellis could meet someone like Angela,' Lavender said. 'Someone who gives of herself all the time and isn't ambitious.'

'Angela is almost suicidally unselfish,' Davy agreed. 'But give this thing time, Lavender. Ellis and Georgie have only known each other for a few weeks.'

'Time is getting to be a bit of a luxury, the way things are at the moment,' Lavender said. She had a confiding look on her face which disappeared as Eliza clattered into the room. She was almost as tall as Ellis and had the same tough jaw. Beside her, Georgie looked fragile and childish.

'You'd be surprised at how well this one rides,' Eliza boomed. She sounded rather put out.

Georgie said, 'My parents had a riding school of sorts. A failure like most of the things they did. You could say that my father died of failure.'

Lavender and Eliza did not care to hear such harsh truths at breakfast, or indeed any other time. They began to fuss with the toast rack and gave small sighs of relief when Angela came in, walking towards the coffee pot with her easy stride and then standing up to drink her coffee in that comfortable way of hers, leaning back a little. Her large-boned, creamy beauty had a soothing effect; she was, so obviously and uncomplicatedly, a woman who had no dark corners.

Angela stretched out her strong hand and touched Georgie's tweed jacket, which seemed only slightly larger than one of Elsie's. 'What a pretty tweed,' she said. 'You don't often find one this soft.'

'I've had it since I was twelve. I didn't grow much after that, so it still fits.'

Georgie will be my first small woman, Davy decided, cracking open the newspaper. How lovely her wrist-bones are, shining through her skin like pearls.

'Where are the rest of the chaps, I wonder,' Lavender said.

'We saw Ellis and Jared sneaking off somewhere in the Land Rover,' Eliza said, sounding pleased with herself.

'I expect they were going to the farm,' Lavender said coldly. 'It's a busy time of year, as you know. It was your father I meant. The wind is getting up and I don't want him walking across the fields without his jacket.'

'Simon's giving Ben Cantalupo a tour of the Edwardian wing,' Angela reassured her. 'They've found some rather interesting mould. Shall we head for the garden, Lavender? There's so much I want to do, and it looks as though it might rain.'

Eliza crunched a last slice of cold toast and reluctantly returned to her own house on the other side of the valley. She was homesick for Hayden as soon as she turned out of the drive. Ellie Cantalupo had left a message with Lolly, who had finally brought in some more coffee, that she had gone to an auction of old bibles in Hay-on-Wye. She thought one or two would look attractive on her slate table.

'I'd like to go somewhere with you,' Davy said to Georgie.

'I'll change into something grown-up then,' she said.

He drove her between sharp hills to the ruined priory where, last summer, he and Angela, to escape one of Lolly's uninspired lunches, had brought Elsie and Maud for a picnic. Davy had thought it was the most romantic setting in the world, quite the wrong place to bring two little girls who giggled and shrieked and threw their Frisbees into the air.

This morning the black stone arches were wet with rain; within their frames, grass melted into sky and the fluting sound of blackbirds, rich and dreamy, wove between the stony pillars. The broken statues lining the crooked path where he led Georgie had raindrops hanging from their ears like crystals. He held her lightly against a crumbling wall and began to knead her cheek-bones with his warm fingers.

'I'm damaged goods, Davy,' Georgie murmured, but, by then, he had started to push quick kisses on her mouth and it was too late to stop.

'Round one to Jared then,' Davy said in the car going home.

During Sunday lunch, when they were all bored by Ben Cantalupo's detailed descriptions of the villa in Portugal where he and Ellie were going to spend the summer, Ellis had said, in a rather quiet slithery voice, that he was giving some thought to cruising around the Greek islands in a boat that some friends of his had chartered.

One look at Jared's lustrous eyes and Angela knew at once that the vague 'friends' could only be him. The Peregorys had obviously reached the same conclusion. Simon's lips were pinched, making his face look engraved; Lavender had gone a little white around the forehead, while Eliza had brazenly smirked.

'More like round one to Eliza,' Angela said, remembering the detestable expression on Eliza's face. 'The thing is that Simon is quite seriously ill. Lavender told me while we were planting out the sweet peas. He doesn't know; nobody does. Lavender insists on keeping it secret.'

'Except from you, it seems,' Davy said, increasing his speed as the Audi nosed into the London-bound motorway.

'At a time like this Lavender needs my support,' Angela said mildly.

'Who doesn't?' Davy said, almost to himself. The two small shadows at the corners of his mouth deepened.

Angela looked at her watch. 'I hope Ma and the children are already in London,' she said. 'I've missed my baby girls the whole weekend.'

'Me too,' Davy lied.

CHAPTER THREE

GEORGIE WELLIVER SAT IN THE CRISP white bedroom of her flat in Hanover Terrace, listening to the lions roaring in the nearby zoo and thinking about Davy Stearns and how he had changed the way that she looked at the world.

Her childhood had left her permanently on the alert for disaster. It had been relentlessly miserable, growing up in a bleak and collapsing manor house in Shropshire, where her father, Gomer, had raged crazily against a postwar England in which he had no place, and her mother, Gillian, had handled the crises that Gomer's anger brought down on his family with a grim pluckiness that made everything worse.

Although Georgie was now one of the most successful publishers in London, she had still thought of herself as severely damaged, somehow fated to lose, crippled by the legacy of Gomer's tragic failure. Everything was different now. Davy had put her in touch with light. As spring gave way to a glowing summer, he had convinced her that she was someone very fine who had large gifts and could do whatever she wanted.

He would be with her soon. For the last fortnight he had been staying with his wife and children at the Cantalupos' rented villa in Portugal. Angela and the little girls were staying on, but Davy had to get back to work, and to Georgie.

His key clicked in the lock and she pulled her hair behind her ears. He picked her up, held her high above his head and dropped her onto the bed.

'Happy landings,' he said.

'Happy landings,' Georgie echoed. It was what they always said to each other when they met and when they parted, part of the secret language that belonged to the passionate hidden-away life they shared.

Davy snuffled happily around Georgie's flat which bristled with gadgetry: a Bang & Olufsen television the size of a small cinema screen, a complicated and powerful sound system and a more up-to-date and expensive computer than the one in his office. Georgie was the most orderly person he had ever known. Everything she owned was stashed away in built-in cupboards according to various methods that she had meticulously devised, sometimes alphabetically (files, CDs), sometimes by size and colour (crockery, cardigans).

Until she met Davy, her neatly arranged possessions and costly appliances had helped to keep the panic of emptiness at bay. She had not had any success with men and had not expected to. She was too strong, too opinionated, too shy. Unsure of the rules of ordinary conversation – at Utley Manor days might go by when the only voice to be heard was Gomer's, as he railed at his wife and children in helpless fury – she would lurch giddily into speech. The results could be embarrassing and charmless and her awkward silences seemed judgemental. This was before Davy had brought her to a ruined abbey where the sky hummed with the sounds of blackbirds, and kissed her more times than she could count. Since then, Georgie had found that she could lead with her heart.

She tapped the tips of her fingers on Davy's chin and said she would ring for some pizza to be delivered. In spite of her brushed-aluminium kitchen fitments, her double oven and her ravenous appetite, Georgie had never learned to cook. She ate out most of the time with authors and literary agents and at weekends, which she spent alone reading manuscripts, she scoffed chocolate raisins, salami and home-delivery pizzas.

Davy took hold of her wrist. 'Later,' he said, and they began to snap and click their way out of their clothes. Georgie's small body, precise and alive, was Davy's delight. He had missed her dreadfully for the last two weeks, most of all when he was making love to Angela. He had begun to feel that there was too much of his wife: those large glistening teeth, that luscious, heaving cleavage, that thick mane of lemon-blond hair, those rounded arms. He had stayed awake, as he always did, until she fell asleep, and then groaned into his pillow, aching for Georgie; to become skin upon skin with her as she lay, sharp and cool, on her cold white sheets.

Angela's cheerful candour made him wince, as she laughed and chatted with the Cantalupos and their other guests, talking easily, saying whatever came into her mind, words filtering softly and pleasantly through her lips. How unlike Georgie who had no social graces and remained distinguished in her loneliness, admirable and rather forbidding.

Now Georgie's cool cheek lay on his chest; their breathing kept time with the lions roaring. He dozed and woke to the sound of Georgie's quiet but commanding voice ordering pizza.

While they ate, and drank the purple-red wine he had brought back from Portugal, he was conscious of Georgie watching him with an attentive tilt of her head. It made Davy feel that she saw him in all his interesting detail. He began to talk about the trip to New York he was trying to organize, in the hope of getting a contract to provide the campaign buttons at the next Democratic Party Convention. He could tell that Georgie was listening very hard, as she always did when he told her about his plans.

'Tell you what, my darling Georgie,' he said, 'why don't you come to New York with me?'

Georgie prodded some olive stones into a neat circle on her plate and said that she would.

'Jared, put that table down exactly where you found it,' Angela said. 'Elsie's going to dance for you to cheer you up.'

Jared had arrived unexpectedly at the Stearns's house the night before, his face the colour of fine brandy, but with exhausted sunken eyes. Even his glossy hair seemed dulled by disappointment. Now he was brooding forlornly in Angela's sitting-room, rearranging the sofa cushions when he thought she wasn't looking. Once again Ellis Peregory had let him down. At the last minute, when Jared was already on board the yacht he had chartered, Ellis had decided not to join him. He had probably never intended to.

So why, Angela thought, as she scraped Elsie's hair into a tight coil, did he suggest that he might, in front of Simon and Lavender? Because he liked having the power to make people unhappy she decided, pushing hairgrips into Elsie's slippery hair; because he was malign and manipulative, betraying those who loved him and then watching them crumple, while he smiled, like an amused serpent.

Earlier that day Angela had gone into the guest bedroom to tidy it up. Smoothing the pillow on Jared's bed, she saw the edge of a familiar Viyella shirt crammed underneath it. She fished it out and held it to her face. Ellis's shirt. It smelled of hay, dogs and wood-ash. Angela put it back underneath the pillow and walked out of the room, badly shaken by this evidence of Jared's morbid, destroying love.

'Now then, little one,' she said to Elsie, 'you look like a proper ballerina. Let's get going before Jared has moved every piece of furniture to another room.'

She put on a tape of 'Air on a G String' and Elsie performed the dance that had put her at the top of her ballet class. In her white leotard, gracefully stretching her arms, she looked, Angela thought dotingly, like an animated strand of spaghetti.

How lucky I am to have my baby girls and my pretty house and Davy too, of course, although in Portugal, he was looking a bit used up. I hope he's not working too hard in New York.

When Elsie had finished her dance, drifting down to the carpet in a deep curtsey, Angela kissed the nape of her neck fiercely before unwinding her pale silky hair and brushing it loose. Jared had scarcely noticed Elsie's performance. That is the tragedy of obsession, Angela thought. It pulls you away from the rest of the world so that you find no joy in it. Blind and deaf to joy, you become locked ever more horribly inside your obsession. Poor Jared. She felt overwhelmed by pity for him and squeezed his shoulder as she strode into the kitchen to start supper.

Orly arrived with Maud. They had been to Knightsbridge to buy Orly a new outfit to wear on a television programme in which she was going to appear as an expert on sexual behaviour. Orly claimed that she got better service in shops when Maud was with her wearing her quaint school uniform – a flower-print dress with a white collar, a straw boater and tiny white gloves, all smacking of hefty school fees. 'The salesgirls let me finger stuff for ages when Maudie comes along,' Orly said, 'thinking that I'm a mother of substance.' She had bought a slate-grey dress and jacket at Emporio Armani, which brilliantly succeeded in being both sexy and demure. She gave Angela a bottle of expensive extra-virgin olive oil. Sighing quietly, Angela put it on a kitchen shelf already crammed with similar bottles.

During supper, Elsie said, 'I wonder what Daddy is doing now.'

She hated it when Davy wasn't there to read her a bedtime story, stretched out beside her on the bed, looking tired, with grey bristly cheeks that Elsie could play a raspy tune on by rubbing the palm of her hand against the stubble. She would fall asleep with the sound of her father's velvety voice in her ears.

'Working his fingers to the bone in New York so that you two little baggages can go to posh schools and Mummy can be the last of the full-time mothers,' Orly said, helping herself to chicken risotto. 'What are you doing in London, Jared? Weren't you supposed to be sailing in swinish luxury on a deep blue sea?'

Jared looked at her with maddened eyes. 'I came back,' he said dramatically, thrusting out his chin.

Maud was playing with Orly's plaited gold ring which fascinatingly unwound into three hoops when you took it off, and closed up into a single band when you put it back on your finger. 'Why aren't you married to someone, Orly?' she asked.

'Because I'm unhappy enough already, my precious,' Orly said.

Elsie's lower lip shuddered. She flung her arms around Orly, who realized that she had gone too far; children didn't appreciate irony. 'I'm only teasing, Else,' she said. 'The real reason is that I'm wedded to my career. This television programme might be turned into a series, you know. Then I'll be rich and famous and shop assistants will be all over me, like maggots on a chop, even when Maudie isn't with me.'

'But I'll still come,' Maud offered. 'I like going to the animal shop afterwards.'

Jared said he would read the bedtime story. '*Nurse Matilda Goes to Town*,' Maud wheedled. She and Elsie gave each other slithery looks; it was their longest story-book.

'Pas de prob,' Jared said and allowed himself to be yanked into the children's bedroom.

'Well, aren't you going to tell me what happened?' Orly asked, flipping plates into the dishwasher.

'As usual, nothing,' Angela said. 'Having more or less promised to join Jared on the boat, Ellis didn't. And, of course, Jared hadn't invited anyone else, wanting Ellis all to himself, so he was left high and dry.'

'Or rather low and wet,' Orly sniggered unkindly. 'Some people might not have been averse to being on a luxury yacht with a crew of handsome Greeks, but Jared always was spoiled. He walks on a golden carpet of advantage.'

'What do you make of Ellis Peregory, Orly?'

'Very uppish,' Orly said. 'Aloof. Disconnected. Sexually agonized would be my guess.'

'Sometimes I wish he would marry Georgie Welliver and put Jared out of his misery. It would be a convenient mating of two emotional misers.'

'Georgie who?'

'The latest decoy woman. Very serious and unforthcoming; she makes no effort at all to like or be liked.'

Orly gave a slight shiver. 'Watch out then. Those acid-hearted types are the very devil when love catches up with them. They don't know how to handle it. I've seen a few professionally, but by the time they come to see me it's usually too late; they're almost suffocated by emotion.'

'But is that to do with sex?' Angela asked. She had planted herself in front of the dresser, her hands resting comfortably on her stomach, secure of her hold on the world.

'Everything's to do with sex,' Orly said.

The room that Davy had booked at the Algonquin hotel turned out to be a suite, filled with flowers sent to Georgie by an American author she published.

'I made a phone call,' Georgie explained. 'They know me here; I always have this suite.' She tucked her hair behind her ears, frowned at the winking light on the telephone which indicated that messages had been left for her, then picked it up. Davy, unpacking in the bedroom, could hear her quiet commanding voice discussing contracts. After a while she came and stood beside him as he sat on the bed and he knocked his head affectionately against her hip, then pulled her down on his lap. Her wolf-grey eyes glittered.

'They're going to offer me the New York job,' she said.

She might as well have stabbed him in the heart. He could think of nothing but the few clothes he had left in her austere white-painted flat: a red flannel dressing-gown, a T-shirt with his company logo printed on the front and 'Novelty Value' on the back, an old pullover. He might never see them again, or throw himself on top of Georgie's narrow ribcage while the roar of hungry lions floated through the air.

'I won't take it,' Georgie said. 'I have to live where *you* are. Naturally I shan't give that as the reason. The board would think I was a little eerie. I'll say that I have to get the London office in good shape first. That's the only kind of language they understand.' She nuzzled Davy's ear with her small flat nose. 'It was the only kind of language *I* understood until you taught me a different one.'

'You are the night's morning,' Davy said.

'Men always say soppy things to women in strange cities,' Georgie said, taking hold of his curly hair so that she could pull his face nearer to hers.

I want to be two people at once, Davy thought, watching Georgie sleep. I want to cut myself in half so that part of me can take care of Angela and Maud and Elsie and the other part can be with Georgie who doesn't need taking care of, only to be loved.

He looked at his watch. Four o'clock. They had made love for half the afternoon and there were things to be done. He pulled the blankets off Georgie's shoulders. 'Wake up, dearest love,' he whispered. 'We have to go and choose a birthday present for my wife.'

Georgie yawned widely. 'Tiffany's then. It's quicker than any-where else.'

Davy was enchanted by the shop's many windows in which pieces of jewellery were displayed as part of gorgeous still-life arrange-ments. Georgie pushed him inside. 'What?' she asked briskly. 'Bracelet? Ear-rings? Sterling silver bookmark with her initials?'

'Well, maybe a bracelet.' Davy hesitated. He wanted to mooch around for a while among this fabulous glitter, see if he could pick up a few ideas for novelties, but Georgie had already raced to a counter. Bracelets were clasped over her tapered wrist.

'Which one?' she asked impatiently, flicking her arm in front of Davy's face.

'Don't you have any ideas?' he pleaded. His eyes were swimming in the dazzle. Jewels jumped and danced in the brightness of the display stands, making him blink. He opened his eyes to see Georgie in her severe black dress, waving her pale arm like a frond. A bracelet was clamped around it; a heavy gold cuff in which bright bands of blue enamel had been worked. 'Yes, that one; it's completely marvellous,' Davy said. 'And now, what about you, my sweet-heart? Would you like some ear-rings, perhaps?'

Georgie shook her head. 'No thank you. I have a curious allergy; I can't tolerate precious metals touching my skin for any length of time.'

'What can I buy you then?' Davy asked. He looked wildly about the shop and saw gold, silver and platinum everywhere he looked.

Georgie pulled at his sleeve. 'Come on. Let's go to Central Park lake and you can buy me a hot dog as big as the Ritz.'

'I closed the deal,' Davy shouted, bursting through the door of their hotel suite. They were flying back to London that evening and he swerved past suitcases on his way to the bedroom. 'Buttons, balloons; I've got the contract for the whole damn shoot. They thought my ideas were cute.'

He suddenly noticed that Georgie was sitting on the edge of the bed, pulling at her hair with both hands and moaning quietly. He prised her hands off her limp hair and stroked it, pressing her head against his heart. 'What is it, my love?'

When she looked up, her grey eyes were as dark as wet slate and her lashes clotted with tears. 'You stay awake until you think I'm asleep, don't you?' she asked. Her voice was desperate.

'I'm sorry,' Davy said. He was mortified to think that Georgie had fooled him into believing she was asleep when she wasn't. 'It's a stupid habit of mine, watching over people I love.'

'That's just it,' Georgie said. Tears were falling down her cheeks now, plopping onto the carpet. 'Nobody's ever watched over me before. You are the first person who's made me feel that I'm more important than anyone else.' She gave a deep shuddering sigh and then squared her thin shoulders. 'Only, of course, I'm not. I know that,' she said.

Davy mopped her face carefully with his handkerchief. 'This isn't the moment I've been waiting for,' he said. 'You know I'd put you first if I could.' His mouth went dry. He thought she might say that she never wanted to see him again. Instead she gave him a sharp look.

'I can probably put up with having to share you as long as I'm not just one of your indiscriminate enthusiasms,' she said. 'No, don't bother to lie. Chicky Smeaton designs book jackets for me.'

Davy groaned. He had mean, clouded memories of his affair with Chicky Smeaton, a woman who, in spite of her loud merry laugh, had turned out to be intensely melancholy. His secretary, Joyce Arledge, had come to dread Chicky's wistful telephone calls after Davy had grown tired of her manic laughter and the despair that was behind it.

'It's different with you,' he said, stricken.

'It had better be,' Georgie said sternly. She gave her hair a final pull. 'Let's bash on, shall we? I'd like to go to the Frick one last time before we have to leave.'

Their plane landed at Heathrow at seven in the morning. Both of them had arranged to go straight to their offices, to seek out the dubious consolations of work. 'Happy landings,' Davy whispered in Georgie's ear, brushing her neck with his warm lips as he undid her seat-belt.

'Happy landings,' Georgie said, buttoning her jacket in a composed way.

Evelyn Dimont was giving a birthday party for her step-daughter, Angela Stearns, who was five years older than she was. Nora Dimont was unperturbed.

'If Evelyn thinks it will put my nose out of joint, she's very much mistaken,' she told Angela. 'I spent far too many years being a hostess not to know that it suits me much better to be a guest. I intend to bask in the sun on one of Ted's idiotic lounger things, drink his booze and not do a hand's turn to help.'

Ted and Nora had spent twenty years of their married life in a tall terraced house in Regency Square, which overlooked the sea front at Brighton. It had a stone-flagged kitchen and a balconied high-ceilinged drawing-room on the first floor. Neither of them missed the house when it was sold after their divorce. They realized, too late, that they had put up with its chilly staircases and insatiable boiler because each had thought the other enjoyed living in Georgian splendour. The night before Ted left they had given a large dinner party to celebrate their thirty-second wedding anniversary, an uncomfortable affair since Nora and most of the guests knew that Ted's infatuation with a red-haired florist was getting serious. It was the sight of his friends' concerned and ageing faces that had made Ted decide to leave. He was still quite fond of Nora, but life with her in their elegant house in which they entertained retired professional couples much like themselves offered at best only a dull contentment on the way to death.

While he was packing Nora had shouted bitterly, 'I can understand your leaving me, but how can you walk out of your house like this?'

Ted had paused in the middle of folding his dressing-gown – he had left all his pyjamas in the chest of drawers, Nora noted – and had said, genuinely perplexed, 'My house? I always thought of it as your house.' That morning the house smelled of wine dregs and ashtrays. Moments after Ted had departed in a taxi, Nora had made an appointment with an estate agent.

With his second wife, Ted lived in a large bungalow with its own swimming-pool and tennis court and views of the South Downs. Evelyn was chaotic in her housekeeping as in everything else. Nora, arriving for the birthday party with Orly, noticed a much-used hairbrush beside the glass bowl of strawberries set out on the wrought-iron table on the terrace, and that Evelyn's yapping dog had a half-chewed American Express card in its basket. There was no sign of Evelyn. 'Busy getting herself undressed,' Orly muttered, loud enough for Ted to hear as he made up a jugful of Pimms. His face twitched with embarrassment. Orly is a savagely critical girl, he thought. Thank the Lord for Angela who takes a more kindly view of our failings.

He felt full of gratitude towards his older daughter who under-stood how all of them, himself and Nora and Evelyn, his children and grandchildren, were helplessly intertwined and must somehow make the best of it. Here she came now with Davy, swinging Elsie along the lawn while solid little Maud clomped along behind, clasping a mauve and white inflatable ring with a duck's head.

Angela greeted her parents in her sunny voice and immediately began to get the barbeque ready. She was wearing a linen dress of the same hot blue as the sky reflected in the swimming-pool; as she bent over the charcoal grill, her creamy back looked firm and luscious.

Evelyn came tearing out of the house, tying a flower-splashed sarong over her bikini, in danger of tripping up on her high-heeled, gold-thonged sandals that revealed cyclamen-pink toenails. The dog's tail ticked back and forth as he lunged at her teetering ankles.

'Happy birthday, happy birthday,' Evelyn shouted, hugging Angela, and then, grabbing a glass of Pimms and raising it, 'Hup-ya-bum.' She giggled and winked before bouncing down on one of the cushioned sun loungers on the lawn.

'Hup-ya-bum,' Maud and Elsie chanted, swinging their glasses of orange juice and waggling their hips, until Davy threatened to make them sit in the car until it was time to go home. He went back and forth over the rather lurid grass, carrying the birthday cake, extra swimsuits, piles of birthday presents, including the pale-blue Tiffany's box containing the bracelet he had bought in New York. Elsie and Maud got into the pool and began to practise the breast-stroke. Their small hands pushed the water away from their chins and then gathered it to their chests.

Nora, screened by her sunglasses, watched Ted slip his veiny feet out of gleaming white canvas espadrilles and wade into the pool. He stalked warily through the blue water, scooping it up in his hands and wetting his arms before throwing himself beneath the surface. Did he always do that, Nora wondered, and did I purposely not notice him wetting his arms or a thousand other minor annoyances for the sake of marital harmony? How could I have stayed interested in Ted for so many years? She closed her eyes behind her dark glasses and stretched out her legs. No longer, thank heavens, she thought. Now I'm even bored by women who are still interested in men because I've forgotten how to be.

Since Evelyn appeared to have fallen asleep in the sun, Davy and Angela began to grill pieces of marinated chicken on the barbeque and the smell of smoke and rosemary twigs wafted over the garden. It was hot work. Davy's eyes smarted. He thought of Georgie's hard cool shoulder under his chin, and guiltily filled a plate with chicken and salad and took it over to Nora.

She had taken off her sunglasses and her pale turquoise eyes, very open and candid, were fixed on Evelyn, who had suddenly woken up and was running towards the pool, her blazing hair cascading down her back. She was carrying an enormous, slightly grubby towel for Ted to dry himself.

'It's all too wonderful,' Nora said, taking the plate that Davy held out to her. She had cultivated an air of imperturbable aplomb that Davy admired very much but found heartbreaking.

When it was time for Angela to open her presents, everyone moved on to the terrace which was sheltered from the early afternoon glare by a retractable awning. There was a cheque from Ted to pay for the Amdega conservatory Angela had chosen, another from Nora to buy a pair of eighteenth-century lead planters. Maud and Elsie, under Orly's supervision, had made lumpy clay pots which they had planted up with geraniums. Orly herself gave Angela a cream clematis, Mrs George Jackman. It was too late in the year to get it established and it was a flower that looked its best against a shady wall, which Angela's garden lacked. She thanked Orly effusively. Evelyn thrust a glossy carrier bag into Angela's hands. 'This is for when you're not in the garden,' she said conspiratorially. Inside the bag was a chiffon nightdress, flesh-coloured, transparent and trimmed with black lace. Angela blushed. 'It'll be totally adorable on you,' Evelyn insisted. 'You wait and see.' She winked happily at Davy.

Angela had left the Tiffany's box until last. The wide gold bracelet gleamed as she tried to slide it over her rounded arm. Hard metal edges bit into her flesh and would not yield. It was impossible; the bracelet was designed for someone with very slender arms. Even as Davy was saying, 'I'm so sorry, angel; I'll see if I can change it at the Bond Street Tiffany's,' Angela had a sudden vision of a delicate white wrist with a pronounced and pearly bone. Georgie Welliver's wrist. Nothing could be more unlikely than that Georgie Welliver had tried on the bracelet Davy had given her, and yet Angela knew that she had. She struggled to keep her voice from sounding thin and distant as she thanked Davy. She put her arms on her daughters' shoulders.

'Here's what we'll do,' she said. 'We'll all choose another bracelet *together*.' She felt that the light must have drained from her face and that her voice rasped, but nobody seemed to have noticed.

She would hold on. She would keep what Ted had so recklessly thrown away. My children deserve to grow up with two parents, she told herself silently. And Davy has to be saved from himself. I won't let him become an abashed and pathetic figure like Daddy, just because of one wrong move. She put her arm through Davy's and kissed his cheek. At the same moment the sun went in.

CHAPTER FOUR

'MORGANE SAID I WOULD FIND MY heart's desire only by escaping it,' Jared said. He had been doing the rounds of astrologers and clairvoyants before deciding on his next move. The latest soothsayer, Morgane Landemare, an exotic-looking woman who wrote the horoscopes for a glossy magazine, seemed to be suggesting in a cryptic way that Jared should leave the country; convenient advice, since Jared would have to pay income tax if he stayed in England much longer.

'So I thought China,' he went on, 'and then, perhaps, Mexico for the winter. I might even learn to paint. Angela, you're not listening. What are you thinking about? Come on, reveal.'

Angela blinked and shook her head. She felt blurry and unreal, as though she were going out of focus. During the last few days, Jared, distraught over Ellis's coolness – he had barely apologized for his failure to show up in Greece – had convinced himself that Georgie

Welliver was the cause of Ellis's treachery. He had heard all kinds of stories about her ruthlessness: the sacking of loyal and long-serving editors; authors lured away from other publishers; the foreign fiction list slashed. A woman like that could bend Ellis – who Jared still perceived as a tortured soul, easily crushed – to her will, with no trouble at all.

As he catalogued Georgie's merciless acts, Angela wanted to put her head in her hands and howl. If Georgie were really that crafty, that treacherous, Davy was as good as lost. She ached to tell Jared the truth, that Georgie Welliver's interests lay elsewhere; it would have put him out of his misery at once. But she knew that, although Jared's black eyes would become moist with sympathy, he would not be able to hide his relief that it was Davy, not Ellis, that Georgie had set her hard heart on, and she knew she would not be able to bear that relief.

She blessed Morgane Landemare for convincing Jared that he should go away, for Angela had her own reasons for wanting Jared gone. She had decided to completely redecorate and refurnish the house and she was determined to involve Davy in this. It would be impossible if Jared were in London. He would take over the whole project, nipping about auction rooms, insisting on paying for pieces of furniture that Angela considered overpriced, making Davy feel like a clumsy stranger in his own home. She smiled at Jared.

'China's a wonderful idea,' she said. 'I'll miss you though. When you're not here, life seems to consist only of dull needs.'

Surely Angela never used to be like this, Davy thought crossly, on the way to choose curtain material at Peter Jones. Surely she wasn't always so trivial, twittering on about interfacings and tie-backs, as though their lives depended on having perfect soft furnishings. Admittedly it had been a long time since Angela had shown much interest in the state of the universe; she was contentedly absorbed in her children, her house and her many clamouring friends. And by me, Davy would have liked to have added, but it wouldn't have been true. He was not of much concern to his wife. Her lack of anxiety about him was what had made him fall in love with her. She had accepted everything he did with a sleepy serenity, quite unlike his parents whom, Davy had been made to feel, worried about him constantly. He was expanding his business too quickly, borrowing too heavily, living too handsomely. When he visited them he noticed how years of anxiety about him had shadowed their eyes; sleepless nights made their relentless questions sound almost hysterical from fatigue. How wonderful it had been to return to Angela's sunny voice and lazy chatter. From the beginning, she had treated him with a loving detachment. She had never been in any doubt that he could take care of himself and was bound to prosper, and this had calmed him and boosted his confidence in himself.

But now her tranquillity had turned into an irritating shallowness. She switched off the radio when the news began, saying it was too depressing, and read nothing but *The World of Interiors*. Sometimes Davy caught her looking at him in a strange way, her kind blue eyes more than kind; forbearing was the word they made you think of. When he objected to her plans – the latest one was to spend this golden September morning among the fabric bolts in Peter Jones – she gave him a brave resigned smile that thoroughly got on his nerves and then made him feel so guilty that he agreed to do what she wanted, but with bad grace.

The truth was that he had stopped loving her and found nothing much to like. He ground his teeth as they drove slowly around Cadogan Square looking for a parking meter. Sitting beside him, Angela wanted to say that she had made a mistake; she should have chosen the curtain material by herself. She shouldn't be trying to draw him closer to her by making him take part in her decorating schemes. She had realized how foolish this was when Ellie and Ben Cantalupo had come over for dinner and discussed her plan to put French windows in the dining-room. Ben had given the Victorian mouldings a pained look. 'Quite frankly, this room will be *nothing* unless you do something about the skirting,' he announced in his definite way. Davy had ground his teeth, just as he was doing now, making an insistent gnawing sound that Angela hated, and changed the subject to the redevelopment of the South Bank for which Ben's architectural practice had submitted a proposal.

What would Ben do about the derelicts, Davy wanted to know, his tone rather belligerent for such a good-tempered man. What could be done about those sad wasted lives spent in the shadows of seeping concrete walkways? Changing the South Bank from the terrifying and squalid place it was seemed to him beyond design, more a question of changing society.

Ben Cantalupo had smiled smugly over the rim of his wineglass. 'You'll see. You'll be surprised at what architecture can achieve,' he said.

'All the same,' Davy said, more amiably, 'a bit like putting lipstick on a corpse.'

Angela, in the kitchen, getting the vanilla soufflé out of the oven, overheard, and felt certain that, in his heart of hearts, Davy wasn't referring to a building scheme but to her futile strategies to revive their sinking marriage. Blinded by tears, she knocked her arm against the oven door, burning it quite badly. When she appeared with an angry red lozenge on her tanned forearm, Davy thought, What's up with Angela? It's unlike her to be so clumsy, she always moves about with such an easy certain grace. Angela assured everyone that her arm didn't hurt and served the soufflé which, unlike the rest of the evening, was a success.

'There's one,' she said, and Davy eased the Audi under a plane tree. They smiled at one another over the small triumph of finding a parking meter on a busy Saturday morning in London, and linked arms as they walked towards Sloane Square.

How easy it is to stop being happy, Angela thought, keeping step with Davy. How easy to stop making love. Once you got out of the habit you stayed out of it; that's something I would never have thought possible. She felt so exhausted that she now went to bed earlier than Davy did and was fitfully and unhappily asleep by the time he came upstairs. He didn't wake her up, didn't make love to her, didn't watch over her until he knew that she had gone back to sleep. That was all over. No wonder she was tired; there was nothing more draining than putting on an act, which she now did all the time. Everything was an act, even her own forbearance; especially that. She felt that every morning carried an unbearable burden for them both.

She squeezed Davy's arm and said chirpily, 'Isn't this exciting? I've got my eye on a dark terracotta linen, picking up the colour of the bricks outside. What do you think of that as an idea?'

'Anything you want, angel,' Davy said, and then added unkindly, 'it's all the same to me.'

At Peter Jones, he paid for everything they bought and folded the receipts carefully in his wallet. In the event of a divorce it would be important to establish who had paid for what when splitting up the household goods. Davy hated himself for acting so shabbily, but he didn't know how long he could bear to go on living with this new detestable Angela, who swung between a jarring effusiveness and a soggy resignation which was equally jarring. He could see a time coming when he would have to tell her that he was leaving her for Georgie Welliver. Angela would get over it. Nora and Orly would rally round. Ted would help her out financially and all those people who'd leaned on her shoulder so often that they'd probably left a dent in it – Jared Dauman and Lavender Peregory to name but two – would have the perfect opportunity to repay Angela for all the selfless and unstinting sympathy she'd squandered on them for years.

As for him, the future held a lifetime of happy landings with Georgie. How he loved her adorable neatness, the way, when she ate an artichoke, she arranged the nibbled leaves in a perfect circle on her plate. Even better was the devoted and serious way she made love to him. In just about everything she did, she made him feel important, *nourished*, because she completely approved of him. His ability was a constant source of pleasure to Georgie – he could tell by the way she listened to him talk about his plans for his company. Because her early life had been blighted by that brute of a father who turned everything he touched to dross, Georgie respected success, whereas Angela, always cherished by prosperous parents, took it for granted.

While Angela was looking at an electric wok in the housewares department, Davy day-dreamed about a lovely thing that Georgie did when they were lying side by side in her cool white bed: she drew up her knees and clasped Davy's penis between her small thin feet. The sensation was exquisite.

'Davy,' Angela asked. 'Do you think we need an electric wok?'

'It's bound to change our lives,' Davy said, reaching for his cheque-book.

'Poor baby,' Lavender said. 'In her pram, in the hall, wearing only her nappy, and the central heating doesn't go on for another fortnight.'

Eliza ignored her. Her baby, Marianne, slept warmly in the sunshine that poured through the hall's great windows, twirling wide bands of airborne dust. It was a perfect day in early autumn. Soft-edged clouds melted in an airy sky above the river which looked sleek and sun-warmed. Outside the kitchen window, where Lavender and Eliza were eating cheese on toast, sated wasps drowsed happily on the ripe figs lying in the grass. Marianne's cheeks had the translucent flush of a rose petal. She had inherited her father, Warner's, deep round head and Eliza hoped she would take after Warner in other ways too rather than the more flamboyant Peregorys, although her own square chin and Ellis's large shapely ears might look distinguished on the boychild that Eliza was determined to produce next.

She had driven over to Hayden to talk to her mother about Simon.

A week ago, when she and Simon were halfway to Hereford to see a demonstration of a new computer system to register milk yields, Simon had suddenly pulled the Range Rover into the side of the road and slumped over the steering-wheel. When he raised his head, his hooded eyes looked puzzled. 'I can't think why, but my head is in quarters,' he said. 'Better drive me home, dear girl, if it's all the same to you.' He gave his head a toss and the movement made him wince with pain.

Since then Eliza had suggested several times that he should see a specialist, but he had refused and Lavender, usually so solicitous where Simon was concerned, had backed him up.

'Daddy had his annual check-up with Dr Kirkland only last month,' she told Eliza now. 'He's just been overdoing it, as always. I made him stay in bed this morning and he's blissfully quiet. Best not to disturb him, I think.'

Eliza thought that her mother's voice sounded cagey and strange, as though she were repeating lines that had been rehearsed earlier. 'I thought Daddy looked deathly ill the other day,' she persevered stolidly.

'Probably a migraine attack,' Lavender said. 'Ellis bought some rather wonderful claret at a wine auction in Bristol and Daddy couldn't resist. I expect that's what it was.' She would rather have had her head torn from her shoulders than tell Eliza the truth: that Simon was suffering from a rare blood disease for which there was no known cure.

This had emerged at his routine medical check-up, after which their family doctor had asked Lavender's advice about the best time to tell Simon that he had, at most, two years to live. Lavender had sat in the familiar surgery, drinking a glass of sherry, thinking about all the other times over the last forty years that she had sat in the same armchair, upholstered in mushroom-coloured plush, listening to Dr Kirkland's soft. rumbling voice confirm what she had expected to be the case: her four pregnancies, a rather troublesome bout of bronchitis, a touch of rheumatism. There had never been much wrong with her or any of the Peregorys with their high-coloured faces and long supple bodies. This was different. Dr Kirkland, who was the same age as Simon and one of his closest friends, was visibly upset, blinking and rubbing his forefinger hard against the bridge of his nose. He put his hand over Lavender's; she gave it a brisk dismissive pat.

'There isn't a best time,' she said. 'If there's really nothing that can be done, we must keep Simon in the dark. In a way I'm quite relieved that chemotherapy isn't the answer. He is so vain about his hair.'

'Won't he wonder why he is starting to tire so easily and gets sudden headaches?' Dr Kirkland asked.

'Simon isn't the speculating type. He will just assume that old age has come as a rude surprise, and I shall convince him that is the case.'

Simon wasn't the speculating type, that was true enough. But Ellis and Eliza were, and Lavender dreaded the day when she would no longer be able to deny that Simon was dying. Both of them badly wanted to inherit Hayden. That each knew the extent of the other's desperate desire made them the more determined. Ellis and Eliza were, had always been, almost morbidly competitive with each other. As children they took part in pony shows only to prevent the other from coming first, cantering around the ring with tense striving faces and usually coming a joint second, the winning rosette awarded to a more equable-looking child who didn't make the judges feel uncomfortable. Grown up, they brought their joyless rivalry to sheepdog trials and fishing competitions – and the tussle over Hayden.

There would be no tussle if only Ellis were to marry. Even Eliza would see the rightness, the convenience of primogeniture: eldest son inheriting from eldest son in uncomplicated sequence. But as things were ... Lavender stifled a sigh and got up to make Eliza some coffee. Disloyally, she much preferred her two younger children,

Anabel and Oliver, who thought their childhood home a nuisance of a place, a chill and lonely castle set in a damp valley. They had shot off to London at the first opportunity and were happily embroiled in city life. On their brief visits to Hayden they complained good-humouredly about Lolly's dreary cooking, the rain, and their parents' uneventful social life. After dinner their mouths cracked into huge yawns, and soon afterwards they went to bed, glad of some restorative early nights before plunging back into their demanding jobs and hectic party-going. They adored Lavender, showing their affection by teasing her mercilessly. How she wished that Oliver and Anabel were with her now, sitting by the kitchen window, talking excitedly about a new play they had seen, a Mexican restaurant they'd discovered, a bakery in Brick Lane where you could go for a bagel and cream cheese at three in the morning. Instead there was Eliza, stirring her coffee in a maddening way and persistently asking questions.

'Mother, have you and Daddy thought about what you want to do about Hayden after, well . . . ?' Delicacy was not in Eliza's nature. Her face reddened and she lowered her knuckly chin in what might have been shame.

This brusque request for forward planning was another reason to keep the truth about Simon's headaches from Eliza. Planning was something Lavender couldn't think about at the moment. Coasting along each day took all her strength.

'I think you'll find that your father knows what he's about, and there's no particular hurry,' she lied crisply, taking advantage of Eliza's discomfort. To Lavender's relief, Marianne woke up and began to cry eloquently. Reluctantly, since she hadn't managed to find out what she wanted to know, which was, in view of her marriage to a competent and successful farmer, her proven fertility, her impressive qualifications in estate management, was she going to inherit Hayden, Eliza snapped Marianne into a pink Babygro and drove home.

*   *   *

Davy parked the car, flipped his raincoat over his shoulder and ran down the street past houses that swirled around a crescent. In the hazy early-evening rain, the houses looked made of smoke. Up the ninety-nine stairs and into Georgie's orderly flat. He held her high above his head and she stretched out her legs like a dancer. He lowered her gently to the ground.

'Happy landings.'

'Happy landings.'

'Here's a rather odd thing,' Georgie said, waving a letter at him. 'Ellis Peregory has invited me to Hayden, even though Jared is in China, so there's really no need to put on his usual charade. What can he be up to?'

'Must we always assume that Ellis is up to something?'

'Most definitely.'

Angela would have said the same, Davy realized. Maybe part of Ellis's problem with women, and there certainly was a problem, was that he hadn't developed the knack of getting them to trust him.

'Ellis doesn't have your gift for spontaneity,' Georgie said, 'so this invitation is part of some master plan. I'll accept though. He's just bought a new hunter which I'd like to ride.'

Davy suddenly realized the point of the invitation. Ellis must have twigged that Simon was dying; parading Georgie at Hayden was part of his bid for the inheritance. Some hopes, Davy thought. Georgie was the most straightforward person in the world; she'd never participate in Ellis's charades, as she called them. What an arrogant bastard Ellis Peregory was. That he should think that Georgie would throw in her career, her London flat and Davy himself (although Ellis wasn't to know how happy Georgie was with him) to moulder away in the country, which she had been only too glad to escape. Wait until he told Angela about Ellis's blundering attempts at courtship, although, of course, he couldn't, not without revealing that he'd been seeing Georgie.

An hour later, Georgie said, 'You are totally unabashed by excess, Davy.'

Davy murmured against her shoulder, 'I just like to complete the full programme once I start.'

He could have stayed in her bed for ever, feeling Georgie's cool flesh on his fingertips, listening to the roar of hungry lions sift through the treetops outside the window.

'I must go, my darling Georgie,' he whispered. But Georgie, sated with sex, was already asleep.

When he came home, Nora, who was staying in London for a few days, thought he looked worn out and disordered by the punishing hours he worked. She didn't like the look of Angela either. She had put herself together in a way that was flawlessly statuesque; her hair was piled into a French pleat and she was wearing a sharply cut cream suit and high-heeled shoes, far too smart for taking the children to school and making tea for the builders. She was smiling too much, showing all her magnificent teeth, but the skin under her blue eyes drooped. Nora was greatly troubled by this. She wondered if Angela were having an affair, but dismissed this notion at once. Angela would never do anything messy; that was her great strength and also what made her rather an annoying person at times. Nora sometimes felt that her elder daughter delighted in secret and delicious feelings of superiority. Perhaps it was just that the builders were getting her down. They were a gang of South Londoners who played Radio One very loudly and forgot to flush the lavatory. She was about to suggest that they all go back to Rottingdean with her for the weekend when Lavender Peregory telephoned, inviting them to Hayden.

'Nora too, of course,' she said, when Angela explained that her mother was staying with them, 'and those delicious little girls. The more the merrier. Ellis has invited that strange young woman, Georgie Welliver. To tell the truth, I find her very hard going. She's so tense and withheld, I'm frightened she's going to suddenly pounce and strip me to the bone. Do come. The salvia *guaranitica* is bluer than blue can possibly be and Simon and I can do with a dose of the Stearns's tearing high spirits.'

Nora, guessing the gist of the conversation from Angela's soothing murmurs, nodded her head enthusiastically and Davy shrugged acceptance, making Angela feel clouded and betrayed. She swallowed hard and told Lavender that they would all love to come.

How could she survive this? Staying in the same house as Georgie was unthinkable. Her shoulders sagged defeatedly inside her new jacket which Davy hadn't even noticed. She felt quite leaden, and looking at Davy's stubbly grey cheeks, didn't think that his spirits were at their highest either. She wondered what he and Georgie found to talk about; that it might be her own shortcomings gnawed at her heart. Angela beamed at Maud and Elsie who had crowded onto Davy's lap, Elsie winding her hair and sucking the two middle fingers of her right hand; Maud, sensing that it was bedtime, eating an apple in tiny nibbles to make it last. 'We're all going to Hayden,' Angela said. 'Won't that be bags of fun?'

They were shocked at the change in Simon. He walked slowly out of the house, calling hoarsely to the dogs who were leaping at Davy's car in a frenzy of welcome. Simon shielded his eyes from the harsh sunlight – an old man's gesture – and when he lowered his hand to kiss Angela's cheek, she saw that his eyes had dimmed and his neck grown weak, softening into wattles.

He held out his hands to Elsie and Maud, who were particular favourites of his. 'I hope we can count on you for a bit of boisterous company, my dear old chaps,' he said. 'This place is quiet as a tomb, you might say. Quiet as a tomb. Do you chaps want to come along with me to feed the pony?'

He went off with the two little girls bobbing beside him, clutching the sides of his jacket. His soldier's stride, arbitrary and efficient, had become a tremulous shuffle; his feet were cautiously splayed. Watching him, Angela and Davy instinctively moved closer together. Tears glistened in Angela's eyes. She knew that for Simon's sake they would rise to the occasion, put on a performance as the amusing, high-spirited Stearns. It was the least they could do to ease Simon's way along the terrifying path towards death. Angela leaned into Davy's chest and he put his arm around her and stroked her shoulder. Nora, noticing, thought that nothing seemed to be wrong between them after all; they were getting on perfectly well.

Deception is hard work, Davy thought, as they sat around the dinner table eating tough braised partridge and unidentifiable cubed vegetables. Simon knows he's dying but is keeping it a secret from Lavender, who is keeping it a secret from him. Ellis and Eliza know something's up, but the rules of the game require them not to notice Simon's shaking hands and that terrible rattly sound he makes when he breathes. How tragic it all is, but what a farce.

Their eyes averted from the difficulty Simon was having raising his fork to his lips, they made strained conversation. Angela, in a ridiculously over-animated way, described the new unfitted kitchen she was installing in Fulham and Eliza hooted that it was all right for some, but people who lived in the country thought that the country look was a bit poncey. She was in a particularly graceless mood, her eyes flicking about in a suspicious way, especially when they rested on Ellis.

Suddenly Georgie leaned over the table, and taking Simon's knife and fork out of his weak grasp, cut a slice of meat that he was having trouble with into neat squares. Red blotches sprang up on Lavender's neck, but Simon gave Georgie a grateful smile. She smiled back at him, the corners of her mouth curving in that way which made Davy's heart kick against his chest.

Embarrassment made them reckless. By the time Tom Ward brought in the trifle, topped with glacé cherries seeping into packet custard, everyone, except Georgie, had drunk too much and was talking in a boozy, mindless way.

Ellis, who was as secretive about his love of farming as about everything else in his life, was telling Georgie about the sheep he bred and how he could tell where they had been grazing by the colour of their fleeces. Georgie listened to him attentively, her head tilted to one side. This put Davy in a state of such maniacal jealousy that he wanted to smash in Ellis's clever narrow head, right between his flaring ears. Instead he threw himself into a discussion about European monetary union with Warner Jones, a sensible chap who deserved better than his strident wife.

Lavender, anxious that Ellis might be making a fool of himself, led them rather unsteadily into the drawing-room. 'Won't you play the piano for us, Davy?' she wheedled. 'Oh do.'

Davy's parents had insisted that he had piano lessons and, before he could master the simplest scales, had bought a mahogany upright which his mother polished with Min once a day. The lessons didn't last long since Davy refused to practise 'Dolly's Funeral' and 'Au Clair de la Lune', but, before they stopped, he had discovered that he could play by ear. He would stretch his fingers over the keys of the upright and imagine that it was a concert grand and that he was George Shearing, Noel Coward, Elton John. As he passed from his teens into his twenties, he realized that this gift he had for being able to produce any popular song he happened to hear was as attractive to women as his long grey eyes and dark curly hair. He had ensnared more than one girl by hunching over a piano stool and singing Kurt Weill's 'It Never Was You' in his velvety baritone. Years later, he knew he had a chance with Angela Dimont, even though, at the time, she was being pursued by a personable barrister who was the younger son of a duke – a pursuit encouraged by Jared Dauman – when, at a party in Eaton Square, she walked gracefully towards the piano while Davy was playing 'Honeysuckle Rose' and beat time on his shoulder.

'Oh do, Davy,' Eliza joined in. 'And Georgie, you can sing whatever it was you were singing to Marianne this morning. It put her to sleep like a dream.'

Lavender realized at that moment that her daughter must dislike Georgie very much to push her into the limelight like this. She foresaw trouble ahead. Georgie was half hidden in the deep-sided fireside chair. Ellis had pulled up another chair beside it, but they didn't seem to be having any kind of conversation. Nora, sipping her coffee, thought that Ellis and Georgie were well matched in their creepy self-containment. Both seemed wrapped in an intense impenetrable privacy. An odd pair.

To everyone's surprise, Georgie moved rapidly towards the piano. 'The song's called "I Know Where I'm Going",' she announced and hummed a few bars so that Davy could pick out the tune. Then she started to sing in a warm rich voice; a voice you wouldn't expect from such a small and slightly built woman:

> I know where I'm going
> And I know who's going with me.
> I know who I love
> But the devil knows who I'll marry

she sang. Angela had no doubt that the words were directed at her. What chance did she have against those flinty grey eyes, that determinedly tilted chin? She had no idea where she was going or who was going with her. She had no weapons to deploy against Georgie Welliver, who seemed to have stolen her husband by being so resolutely uncharming; her refusal to charm making her irresistibly appealing to Davy in a way that Angela could not fathom. It must take courage never to be pleasing or accommodating; perhaps it was this defiant bravery that left Davy weak-kneed. Georgie finished singing and Angela applauded hard, the bracelet which had been changed for the smaller one brought back from New York clanking on her arm, her face radiant. At least I'm going down with a smile, she thought.

CHAPTER FIVE

Even in the narrow streets known as The Lanes, several yards behind Brighton's sea front, the air smelled strongly of suntan oil and brine. It was the end of September but the weather had settled into a blazing Indian summer. Sunbathers stretched out on the shingled beaches, their stomachs tanned and leathery from the weeks of unbroken heatwave.

'Just look at those library steps, aren't they ravishing,' Orly said, and she and Angela went inside an antique shop that was pitch-dark to their sun-dazzled eyes. The mahogany library steps had two slant-eyed lions as supports; sitting on their haunches, their flowing manes indicated by beautifully carved scoopings in the wood. Orly began to make arrangements to have them delivered to Harley Street.

Angela picked up something that was glittering sharply in the window. It was a heart-shaped Victorian pincushion, a Valentine made of horsehair covered over with faded plush, in which glass beads threaded onto pins were arranged in formal patterns. In the centre a fraying scrap of silk carried the embroidered words: 'Your love my happiness – evermore.' Orly, putting away her credit card, saw Angela's shoulders heave. She marched her into the sunlight. 'We are going to have a drink on the terrace of the Metropole, and you are going to tell me what all this is about,' she ordered.

'Well that's the game,' Angela said, when she had finished. 'What do you think I should do? Tell him that I know? Try to lure him back by wiggling about in that transparent nightie Evelyn gave me? Pack my bags and go home to mother?' She couldn't go on with this ridiculous performance. Slumping over the wrought-iron table, she gave in to great shuddering sobs. 'We're still sharing the same sheets and towels,' she wailed; 'that's what's breaking my heart.'

Orly kicked off her shoe and jiggled her foot up and down. She looked at the subtle lustre of Angela's hair, the tears drying on her wide golden cheeks. She remembered how persistently Davy had pursued her, his persistence causing the well-born barrister and several other men besotted by Angela's beauty and sweetness to melt away into oblivion. Orly's experience of men had taught her that for most of them, like Davy, pursuit was the better part of love. She scowled into her glass of Kir Royale. 'This isn't about *you*, Ange,' she said. 'That's another heartbreaking thing you have to realize; for the time being you're just a sideshow. This is all about Georgie Welliver. She sounds like a pissy little bitch to me; I can't see it lasting. Only don't confront Davy with anything; no outrage, no injured innocence – that could push him into her skinny little arms.'

'I can hardly make a scene,' Angela said; 'half the time I don't even know where he is.'

'Could I move in with you as soon as Elsie's taken her Grade One ballet exam?' Davy asked Georgie. 'We're all a bit at fever pitch until then.' He was trying to keep his voice steady but the words fluttered in his mouth; he was so excited at the thought of his new life waiting just around the next corner.

Georgie pulled an electronic personal organizer out of her shoulder-bag. She pressed some buttons which gave off restrained beeps, then nodded her head. 'Excellent timing.' She took Davy's hand and pressed it against her cheek. Love fizzed up like champagne and filled her heart.

They were walking beside a canal in Bruges. Georgie was paying for this excursion. She had just been awarded a performance-related bonus and was giving Davy a treat: three days in a magical city with a lingering kiss at every stone bridge, delicious dinners at Le Duc de Burgoyne, devoted lovemaking in a bedroom at L'Orangerie, while the glittering river outside their window shot spangles of light onto the ceiling. The trip had been easy to arrange. Davy was supposed to be at a trade fair in Amsterdam and had spent two days there, drinking too many beers with suppliers, cracking jokes, playing the piano in the bar, closing deals at breakfast when they had all been hung-over. Then he had hired a car and driven to Bruges where his lover waited for him: a small woman with limp straight hair and a heart that was getting wilder every minute.

Hand in hand, they watched a procession of nuns in grey habits and glazed winged head-dresses cross a meadow in front of their convent, the grass quivering brightly at their feet. The austere beauty of their progress reminded Davy of Georgie's flat. He was very much looking forward to arranging his shirts on the orderly shelves of her built-in wardrobes and hearing the muted roar of lions as he lay, stretched out, on her cool starched sheets in a bedroom that was as unadorned as a nun's cell.

There was something deceptively nun-like about Georgie herself. Today her hair was tied back with a narrow blue ribbon and she was wearing a long stone-coloured tunic that hardly grazed her body. No make-up, no scent, no jewellery, not a sign of sexual availability. Not many men would have guessed at the erotic writhings Georgie was capable of, or the ardour that she kept hidden under her unbecoming clothes. Not many men, but he had. Davy congratulated himself for his shrewd instincts. He thought of the way that Georgie flung kisses on his thighs, of the rich silence of their two bodies after sex. Georgie brought him joy from the deepest recesses of her spirit. Before he met her, his life had been unsweetened. Georgie gave a slight shiver and he took off his jacket and wrapped it around her shoulders, and wrapped her cold hands in his.

'Come on, troops,' Nora said. 'It's hot enough for a picnic on the beach.' She tied the straps of Maud's smocked sun-dress into bows and flicked the ends. She had sent Orly off to The Lanes with Angela with strict instructions to find out what the problem was. Angela had been acting in a brittle, breezy way for weeks. Ted had behaved in the same ghastly manner just before he'd finally decided to leave home. At a time when talking might have saved their marriage Ted had retreated behind jovial banter and silly jokes. Because he hadn't *wanted* to talk, Nora could see that now. With a stubbornness that was practically insane, he had claimed the right to make what might turn out to be the worst mistake of his life with no prior discussion. Now here was Angela displaying the same foolishness – you simply couldn't get near her these days – and Nora wasn't going to stand by for a second time in embarrassed terrified silence, full of foreboding, watching someone she loved falsely sparkling while some terrible secret was festering away inside.

'I never thought I'd hear myself saying this,' Nora admitted to Orly, 'but I rather wish Jared were around. I can tell you this, his complete lack of emotional restraint would clear the air in no time. Anyway, do what you can; it's all too silly.'

The little girls ran down to the beach, their sandalled feet making chirring sounds on the shingle. At the end of the breakwater, waves pleated themselves neatly on the shore. Nora unfolded a canvas chair and sat in it for a moment to feel the sun on her eyelids, before setting out the cold sausages, plastic-wrapped squares of cheese and the seeded grapes that Maud called spitty fruit. She closed her eyes.

'Grandmother's asleep,' Elsie said. 'Don't make a noise.'

'I'm going *up* on the wall, *up* on the wall, *up* on the wall,' Maud sang.

'We're not allowed,' Elsie said primly.

Maud had been teasing, but Elsie looked so shocked that she wanted to give her something to be shocked about. She climbed up on the breakwater and ran towards the sea, wheeling her arms from side to side. Far out, the waves had a jellied look and were moving slowly towards the beach. Elsie, giving a responsible sigh, clambered up after Maud to bring her back before Nora woke up. She was almost within touching distance of Maud's wheeling arms when she tripped over the trailing strap of her sandal. She thudded onto the sharp stones and was perfectly still.

The receptionist at the hotel in Amsterdam where Davy was supposed to be staying said that he had checked out three days ago. Orly put the receiver down thoughtfully, deliberated for a moment, and then rang Joyce Arledge.

'Elsie is in a coma,' she said. 'Wherever he is, please get him back.'

In the hospital Angela watched green lines wiggle across terminals, proving that Elsie was still breathing.

'Davy's on some junket on a boat on the canals; the hotel is tracking him down. He'll be here soon,' Orly lied.

Joyce Arledge had believed Davy when he'd rung her, supposedly from Amsterdam, and said that his mobile phone was on the blink. He'd rung her a few times since then, but she hadn't thought to ask him where from. There had not been a lunchtime liaison for some time. Davy quite often worked right through the lunch-hour, eating sandwiches bought by Joyce from an excellent sandwich bar: avocado and crispy bacon on stoneground bread, goat's cheese and sundried tomato paste on ciabatta, far superior to the soggy wedge-shaped stuff he used to buy from the corner newsagent on his way back from a lunchless lunchtime. Joyce made Davy fresh coffee too, to demonstrate how much she approved of the new leaf he had turned over.

At his desk all day, Davy left the office earlier; five-thirty or six o'clock at the latest. Joyce thought how pleased Angela and the children must be to see him home so soon. In her imagination, Angela ran to the front door as soon as she heard the arrival of Davy's car; she tilted back her long full throat and Davy pressed a kiss on it with his warm lips. How wrong she had been. Davy had merely shifted the time he set aside for adultery; *le cinq à sept*, Joyce believed they called it in France. And now, he'd extended it as well – he'd taken some tarty piece abroad with him.

Feeling colder and wiser, Joyce rang the international car-hire firm where Davy had an account. Bruges. She leafed through *The Good Hotel Guide* on the shelf above her desk and thought that L'Orangerie sounded the most romantic. When she was put through to Davy's room, a woman with a quiet but commanding voice answered the telephone.

'I've booked you a flight from Brussels leaving this evening,' Joyce said to Davy, 'and there'll be someone at the airport to drive you to Brighton General.'

'Thanks a million, Joyce,' Davy mumbled.

'One more thing. I'm resigning.'

'I see.'

'If I had any guts, I'd stay long enough to kick your balls into the middle of next week.'

'Goodbye Joyce.'

'Goodbye Davy.'

Shoes squeaked down a corridor and Davy was in the room. Relief flooded through Angela's tired brain. Now Davy could take over and be her voice in the harsh world. In his Armani suit, even though it was crumpled from the flight, he looked like a man who insisted on being fed on facts. The doctors who had offered her nothing but smarmy and vague reassurances would tell him at once what they had refused to tell her, which was whether Elsie was going to die.

Davy walked over to the bed and stroked the cool softness of Elsie's hair. He spoke to his wife across the webs of plastic tubing and flickering monitors.

'How are you?' he asked gently.

'Sort of riding on the waves of a nightmare. I'm pleased you're here.'

'I'm sorry,' he said, and meeting her blue gaze, realized that she knew exactly what he was sorry about.

'Time and forgiveness are on your side,' Angela said wearily and, although Elsie lay between them, almost lifeless, Davy felt riled by her uplifting tone. His eyes darkened with anger and shame.

Angela said, 'Maud has to go back to school. Can you take her to London tomorrow? Mummy's in a bad way. She wants to stay at the hospital all the time, but she'd be more use going to London with you so that she can look after Maudie in the afternoons.'

'It's OK. Let Nora be wherever she wants to be – it's important for her. I can look after Maud; I'll work from home.'

He thought Angela looked as though she had been bleached, all her creamy beauty dulled to a livid pallor. He stood up. 'I'm going to find a doctor who knows what he's talking about and then I'm going to get some sleeping pills for you and send you back to Nora's to get some sleep. I'll stay here for the rest of the night.'

'Yes, I'd like you to. Just in case she wakes up. All her favourite story-books are in that locker. I read them to her all the time; I know she's listening.'

As Angela drove back to Rottingdean where Nora would be waiting up for her, her face lined and stiff with guilt and anxiety, it crossed her mind that as long as Elsie remained unconscious, Davy wouldn't leave home. That she could think in those terms made her feel sick with disgust at herself.

Davy fumbled in the locker for a book and pulled out *The Mouse and His Child* by Russell Hoban, a harrowing story of a motherless clockwork mouse and his troubled father, joined together in perpetual clockwork motion, threatened by terrors. It was nearly two hundred pages long and he read all of it into Elsie's ear, sometimes stopping to put a hand on her cheek which had a frightening waxy glow. When he had finished, he took out the other books: *The Avocado Baby*, *Peter Pan*, *The Little Bear* series; stories, it seemed to him, that pleaded for the indissolubleness of family life.

He wondered how much his grave-eyed child had noticed about her parents' marriage, the way it had crashed and flowed and come near to crashing again, broken by the dead weight of silence between them. He should have watched over Elsie. Angela, in her kind easy way, would forgive him for his neglect; he might not forgive himself.

After that the days seemed to float away from him. He drove Maud to school and came back to a silent house – the builders had left, the new terracotta curtains hung from heavy cast-iron poles, muffling the noise in the street – to make himself a cup of coffee and get down to work. But he couldn't. Before he had finished his coffee, he would walk heavily up the stairs to Elsie's bedroom, pick up a piece of doll's-house furniture and carefully replace it, brush the felt of her royal-blue school hat, a hideous pudding-basin with a narrow upturned brim. Always, at the sight of the tiny white leotard hanging in her wardrobe, he felt a chill at the end of his lips. Whatever happened he could never leave. The pair of pink ballet shoes waiting for Elsie's square little feet would haunt him always.

Halfway through the week Maud demanded to spend the night with her best friend, Zoe – Zoe's mother was going to take them to Ed's Easy Diner for supper. That same evening, Davy drove to Hanover Terrace.

He reached into his pocket for the key to Georgie's flat, then changed his mind and rang the doorbell instead. He had meant to tell her at once that it must be over between them; that it was dangerous to love someone so much that nobody else mattered, not even your children; that, if Elsie died, he could not abandon Angela and Maud and, if she recovered, he thought he would find it impossible to let her out of his sight again. He had meant to tell Georgie all these things, but his lips bent to hers and they moved dreamily towards her cool white bed. He kissed her fingernails one by one. He kissed her small breasts as though they were two gravestones. He gripped her so hard in his arms that her bones shifted under her skin.

As he moved away from her, moonlight streamed through the window. In its blue gleam, Georgie's naked body seemed made of stone. He told her then, as miserable as he had ever been in his life, banging his fist into his palm to keep himself from weeping. When he had finished, she raged at him until she lost the sense of her own words. At last she pulled at her hair with both hands and screamed at him in a terrible desolate voice, 'Is there no place on earth for me?' As Davy moved towards her, she shrank from his touch, grey eyes like flints, and almost hissed, 'I hope love kills you one day.' He pulled open the door and ran down the ninety-nine stairs to the street, tears streaming down his face.

Georgie washed her face and dried it on a stiff white towel. She took the sheets and pillowcases off the bed, carried them down the ninety-nine stairs and stuffed them into one of the dustbins at the side of the house. She thought that Davy had lied to her; that the reason he had changed his mind about coming to live with her was not because of Elsie's accident but because he had found her love too strong in the end. She would not make that mistake again: loving a man more than he required to be loved. She had just been another of Davy's indiscriminate enthusiasms after all, of no more importance to him than Chicky Smeaton, and all the other Chicky Smeatons that

Davy had amused himself with for a time. It seemed impossible that anyone else would ever love her now; when your luck had run right out it would never come back. Gomer had known that; it was what had driven him mad. The best plan was to do something that would cause the most unhappiness to the person who had harmed you, and Georgie intended to do that. As she slipped a laundered pillowcase, glinting with starch, over the pillow that was still dented by Davy's head, she felt a sudden raw absence. Then her love for Davy turned into a steady loathing. She climbed between the clean sheets and immediately fell asleep.

A casserole had been left on the doorstep by the couple next door, who Davy scarcely knew. The note attached to it read, 'Give Angela our love. Hope you like goulash. With best wishes from Richard and Susan.' It had been like this all week. One neighbour had come in and filled the fridge, another had offered to take Maud to school and bring her back home every day. The answering-machine spoke in voices that Davy didn't recognize, who insisted on their deep affection for Angela. Anything, anything at all, the voices said; they would do anything for Angela Stearns who had, it seemed, at one time or another, practically saved their lives. The last message was from Jared, 'Angel, Ellis sent me a fax. Chin up; your special kind of girlfriend is on his way back. Lots of hugs. Bye.'

One evening in the spring, lifetimes ago, Davy, irritated by having to listen to Angela comforting some whiny acquaintance who had telephoned, inconsiderately, in the middle of dinner, had complained, 'I wish you'd cut this stuff out, being a long-suffering ear to half the country. What are you trying to do, bankrupt the Samaritans by putting them out of business?'

Angela had looked at him out of her clear blue eyes and asked, quite simply, 'What has one to give but oneself?'

Davy had longed to shout, 'But you give *me* nothing, not even in bed. You just accept being made love to, quite pleased about it, but giving *me* a good time is the last thing on your mind.'

He had started his affair with Georgie Welliver by then and had learned what responsiveness was. And because he was being unfaithful to Angela he didn't feel in a position to criticize her. They had finished dinner talking about other things.

Angela's past kindnesses, whatever they were, were being repaid. All her hangers-on were praying for Elsie's recovery. If the prayers of a load of self-pitying, self-obsessed emotionally retarded, pretentious clowns meant anything at all, Elsie would be capering about in her white leotard in no time. Davy put the casserole in the fridge beside several others which Maud had refused to eat, and waited for Angela's nightly call.

It was Maud who kept Nora going. She was a robust, straightforward child who threw her shoulders back and looked straight ahead when she spoke. Having been told that Elsie was in hospital so that the doctors could make her better, she put the matter out of her mind and looked to Nora to provide weekend treats, while Davy and Angela stayed at Elsie's bedside.

Maud had to be provided with fish fingers and French toast, rides on the open top of the cream double-decker buses that trundled along the sea front between Brighton and Rottingdean, hair ribbons and ice-lollies. Maud must be allowed to wiggle her hand out of Nora's clutching one and skip along the pink-paved promenade by herself. Maud had the right to an uncomplicated life – all children had this right – and so Nora must present herself as an uncomplicated woman, rather than one who lived in torment that Elsie might die and that it would be her fault if she did. She let Maud tip purple bubble bath from a Mickey Mouse-shaped bottle into her bath and then stay in the water, playing with the suds that made crispy little explosions, until the skin on her fingers was white and crinkled.

'Out now, Mademoiselle Maudie,' Nora ordered brightly, and

Maud launched herself into the big white bath towel that used to be Ted's.

'Yeuch. Yuck. It's all scritchy-scratchy,' she said. 'What's for supper, grandma?'

'Chicken Tonight,' Nora said and laughed as Maud stomped around the bathroom with elbows bent, flapping her arms, imitating the Chicken Tonight commercials she had seen on television. 'It's not as nice as your mummy's casseroles,' Nora said loyally.

Maud shook her head. 'It must be, it's on television,' she said.

Evelyn turned up at the hospital carrying a Tower Records carrier bag full of tapes of ballet music. Like everyone else in Brighton, she had spent too long in the sun and her bright hair looked rusted, almost burned. Her eyes swept over Angela's and Davy's exhausted faces and tight mouths and Elsie lying between them, as perfect and lifeless as a doll. Evelyn clicked a cassette into the mouth of a neat recorder that swung from a cord on her wrist.

'The Dance of the Sugar Plum Fairy' filled the room, relentlessly bouncy. For the last three Christmases, Davy and Angela had taken their daughters to a matinée of *The Nutcracker Suite*, the children's favourite ballet and their own least favourite; they both thought it bland and banal. Last Christmas, Elsie and Maud had worn very dark crimson taffeta dresses with crocheted lace collars to go to the ballet at the Royal Opera House. They had had supper afterwards at Le Palais du Jardin in Long Acre, where an attentive French waiter had put a cushion on Maud's chair and spread a napkin on Elsie's crimson lap with great solemnity. A painted carousel had been flashing gilded circles in the Piazza, Christmas shoppers had streamed out of Crabtree & Evelyn and the Body Shop. The bright cold streets of Covent Garden had smelled of beer and fried onions and the faint tang of urine. It had been a perfect day.

Angela put her head on the flat pillow. 'Listen, Else,' she said. 'It's *The Nutcracker*.' As Tchaikovsky's music played over them, she began to tell the story of Clara and her mysterious godfather, Drosselmeier, the Nutcracker prince and The Land of Sweets. At some point, Davy walked around the bed and stood beside his wife, rubbing her back. Angela had almost reached the end of the story when a soft blowing sound came from Elsie's lips and she opened her eyes.

'I thought that might work,' Evelyn said. 'I read about it in the *Daily Mail*. Wotcha, gorgeous,' she said to Elsie. 'Hup-ya-bum.'

'Hup-ya-bum,' Elsie said drowsily and moved her hand slowly over the coverlet until she found Davy's.

CHAPTER SIX

To CELEBRATE ELSIE'S RECOVERY, DAVY Stearns took his wife Angela to the River Café for dinner. Autumn had arrived at last, with sharp winds and needling rains that left the trees dripping. They walked through streets of cold stiff houses towards the river.

The restaurant's bright lights streamed enticingly on to the ugly riverside terraces; they ducked through its glass doors and gratefully let themselves be led towards a table alongside the steel counter that stretched like a shiny ribbon along the length of the room. In front of them, on the white wall, the face of a clock was projected, its hands urgently moving their lives onwards.

They were in the mood for something sustaining: polenta, two kinds of pasta, braised fennel and a dark heavy red wine that made their blood throb warmly in their veins. The good food softened them; they relaxed their shoulders and leaned back in their chairs as their wineglasses were refilled. The black shadows at the corners of Davy's mouth were smoothed away by the lively clattering sounds coming from the kitchen, the musky taste of the wine at the back of his throat, his wife's shining hair. This feeling of having come safely into a harbour brought with it a sudden desire to explain why he had done what he'd done: his sense of exclusion from Angela's radiant sympathy, the feeling that he was stranded on the margin of a life which held her at its centre. He wanted to tell her that when Georgie Welliver had picked up one of the hideous umbrellas emblazoned with the stars that symbolized the member states of the EC and exclaimed, 'You mean they're paying you ten quid a pop for these? I'm impressed,' he had felt that he was someone who mattered. He put down his fork and cleared his throat.

Angela said quickly, 'So how are things at work? It must be difficult without Joyce.' She felt that if she didn't distract him, he would start to tell her about Georgie Welliver, and she wouldn't be able to bear that, not yet.

'We muddle along,' Davy said. 'Export orders are holding up well.' He described the recent visit of some Japanese car manufacturers to his office – they had been impressed by a combined key-ring and personal alarm – but saw by Angela's exaggeratedly wide-open eyes that she was already thinking about something else.

I wonder what Georgie was like in bed, Angela thought. She's such a scrappy little thing, everything about her thin and meagre. That time when she'd been out riding in the rain, her hair clumped itself into wet triangles, the way a cat's fur does. That's what she looked like: a mangy little cat. Angela faced the rotten truth: she would have been more understanding if Davy had fallen for a cut-price siren like Evelyn. If he had, it would have been quite easy to have bestowed upon him the lofty forgiveness of a superior woman. That she was finding it so hard to forgive him worried Angela; it put her on the same level as everyone else. She saw that Davy was looking at her in a rather chastened way and she gave him one of her most reassuring smiles.

'No hard feelings?' Davy murmured.

Angela bridled, in spite of herself. 'Yes, lots, actually,' she snapped.

It was exactly the right thing to say. Davy laughed, holding up his hands in mock surrender. There wasn't going to be a scene; they would be able to enjoy their pudding.

They strolled homewards beside the dark river. On its muddy bank, supermarket trolleys pitched over the wall by the neighbourhood vandals, had arranged themselves into a tangled heap which glinted in the light of the moon.

In their bedroom, Angela threw off her dressing-gown dramatically, as though it were a magic cloak that had kept her invisible. 'Da-da,' she said, flipping it over a chair. She was wearing Evelyn's birthday present: the transparent flesh-coloured nightdress, edged with black lace. Its chiffon folds clung to her thighs and pressed against her breasts; her creamy shoulders gleamed above lacy frills. Davy looked at her in utter amazement before they both collapsed in helpless giggles. It was not too late; they were not too far gone in mutual dislike. Davy slid his hands under the lace edging and Angela parted her thighs. Afterwards they smiled at each other, sweat cooling against their spines. He stayed awake until she fell asleep, and for a long time after that.

Ellis Peregory drove into Newport to meet Georgie Welliver off the London train. It was a relief to ease the Land Rover over the cattle-grid that marked the end of Hayden's drive, and to be alone on the country roads on a calm and golden October day.

Dr Kirkland was at the house, his second visit in two days, prescribing medicines for what Simon insisted was a touch of flu. The skin on Simon's face was as thin as paper, with a strange ghostly shine to it, and there were sores around his lips. There was something seriously wrong with him; Ellis knew this and so, apparently, did Eliza. She was there now, demanding that Simon be sent off for blood tests and X-rays and what have you, and thoroughly upsetting Lavender. Ellis didn't know what the deuce Eliza was playing at. She wanted to inherit Hayden as much as he did, in which case it would be to her advantage if Simon didn't get better and died while Ellis was still unmarried, a bad state to be in as far as Simon was concerned. Perhaps Eliza wasn't as tough as she liked to make out. He, on the other hand, was more brutal than he let on. While he reassured Lavender that Simon seemed over the worst – weasely words of comfort that neither of them believed but which touched Lavender as Ellis had intended that they should – while he listened to reports on livestock prices on *Farming Today*, sitting companionably on the edge of Simon's bed and noticing how his father's wasted legs hardly mounded the blankets that covered them, Ellis was making plans.

He had almost decided to marry Georgie Welliver. She was an undemanding sort of girl, the opposite of clingy; the kind he would be able to leave to get on with her own life, while he got on with his. Ellis parked the Land Rover and walked onto the station platform.

A young woman stepped out of a compartment at the far end of the train. She had pale blond hair, expensively cut, and was wearing a cream wool coat, as closely fitted to her body as a riding jacket. A silk scarf, bright with scrolls and swirls, had been settled over one shoulder of the coat, just so. The woman carried a small suitcase and a soft Italian bag on a strap. The woman, Ellis realized as she came nearer, was Georgie, her hair subtly lightened, its full layers contriving to make her face look smaller, and more kittenish.

Ellis was displeased by these efforts at elegance. One of Georgie's attractions had been her indifference to her own appearance; a rare quality in a woman and one that hinted at a refreshing refusal to play by the rules. There was surely something rather striving about her new hairstyle, even a longing for approval. Ellis gave Georgie's cheeks two dry little pecks and took her suitcase. He thought that, all things considered, he would delay his proposal of marriage until after the sheep-dipping.

PART TWO

CHAPTER SEVEN

'ELLIS HAS INVITED *YOU* TO MARIANNE'S christening. How very odd,' Angela remarked tactlessly to Jared, who had telephoned her from Zurich where he was attending an art auction.

'Even odder,' Jared said excitedly, 'the invitation comes from Eliza. Oddest of all, she has asked me to be Marianne's godfather. I've been summoned to stay with the Jones's next weekend for a spot of spiritual bonding with the baby.'

'And they've asked *me* to be godmother,' Angela said faintly. 'What can we have done to have got ourselves into Eliza's good books?' She was rather put out that Jared wasn't coming straight to London to stay with her.

'I think we're being rewarded for not being Georgie Welliver,' Jared said shrewdly. Then, sensing that Angela sounded a bit miffed, added, 'As soon as I come to London, let's go shopping for some ravishing godparent outfits; something that makes a rather worldly statement with just the teensiest suggestion of chastity. The christening party could turn out to be a major kind of event.'

Simon leaned on Georgie's arm as they toured the rooms of the Edwardian wing. Her arm felt surprisingly strong and he put more of his weight on it. Georgie shifted the sheaf of builders' estimates to her other hand; pursing her lips as she studied one for injecting a cementatious waterproofing compound into the walls to prevent future dampness. It ran into thousands of pounds. 'Honestly, Simon, it's chucking money away,' she said. 'It would be cheaper to knock the whole lot down.'

'But my grandfather designed it himself,' Simon protested.

Georgie frowned. 'Ancestors are a menace. They build houses that are much too big, with no thought for their descendants, who have to pay the heating bills and restore the hideous paintings. When we lived at Utley Manor I used to dream of running away and being adopted by people who lived in a bungalow with all mod cons. I still think constant hot water are the three loveliest words in the English language.'

Simon's hooded eyes regarded her keenly. 'So you wouldn't be too happy living somewhere like Hayden?'

Georgie coloured. 'I didn't say that. It would be an interesting challenge to bring it into the twentieth century. If it were up to me, rather than restore this mouldering old wing, I'd spend the money building half a dozen holiday cottages on that field beside the spinney. I did some figures; you'd get your costs back inside of two years.'

'You're very practical, my dear.'

'Dreams cost too much, I've always found.'

From her bedroom window, Lavender watched Georgie's purposeful advance as she led Simon around the grounds, walking slowly so that he wouldn't tire, letting him lean on her arm. Lavender felt the skin on her neck throb hotly as she saw them turn towards the Japanese garden. It was absurd to have qualms about Georgie's regular weekend visits, or the length of time she spent with Simon. Wasn't this what she had always wanted? Ellis quite obviously serious about a young woman – yesterday he had taken her to see the method he had devised for hardening the hooves of his ewes, which was to make them walk on a floor sprinkled with lime – and in all likelihood prepared to marry her. And yet Lavender did have qualms. Georgie Welliver had no cream about her. Her newly lightened hair and fashionable clothes made her look attractively tamed and groomed but couldn't disguise her core of ice. Lavender came away from the window and looked at her watch. Very soon, Angela would be at home in Fulham, giving Maud and Elsie their tea. Perhaps she would telephone her and explain how she felt about Georgie. Angela was so wonderfully sympathetic, so warm-hearted that you felt that you could easily roast yourself at her feet. Lavender looked forward to hearing Angela's sunny coaxing voice saying, 'Tell it to me quietly,' and then listening without interrupting until Lavender had blurted out all her confused anxieties. Lavender thought for the thousandth time: if only Ellis could meet someone like Angela. She changed into her corduroy trousers and sailcloth smock and set off for the herb garden where she intended to plant alliums and parrot tulips. Simon and Georgie were seated on a stone bench at the entrance to the box-lined walk. 'Care to help?' Lavender shouted across to Georgie, waving a trowel.

Georgie shook her head. She had hateful memories of gardening, staking the tangled borders with her mother in mutual unspoken despair. They had been reluctant to leave the garden even when the wind started to blow high and cold across the valley. Rather shiver in their thin clothes than go back to the house and Gomer's eyes like ice-picks.

'I have some proofs to read,' she apologized and walked away with rapid steps along the silky grass paths.

'Works like a Trojan, you might say,' Simon observed, watching Georgie's neat head disappear between rows of sculpted box trees. Lavender thought that he sounded ridiculously doting.

'That's certainly true,' she said sharply. 'It makes her a rather limited person, in my opinion.' She shook some bone-meal into the soil and began planting the tulip bulbs. The set of her shoulders looked angry as she bent over the trowel.

'It might be the best thing, you know,' Simon ventured, and then looked across the garden, surprised, as Jared came sauntering across the grass, carrying a handsome terracotta oil jar, whitened with age.

'Good Lord,' Simon said. 'I'd no idea Jared was staying.'

'He's not,' Lavender said, sounding rather pleased with herself. 'He's staying at Eliza's. The two of them are frightfully pally these days.'

She got stiffly to her feet as Jared approached. He held out the jar to her. 'For you, Lavender. I thought that vividly pink verbena would look rather fine in it.'

'My Sissinghurst? Why, so it would, Jared. Thank you.' To Simon's astonishment, she kissed Jared's smooth cheek.

'I thought we'd go over to Eliza's,' Ellis said. 'I'd like to see how Warner's managing with the apple harvest.'

Georgie went upstairs to change out of her riding clothes. Eliza had not joined her for a Sunday morning ride in weeks; strange, since she had a proprietorial attitude towards Ellis's horses, even though she contributed nothing towards their stabling. Georgie hadn't missed Eliza's company. Eliza was a petulant woman who'd never got over the injustice of being the second-born, and female at that. She and Ellis lived in a state of snarling rivalry because of their determination to inherit Hayden. Such a stupid longing, Georgie thought, tucking a silk scarf around her throat. Hayden is a rather insignificant estate and a not particularly distinguished castle, its profitability by no means assured. She was surprised that Ellis wanted to visit Eliza. Perhaps, Georgie thought, smirking at her reflection in the dressing-table mirror and running her fingers through the beige, fawn and honey-coloured strands of her hair, Ellis wanted to show her off, parade her as his prospective fiancée. Georgie was certain that Ellis intended to ask her to marry him, just as she was certain that he didn't love her. Without ever talking about it, they understood each other perfectly, knew that each intended to use the other. Ellis would marry Georgie to ensure that Simon would leave him Hayden. Georgie would marry Ellis because anything was better than going back to the life she had lived before her affair with Davy Stearns, a life of hard work, sad peace and proud isolation, a life that had suited her well enough until Davy had shown it up as empty and unrewarding. Better not think of Davy now. Ellis was waiting for her.

Jared was lounging against the doorpost of the Jones's farmhouse. He had quite obviously been waiting for Ellis; his black eyes glittered with noticeable hopes. When Ellis got out of the car, they didn't touch, didn't even shake hands, but Georgie saw Jared's plump lips part slightly, heard his breathing get deeper. She noticed the flush on Ellis's thin cheeks. She thought she might go mad with shame.

Eliza appeared with Marianne nuzzled into her hefty shoulder. 'Stay for lunch, do,' she said. 'This little bag of tricks has been asleep all morning, so there's roast venison and a lemon meringue pie; that's your favourite, isn't it Ellis, aren't I right? Georgie, you're shivering. Come in by the fire. You chaps might give Warner a hand with the Emperor Alexanders. A huge crop this year, more than we'll be able to sell.'

Georgie hoped Ellis would say that they had to get to Hayden by lunchtime, Lavender was expecting them, but he slid his tongue over his lips. 'Ah well, Lizzy,' he said, 'if you've really cooked a lemon meringue pie.'

Eliza smiled complacently, stretching her large chin. She put a

97

hand between Georgie's shoulder-blades and steered her into the house. Georgie could hear Jared murmur something to Ellis and Ellis's responding laughter as they climbed into the Land Rover.

'So what should I do next?' Georgie asked . . . She was speaking to her uncle, Harry Welliver, the former Labour MP for Chipperton, recently elevated to the House of Lords, and his wife, Zanna.

Jared turning up had changed everything. Georgie knew that he planned to take Ellis away from her and she didn't intend to go back to Hayden until she was able to do battle and be certain of winning. She had come to Utley Lodge, just a few miles from where she had grown up, and explained everything to Harry and Zanna, quite unemotionally. Georgie had discovered that she had iron in her character and couldn't be bothered to hide it. Harry and Zanna, more than anyone she knew, didn't take her refusal to be charming as a personal insult.

'So,' she repeated the question in a challenging voice, 'what do you think I should do next?'

Zanna's crooked, arthritic hands were curled on her lap. She had been a beauty in her day, would be still were it not for her wizened hands and the lines that bit deeply into her forehead. Beneath them her purple eyes still gleamed brilliantly and her hair, once the colour of marmalade, shone too, pewter-coloured, and coiled into a tight French pleat.

Zanna raised her arched eyebrows at her husband and he gave her a rueful look. Georgie reminded them, disturbingly, of Gomer, Harry's late elder brother; the way she got hold of an idea and wouldn't let go of it. They had noticed years ago that her determination left her at odds with the world and sometimes made her enemies. Zanna had caught a whiff of vengeance in Georgie's story. Could her pursuit of Ellis Peregory have something to do with paying off old scores? If that was the case, Georgie was truly her father's daughter. Gomer had gone to any lengths to avenge himself for the slightest disregard. Harry, seeing Zanna's eyes darken, knew the direction her thoughts had taken. He came and sat beside her on the blowzy old sofa and took her crabbed hand in his. They could remember a time when Gomer, maddened by Zanna's taunts and teases, had come close to destroying their happy, ardent love affair.

Zanna straightened her spine and considered Georgie's question. 'You say Ellis had three helpings of Eliza's lemon meringue pie?'

'I can't see what that's got to do with anything,' Georgie said, 'but, yes, he did. It *was* delicious and what he gets at Hayden is pretty miserable. A wretched old biddy called Lolly Ward cooks in a put-upon sort of way and her husband shuffles around the table, presenting the muck she's dished up with this look in his eye, as though he's daring you to enjoy it. Nobody does; I'm the only person who really tucks in because I'm always ravenous.' Georgie reached for an apple from the shallow blue bowl on the window-sill.

'But why don't the Peregorys get rid of their lousy cook?' Zanna asked, thoroughly intrigued now. 'From what I've heard they are seriously loaded. Seems a shame not to eat well.'

'Oh, they're complete wimps,' Georgie said bitterly. 'When Ellis made the mildest complaint about finding congealed lumps of flour in the gravy, Lavender said how difficult it would be for Lolly to find another job. I'd have had her packing her bags before you could say Marco Pierre White.'

Zanna gave a little bounce on the sofa. 'That's it. That's the answer. *You* have to take over the cooking.'

'That's a laugh,' Georgie said, crunching her apple. 'I can't boil an egg.'

Harry was gasping and wheezing with laughter, his chest bent over his thin old legs. 'Oh that's rich, Zanna, coming from you. You can't boil water.'

Zanna smiled widely at him. 'You never minded that,' she said. 'Anyway, I had other tricks in my repertoire.'

'I should just say you did, my love,' Harry agreed, chortling into her shoulder.

'The first rule of seduction,' Zanna said, ignoring Harry, 'is always give a man exactly what he wants. In Ellis's case, it seems to be edible food. Now what you don't know, Georgie, is that Ivan and Clemency have taken over Lucullus. Lawdie-gawdie, that's what I call fate lending a helping hand.'

Lucullus country house hotel and restaurant stood solidly on the remains of what had once been Utley Manor, the Elizabethan mansion that had burned to the ground thirty years before, its flames killing Gomer Welliver and making worthless all his damaging secrets. Lucullus had been built in the Georgian style by the restaurant's first owner, Dominick Byrde. The squarish house had looked like a raw and unconvincing imitation of a Regency buck's country seat but, over the years, the wisteria tumbling down the stone walls, the splashes of lichen on the terrace and the landscaped garden had given it an attractively settled look. The restaurant had changed hands many times, restaurateurs having fickle and restless natures. Ivan and Clemency Fadge had owned Lucullus for the last year. They had built on ten well-proportioned bedrooms and introduced to the restaurant the rather quirky Provençal-inspired cooking that had made their London bistros so successful. The bistros had been sold to an American chain for more money than Ivan would have believed possible. He invested part of it in Lucullus because Clemency liked the idea of hospitably queening it in a hotel and of bringing up their children in the country. A month before, Lucullus had been awarded its first Michelin star and Ivan had bought each of his four children a pony.

'Hallo Aunt Zanna, Georgie,' Ivan waved his cigar in greeting. He was the eldest son of Zanna's late sister and brother-in-law Minetta and Geoffrey Fadge and had been quite a worry to them in his younger days, a sulky idler in a leather jacket, who modelled himself on James Dean. His parents would have approved of him now, Zanna thought; Ivan had grown into Geoffrey's sleek and prosperous glow, he even flourished his cigar the way Geoffrey used to, in the expansive gesture of a man who is handsomely in profit. It was arranged. Georgie would take a fortnight's holiday and spend it with Clemency in Lucullus's orderly white-tiled kitchen, where rows of knives glinted on built-in racks and starched white coats were stacked on scrubbed shelves.

'Two weeks is time enough to learn the basics,' Clemency said. 'After that a few good cookery books and your own appetite will see you through. It must be upsetting seeing your childhood home so changed,' she added sympathetically.

'Far from it,' Georgie said. 'Any change would have been for the better.'

She drew her finger around the rim of a spotless sink and remembered the cracked and mottled version that used to be there, the smell of drains from its plughole, the tap banded with an old and insanitary rag to muffle its leak, the march of silverfish on the stone flags below. She shuddered.

Clemency, noticing the shudder, remembered that Georgie's father had died rather horribly in the old house – A suicide? A fall? – and was stricken.

'I'm so sorry,' she said. 'I'd forgotten . . . your father . . .'

'Don't be,' Georgie snapped. 'My father died of failure years before he was burned to a crisp. Never being able to have what he wanted was what really killed him, And, quite honestly, there wasn't much point in him being alive. I found him impossible to mourn.'

'Georgie is a bit of a worry, don't you think?' Harry Welliver asked his wife as they were getting ready for bed that night. 'Such a driven girl. Lord knows, my darling, you and I were ambitious enough when we were younger, but surely not so narrow.'

'We were lucky,' Zanna said. 'We had each other, and we didn't have Gomer for a father. Georgie has a horror of failure; that's understandable. She won't allow anyone the right not to succeed, least of all herself.'

'But why should she be so hard on herself when she's doing so well in publishing? And why go after this Ellis Peregory in such a desperate way? He sounds like a very duplicitous type.'

'That's easy to explain,' Zanna said, 'she's in love with somebody else.'

On Lolly Ward's Sundays off, she overcooked a joint for the Peregorys to eat cold with tinned potato salad for lunch. This Sunday, returning from a visit to her sister in Abergavenny, she found the joint of beef untouched. The kitchen smelled of olive oil, saffron and oranges, and in the larder, in an earthenware bowl she had not seen before, were the scant remains of a fishy broth. Fleshy chunks of lobster, mullet and crab and other fish that Lolly could not put a name to, sat in a liquid that was a colour somewhere between yellow and rosy pink.

'That Jared Dauman's been poncing around my kitchen, must've been,' Lolly hissed to Tom. She tipped the soup into the waste-disposal unit, which she let whirr for longer than was necessary. She scoured the bowl with a Brillo pad, scratching the glaze, rinsed it under scalding water, dried it and hid it at the back of the highest shelf in the crockery cupboard. Then she marched into the drawing-room to bully Lavender.

The curtains had already been drawn against the dimming hills but the lamps had not been switched on; the room was in firelight. Georgie sat in the high-backed armchair; Ellis knelt beside it, his hand on Georgie's knee. Georgie saw Lolly standing in the doorway and snapped on a light, making Lolly feel foolish. Ellis pretended to examine the nose of the bellows for dents.

'I was looking for Madam,' Lolly said.

'A problem?' Georgie prompted. She held out her left hand towards the rustle and crack of the burning kindling. The room was bright enough now for Lolly to see the large flat diamond on her finger. Lolly's eyes swung from its icy sparkle to Ellis, still on his knees in front of the fire. Her mouth felt dry. She had never taken to Georgie; her rapid buzzing step as she rushed towards Ellis's office to collect her faxes; her scrutinizing eye falling on a crease in a table napkin or a smeary doorknob. She was the sort of woman who would be into everything given a chance, which the diamond engagement ring pouring out light provided. Lolly squinted at the ring again. Its heavy scrolled setting weighed down Georgie's small finger which had become red and puffy around it.

'Should I be saying something in the way of congratulations?' Lolly asked unenthusiastically.

'Goodbye would be the best thing,' Georgie said. 'The bouilla-baisse I made for lunch achieved the most satisfactory results, so I shall be doing the cooking from now on. I shall provide you and Tom with faultless references and six months' salary in lieu of notice.'

Lolly looked at Ellis helplessly, but he had turned away from her to feed the already blazing fire with another log.

'I take my orders from Madam,' Lolly insisted dully.

'This is what we ate after the bouillabaisse,' Georgie said, ignoring her. 'Braised chicken stuffed with noodles with a lemon salad, and then a frangipani tart. Lavender said she had never eaten so well in her life. She's rather come around to my point of view. She's out, by the way. Decided to visit her granddaughter to give me a chance to make arrangements.'

'Taking advantage,' Lolly sniffed. But she was calculating six months' salary in her head, that, and what she'd managed to put by from fiddling the household accounts. She'd been getting away with it for years, Lavender being so ladylike. Maybe it was time to go, before Georgie Welliver turned her wolfish eyes on the tradesmen's bills. 'I shan't be sorry to stop cooking, to tell the truth,' she said.

'You never started cooking, Lolly.'

Later, after Georgie had fed him on stuffed artichokes Stravinsky followed by some delicate little cakes called Visitandines, Ellis ruffled her hair affectionately, the way he stroked the head of his sheepdog, and suggested that they sleep together. He swung her hand in his as they went up the stairs to his bedroom, a room which Georgie had never seen.

Behind thick brown curtains, the windows were open to the night air; she could hear the ivy ticking against the outside wall. The room was lined with mahogany shelving. Propped on them, in cheap plastic frames, were photographs of men in formal groupings: rugby teams, the officers of the Oxford Union of twenty-three years ago, a delegation of British farmers on a trade visit to Pakistan. Ellis figured prominently in all of them, taller than anyone else, his ears majestically flaring, a fidgety smile on his lips. Beside the framed photographs were the silver-plated cups that Ellis had won for riding, fishing and at sheepdog trials, red and yellow rosettes clustered around them, their pleated ribbons silted with ancient dust.

The effect was of a boarding-school headmaster's study, depressing and slightly scary. Georgie thrust out her chin and began to take off her clothes. In bed, she clung to Ellis, her teeth chattering. His legs were cold under her palms. Davy had been so warm; lying next to him had been like having the sun on her shoulders. Tears fell out of Georgie's eyes.

'Steady on, old thing,' Ellis said, patting her shoulder. 'You'll get used to it.'

He turned away from her and was soon asleep. Georgie pressed her lips together to stop herself from howling with sorrow and, wakeful, waited forlornly for morning.

CHAPTER EIGHT

Tradition is a curse, Davy decided, gloomily eyeing the embroidered hassock at his feet. The design on it – some heraldic animal in danger of being choked by its cruelly restricting gold collar – was the same as that on Simon's evening slippers. In this small church, generations of Peregorys were commemorated by stone tablets, some of them supporting stone busts in which Davy could see the source of Ellis's brutal chin and lordly ears. Few of the enshrined military men and landowners had left their damp valley for any length of time. Neither would Ellis. He would moulder comfortably in the shelter of the hills, afraid to take his chances in the real rough world. Cursed by the cult of tradition, he would not be able to lift his feet out of the past's forceful, confusing imprints. Seduced by spectral ancestral voices, he thought in terms of dynasties, inheritance, carrying on the line; quaint notions that were also harmful.

Pantomime aristocrats, the Peregorys. Look at the baby, smothered in ancient cascading lace, the soft worn christening robes that had covered the limbs of all those Peregorys now sleeping under slate slabs in the adjacent churchyard. Davy had once been grimly amused by the embroidered beasts on Simon's slippers and his almost primitive devotion to the ancestral fields, but that was before Ellis had entrapped Georgie Welliver in his pantomime universe. Sadness swirled in Davy when he looked at Georgie, seated next to Simon in the family pew. Her lightened hair and lipsticked mouth gave her a cold tricked-out beauty, flat as a mask. She wore a suit the colour of butterscotch and a beehive-shaped hat in the same colour, made out of wired bands of glossy ribbon. She reminded Davy of Maud and Elsie's cut-out paper dressing-up dolls, whose dresses were attached to them only by paper tabs so that they always looked slightly detached from the clothes they wore. Elegance was beyond Georgie's scope. In her expensive suit she looked uneasy and rather cross. The gold mount of her engagement ring had inflamed her finger and, from time to time, she scratched it angrily.

While the visiting Bishop, a distant cousin of Lavender's, mumbled blessings over Marianne's lacy head, Davy drifted from memory to memory of the old beloved Georgie with her limp hair and sludge-coloured tunics and the curved smile that made the corners of her mouth fly upwards. She smiled a different smile now. A smile with determined lips. A smile she didn't mean.

The baby was handed to Angela, who held her confidently in her strong arms. Standing comfortably, feet apart, she looked as though she had calmly taken root on the stone floor. She was looking particularly pearly and magnificent today in soft pink tweed and a wide-collared blouse that showed off her lovely throat. How lucky he was to be married to her, he knew that. But it was Georgie who held his heart. More than anything else in the world he wanted to kiss the hot sore skin under the diamond on her finger.

*   *   *

106

When they were back at Hayden, having tea and christening cake in the drawing-room, Jared said to Angela, 'Keep tomorrow free; I've planned a surprise.'

Jared was behaving in a very civilized way, Angela thought; they all were. It wasn't an easy situation for any of them, but the demand for decorum had to be met, for Lavender's sake. They couldn't desert her when she was nursing Simon so bravely. Continuing their visits to Hayden was the right thing to do, however barbaric their feelings. Davy was heading in Georgie's direction carrying a cup of tea. 'Davy,' Angela called, 'do you know where Elsie is, darling? She seems to have wandered off.'

Davy was out of the room at once. Lavender, sipping tea close to the window, could see him take long loping strides across the grass, heading for the stables, his face stricken.

'Elsie hasn't gone to see the horses,' she observed. 'She went upstairs with Eliza to help her get the baby changed. Don't you remember, Angela? She asked you whether she could.'

'How stupid of me, I'd forgotten,' Angela lied. 'How very much better Simon is looking; remarkably springy.'

'He's in remission,' Lavender said. 'Dr Kirkland is quite confounded by it, but I'm not. He has something to live for and, by God, he's going to live for it.'

'Watching Marianne grow up, you mean?'

'Not at all. Watching Georgie Welliver change our lives. He finds it a fascinating procedure.'

'And you don't?'

'I think she's gone crazy mad,' Lavender said, and it struck Angela that she looked crushed and old, in spite of her wind-burned cheeks, 'but nobody else seems to have noticed.'

Jared drove Angela along the narrow road that wound itself through the Black Hills between Hay-on-Wye and Abergavenny. He turned up a sandy track and stopped in front of a stone cottage with newly painted window-sills.

'Home at last,' he said, unlocking the door.

'Whose home?' Angela asked. She could guess the answer by the showy way Jared turned the glittering brass key in the lock, by the way his teeth were biting his rosy padded lower lip.

'Mine. It's my observation post. Come upstairs, Angela-la-la and look out of the window.'

He bustled her into a bedroom with a high-timbered ceiling and drew back the curtain. She could see right across the valley to Hayden. Sun flashed on the water floating down the rocks of the Japanese garden and caught the great useless windows of the Edwardian wing. Feeling like a spy, she turned away. The room she was in was charming; a painted cupboard with oval panels filled an alcove, the brass bed had a canopy of dark blue and white cotton ticking. Jared led the way down dented wooden stairs to a brick-floored kitchen with a lead-lined timber sink, too small to be useful.

'A fairy-tale interior,' Angela said.

'Do you think Ellis will be happy here?' Jared asked, as though it had already been arranged that he would be.

Angela put both her hands on Jared's shoulders. 'Jared, it's over, this thing with Ellis. Get out of the way and move on.'

'But I saw him first, remember. You shouldn't be talking like this, angel. You're supposed to be loyal to your friends.'

'Better to try and stop them ruining their lives. Dear lad, don't be a fool. Come back to London with us.'

'And leave Ellis to be picked dry by the she-devilette? Never.'

'The wedding's in the spring, Jared. Try to be realistic.'

'No I won't. Reality is worse than anything.'

'Jared, dearest, this doesn't make sense.'

'Too late for sense. I'm staying here for ever. Dared and done, angel, dared and done. Why aren't you more supportive? You can't think that Georgie Welliver will bring Ellis anything but misery.

Lavender is terrified of her, you know. She says that whenever Georgie looks at her, she feels that she's being sandpapered by those hard grey eyes.'

Angela sighed. 'Admittedly, Georgie is a hardened giver of offence.'

'Well then, stop being so disgustingly fair to her.'

Angela looked out of the kitchen window at the dark slopes of land under the thin blue winter sky. She would not have thought herself capable of this treachery: trying to drag Jared away from Hayden because she wanted Georgie married, out of harm's way, and out of Davy's. Jared's ruinous optimism disturbed her. His everlasting devotion to Ellis, his determination that Ellis would be his in the end made her feel almost panic-stricken. She rubbed her brow then turned around and cuffed Jared on the arm. 'It's a ridiculous thing to do, moving here; of benefit to nobody except the Inland Revenue. Sometimes you're about as responsible as a bubble. We'd better be heading back. The she-devilette is cooking a special godparents' lunch. If she had any sense, she'd put ground glass in yours.'

'I wouldn't put it past her,' Jared said. 'She does everything with a deadly precision.'

'Pass me the business section, would you, dear?' Ellis asked Georgie. Davy, pretending to read the sports pages of *The Sunday Times*, wanted to pull the lobes of Ellis's impressive ears until the flesh tore. The man had no idea how to love Georgie. You had to love her enough for all the people who hadn't loved her enough: her lunatic father and vague remote mother, and Davy himself, whose betrayal had been necessary but unforgivable. You had to be her escape route from being unloved. You had to understand that to be in the full of her life, she needed to be painstakingly cared for. You also had to convince her that she was an object of allure. Davy had known this from the start; Ellis clearly hadn't. He treated Georgie in a diffident clumsy way, as though she were an old school chum or a favourite dog. If this distanced affection was all that she could hope for she would be ruined. Angela had always maintained that Ellis played ruthless games with people, denying them what they needed most. It looked at though Georgie was his latest victim. Miserably, Davy tried to concentrate on the reported views of a sacked football manager.

Later that morning, pacing the garden while Elsie and Maud were playing dominoes with Simon in front of the morning-room fire, he saw Georgie walking across the fields towards the river, her step rapid, head down, shoulders forward. She was carrying a surveyor's measuring-tape, housed in a leather casing. Davy followed her.

She was staking out one of the prettiest meadows, watched by a composed group of seated cows. Davy wormed himself through a squeaking farm gate. 'What are you doing?' he called.

She turned a white, bitter face towards him. 'Trying to get some use out of this place. I want to build holiday cottages on this site. It would cost less than restoring the Edwardian wing *and* show a profit at the end. But Lavender doesn't like money spent on anything that isn't decorative.' She snorted, her small face a knot of fury. 'Ornamental onions; they're the only kind grown here. It's all going to change. It's going to be my way or no way.' She took a notebook out of her pocket and wrote down some dimensions in it.

'Don't do it, Georgie,' Davy pleaded. 'Don't marry Ellis. He'll diminish you; they all will. Their way of coping with intensity and pain is to pretend they don't exist. It's like being on stage all the time; you'll hate it.'

Georgie glared at him. 'Don't worry about me. I'm a woman of today, which means I can be just as horrible as a man; that is, not interested in anyone other than myself. And, anyway,' she gave Davy a hard look out of her clever wolfish eyes, 'marriage is all about pretending. I don't have to tell *you* that.'

110

He turned to go, so jagged with pain that he didn't know how he managed to put one foot in front of the other as he moved through the stiff grass towards the house.

Georgie watched him go until he was shielded from her eyes by the wall of the stable block. Once she had trusted his warm languorous body; a foolish thing to have done. She took a livid pleasure in watching the defeated slump of his shoulders as he walked away from her.

'We're having a *lovely* time,' Maud said to her father, sounding exactly like Angela, who frequently used that expression. 'Simon's letting us choose his tombstone.'

Brochures from monumental masons were scattered on the table. Simon squared them into a pile and mumbled, 'No need to pretend any more. Ellis is doing the sensible thing. No end of a relief knowing that Hayden will be in Georgie's hands. I'm ready to move on when the time comes, or bash on as she would say.'

'Look,' Elsie said, disturbing the stack of brochures, 'here's one with a little angel on top. How sweet.'

'Stinky,' Maud said, clambering onto Simon's lap. 'Angels are only for babies.'

'Time to find Mummy, my lollypops, and get you both tidied up for lunch,' Davy said. He took hold of Elsie's hands and pulled them gently up and down like bell ropes.

'Worth putting on your best bib and tucker, chaps,' Simon advised. 'Georgie's rustling up something special.'

'We had a *lovely* time,' Maud repeated while Angela was brushing her hair. She thought she sounded very grown-up saying things like that. 'And we're going to have a special lunch,' she added. 'It could be crinkly chips.'

Was Angela having a lovely time, Davy wondered. She had been looking rather subdued since her drive with Jared. Usually, after one of their outings, she was brimming with good humour, brought on

111

by conspiratorial giggles over a cappuccino at the Bon Gout café in Hay, leafing through the latest *Vanity Fair*.

'So how's Jared keeping up?' he asked, thinking, as soon as the words were out of his mouth, that he sounded like, and probably was, a crass oaf.

'He's bought a cottage in the hills, just the far side of Hay, near enough to Hayden to be an enticing and disturbing presence. He thinks he still has a chance with Ellis.'

'About as likely as growing mangoes on the moon.' Davy assured her. Still, he thought, you never know. Ellis has lived his whole life in the deadly undercurrents of deception. He was the unknowable other, like a secret agent. He felt a warm spread of hope that Ellis would not marry Georgie. Guilt followed hope; it was wrong for him to want what Angela dreaded. She had put on a poppy-red dress with a long tight skirt; the Tiffany bracelet gripped her smooth solid wrist. The dress did not suit her. 'You look amazing,' Davy said. Georgie was right: marriage was about pretending.

'Beautiful Mummy,' Maud agreed, and then, because she had overheard Georgie saying the words to Ellis at breakfast time, 'Let's bash on, shall we?'

'Let's bash on, shall we?' Georgie suggested to Dinah Thomas, a puddingy girl with rolling shoulders whom Georgie had spotted unhappily waiting on tables at the Bon Gout café. She had seen at once that Dinah hated working in front of other people, who looked at her with pitying eyes as they ordered portions of quiche and apple pie, as embarrassed by her fatness as she was herself.

Georgie had removed her to the seclusion of Hayden's renovated kitchen, an undisturbed haven of scaldingly white tiles, where, instead of the huge limp smock that had been her waitress's uniform, Dinah could wear a starched white apron, hard as armour, and wield a narrow, formidable-looking knife. She loved the vigorous complications of cooking and, by extension, loved Georgie. She sucked

112

her teeth in concentration as she added butter, piece by tiny piece, to the lobster sauce which was to be served with fillets of sole.

Lavender scuttled awkwardly into the dining-room, astonishingly dressed in a kimono that Jared had bought in Japan. It was made of heavy cream silk splashed with orange dahlias and irises. Jared, close behind her, was still rearranging the stiff loops at the back of the wide woven sash.

'I wasn't sure about wearing this at lunchtime,' Lavender said doubtfully, 'but Jared persuaded me that something special was called for.'

'And I was right,' Jared shouted gaily. 'There's so much to celebrate, is there not? Georgie, what a zippy new hairstyle that is, and a most effective frock. I'd swear it makes you look two inches taller.'

As Maud and Elsie skipped into the room, Jared seized their hands and marched them around the long table, rimmed with spoon-backed chairs, singing:

> What are *little* girls made of, made of
> What are *little* girls made of?
> Sugar and spite and all things slight
> That's what little girls are made of.

Elsie and Maud, weak with delight, flung themselves against Angela's thigh. Georgie, stone-faced, set out bowls of a Turkish soup called Cacik, served ice-cold. With the unvarying geniality he always displayed when others were behaving badly, Ellis guided everyone to their places at table. You have to hand it to Jared, Davy thought, he is quite dauntless. It would be difficult to prove that the several disasters that ruined Georgie's excellent lunch had been planned in advance, but Davy recognized them as Jared's master-strokes: cunning brilliantly disguised as mishap.

It was inevitable that the wide sleeve of the kimono that

Lavender wore so uncomfortably would, at some point, flick a wineglass towards the floor, which it did, pouring its contents over Georgie's dress first – had that been part of Jared's plan too? It was to be expected that, just as the main course was being served, Jared should be urgently called to the telephone and not return for several minutes, by which time the fish on his plate was tepid, its rosy glistening sauce beginning to harden; an excuse for him not to eat it. Always a mistake to serve Jared sole, Davy thought, remembering the evening at Nico at Ninety, when Jared had ostentatiously sniffed his plate. His appalling behaviour that evening had made Georgie's lips curve with amusement. Not today; her eyes were murderous.

When the pudding arrived – a crème renversée à la Cevenole, which Dinah, with much sucking of teeth, had managed to turn out perfectly from its elaborate mould – Jared asked with heavy indulgence, 'So what is this we're guzzling now?' as though it were no end of a hateful duty for all of them to plough through the food that Georgie had cooked. The question sent Georgie deeper and deeper into a rage, which was Jared's intention.

'A recipe of Alice B. Toklas's,' she snarled. 'I thought I'd produce something decent to eat to stop you launching into one of your gastronomic discourses, the way you used to in Lolly's day. You can't imagine how boring it was, eating slushy cabbage while you banged on about the deep-fried courgette flowers you'd feasted on in Perpignan ten years ago.'

'That *Ellis* and I had feasted on,' Jared said reprovingly.

Inside the winged sleeves of her inappropriate kimono Lavender squeezed and wrung her hands, while Simon's voice drifted sadly as he explained the theory of set-aside to a politely listening Angela. Davy felt overwhelmed by a hot sorrow. He sensed that Ellis was up to his old tricks; there he sat, his eyes furtively watchful and rather amused, as Georgie and Jared scraped at each other's words. He was soaring above the occasion with his sharp treacherous smiles, pretending not to notice that Jared and Georgie were out to annihilate each other.

Angela leaned forward in her chair, the expression on her face almost dangerously benign. It suggested that she was ready to help overcome any suffering that might have befallen the rest of them, while being herself out of reach of pain. 'Georgie,' she said warmly, 'lunch was superb. You're spoiling us, you know. Is it true you've resigned from your job? That's a brave step.'

'She'll be here all the time,' Simon interrupted fervently.

'And so shall I,' Jared said, 'or just three miles away as the crow flies. Won't that be neighbourly?'

'Simon is signing his will after the wedding,' Lavender told Angela. 'He could hardly make it clearer that it's Georgie who's to be the beneficiary in all but name.'

'Poor Ellis,' Angela said mildly. 'A bit of a snub.'

They were in the greenhouse, comfortable in their gardening clothes, cleaning out the terracotta pots for the winter. The piny smell of Jeyes Fluid clung to their fingernails.

'Poor Ellis, my foot,' Lavender snorted. 'He knows what he's doing.'

'It's called getting married,' Angela said. 'For years you always complained that he wasn't.'

'But I didn't want him to choose Georgie. I wanted him to marry someone like you.'

'For your benefit rather than his?'

'That's what every mother wants.' Lavender shielded her eyes against the wintry sun that was shining fitfully on the grass. 'There's my future daughter-in-law now, heading for the water-meadows with Ben Cantalupo of all people. For such a short woman, she has a very purposeful stride.'

'And she always knows where she's going,' Angela said.

They were back at the house, absorbed in the seed catalogues, when Simon came into Lavender's small sitting-room and sat down in a rather solemn way, smoothing the wattles on his neck. 'Ben Cantalupo's had another squinny at the Edwardian wing,' he said.

Lavender shut the catalogue she was studying with a slap and straightened her shoulders. In all the years she had known them, Angela had never seen Lavender look at Simon the way she was looking at him now, her face set, her eyebrows strained, and her eyes distrustful with no love in them.

The Edwardian wing, designed by Simon's grandfather, Casper Peregory, an admirer of the work of Sir Edwin Lutyens, had always looked absurdly robust and grandiose beside the delicate glimmer of the twelfth-century castle. The wing had been added at a time when there were dozens of young male Peregorys to be put up during their university vacations, lanky boys who drifted back to Hayden every summer to fish and ride and write stilted poetry. There had been dances then – the Edwardian wing had a ballroom with a maple floor and raised gilded balconies for sitting out – and charades and snooker tournaments. The Edwardian wing, in spite of the serious-ness of its plummy sandstone façade, had been designed and used as a fun palace. The young men who had loved it had all been killed in the Great War, among them Simon's father, whose wedding had been celebrated in the Edwardian wing six months before his death on the first day of the Battle of the Somme, on 1 July 1916.

His young pregnant wife came to live at Hayden and, at her request, the Edwardian wing was closed up. After his mother's death, Simon re-opened the long many-windowed rooms of the wing for a mid-summer ball. Leading Lavender onto the dance floor, he felt the newly waxed floorboards give mushily under his feet. The scent of lilies cascading from ribbed bronze vases didn't quite disguise the smell of wormy carvings and damp plaster. The ball was not a success and the rooms were closed up again. Sometimes, Lavender, passing by the sandstone frontage on her way to the Japanese garden, thought she could hear the heavy bounce of young men's feet on the splintery staircase, their clever talk drifting through the cracked windows. She kept this to herself.

Over the years she had softened the solid bulk of the Edwardian wing by smothering its walls with climbers: Madame Alfred Carrière and Climbing Lady Hillingdon, a magnolia grandiflora. In front of them she planted massed borders of artfully structured confusion, the riotous flowers constrained by edges of blurry grey-green catmint.

'The Edwardian wing,' Lavender said in a clipped voice, 'a lasting monument to the valour of your father's generation. I am very fond of it, you know.'

'The thing is,' Simon said uneasily, 'Ben Cantalupo says it will cost a small fortune to restore. Wet rot and all that sort of thing. It mightn't be such a bad idea to pull it down; get Hayden in some sort of order, you might say, before . . .' He gave an apologetic smile.

Lavender clicked her tongue. 'Georgie's idea, I suppose. She's mad keen on old buildings being razed to the ground, never happier than when she's describing in grisly detail the way Utley Manor burned down. Not much hope for the rest of the house. She'll have it down in no time and replace it with one of Ben Cantalupo's glass wigwams.'

The colour high on her cheeks, Lavender left the room. What a strange thing for Simon and Lavender to quarrel about, Angela thought. The Edwardian wing was cheerless and dull, long fallen into disuse. Lavender had never before expressed any fondness for it. Simon sat with his walking stick clamped between his knees, looking morosely at the door which Lavender hadn't bothered to close behind her.

'Time for tea,' Angela said. 'I'll make it.'

She had not seen the kitchen since Georgie had had it redesigned. Opening the door, she blinked at the expanse of white tiles, which reminded her of bared teeth. Dinah Thomas was wiping down glass spice jars and putting them back on a shelf in alphabetical order. 'Caraway, cardamom, cayenne, cloves, cumin,' Angela read the gilt labels aloud. 'They sound like Elsie's skipping rhymes,' she said, and then noticed how nervous Dinah seemed; her bloated fingers pulled at the dishcloth and her flickering eyes followed Angela's every moment as she put on the kettle and took a tray from a rack. 'Why, how beautifully organized everything is, Dinah,' Angela said encouragingly,'and you keep it spotless.' She began to fling open drawers and cupboards. 'Do you mind? I'm curious about what other people keep in their kitchens. What are these?' She took down a jar of what looked like golf balls in brine from one of the gleaming tiled shelves of the new pantry.

'Pickled goat's cheese. Please try to put it back exactly where you found it, Mrs Stearns. Georgie will get so cross otherwise.' She made a sudden grab for the jar and gave it a furious wipe.

Angela carried the tea tray towards Lavender's sitting-room. How unpleasant the scoured sterile look of Georgie's kitchen was. It made Angela feel quite warmly towards her step-mother, the former Evelyn Coote, who turned a blind eye to bird's nests of hair in plugholes and the necks of ketchup bottles caked-up with darkened hardened goo. Again Angela felt that resentment, heavy and smooth as pebbles, that overcame her when she thought of Davy's unfaithfulness with Georgie. So perverse of him to fall in love with a woman who was tidy to the point of obsession, and so humiliating. Angela looked in the cloudy panes of the gilt-wood mirror in the hallway to confirm her own gorgeousness before taking the tea tray into the room.

'Georgie in a frantic tizzy, is she?' Jared enquired hopefully. 'Having one of her tantrumlets, would that be it?'

'Jared, how could you?' Angela's sunny voice seemed to have faded. 'It was none of your business.'

'Don't be so sure,' Jared smirked. 'Hayden might very well be my business before too long.'

Abetted by Eliza, Jared had written letters to the National Trust and the architectural correspondents of several newspapers expressing concern about the proposed demolition of Hayden Castle's Edwardian wing. This had resulted in an article in one of the weekend supplements which rather wittily put forward the case for an Edwardian revival. It featured photographs of Hayden's Edwardian wing taken soon after it was built, as well as several buildings by Lutyens and examples of Edwardian overmantels, bookcases and dining suites which might be found at auction houses. At the same time Jared had moved permanently into his hillside cottage.

'Actually, Georgie's taken your interference very coolly,' Angela said. She considered her own words for a moment, then added, 'Which is not to say she's not envenomed. The idea of pulling down the Edwardian wing has been temporarily shelved; Ben Cantalupo was a bit fearful of attracting adverse publicity. The really bad news is that Georgie is convinced that poor old Lavender is implicated in your fiendish teases and has devised a new torture for her which is to frequently mention how much she'd like to grow all her own vegetables, if only there were a suitable spot, and then fix her eyes very pointedly on the Japanese garden. The atmosphere at Hayden is fairly poisonous.'

Jared nudged another log inside the cast-iron stove and got up to close the wooden window shutters. Angela shut her eyes. 'It's so peaceful here,' she said.

Jared trundled an ottoman upholstered in Turkish carpet towards her and gently lifted her legs onto it. 'Mm,' she said, 'a veritable sanctuary.'

'A haven for Ellis to escape to when the she-devilette begins to cut up rough. He gets so distressed by displays of temper.'

Angela opened her eyes so suddenly that they seemed to click in their sockets. 'How you god him up,' she said. 'You think he's lost and confused and easily led. That's rot. Ellis is diabolic. He could dig graves in the air. Seeing his entire family in a huff is his idea of fun.'

They looked away from each other while the logs in the stove slipped and tumbled and collided into sparks.

'There you are,' Angela said, after a while, 'he's even got me shrieking at *you*; something I've never done.' She stood up to press her head to his but he moved away from her. Heavy-hearted, she drove back to Hayden under the high mid-winter moon.

CHAPTER NINE

THREE DAYS BEFORE CHRISTMAS THE snow came; solid flakes that flumped onto the pavements in Covent Garden, surprising the pigeons, who rose in the air in a grey flit.

The Stearns came out of the Royal Opera House after a performance of *The Nutcracker Suite* and breathed plumes of white into the coldness. Snow spangled Davy's dark hair as he bustled his wife and daughters along Long Acre towards Le Palais du Jardin. Steam from their coats made a mist around their shoulders as they pushed through the door.

'This is worrying,' Angela said, watching the parked cars outside getting roofed with white. 'Lavender and Simon might not be able to make the journey.' Davy raised his eyebrows in a concerned way. Relief was what he felt. The thickening skies seemed like salvation if they could keep the Peregorys at Hayden. He would be spared Lavender's flustered peevishness and Simon's stoic endurance; thank heaven for large mercies and blocked roads. It had been Angela's idea to invite the older Peregorys to spend Christmas with them, and how could Davy refuse without seeming made of granite? Angela thought that Jared might show up at Hayden; that Ellis might have secretly encouraged him to do so, because Ellis's idea of an entertaining Christmas lunch would be to see his parents caught in the crossfire of enamelled violence as Georgie and Jared fought to the death.

'They'll be company for Ma, too,' Angela had chirped. Her theory was that old people were bound to get on with one another since they had in common the absorbing pastime of watching their bodies flounder. Davy didn't agree. He suspected that the Peregorys' stately disintegration had a deadening effect on Nora's spirit; he'd noticed the way she frowned at Lavender's fluttery hands and the jut of Simon's bony knees breaking the crease in his trousers. And Nora was something of a trial to the Peregorys with her truculent independence and the way she talked about marriage as though it had been a comical mishap in her life. 'Ted, like a perfect fool,' she would begin some anecdote, smiling to show that Ted's foolishness was nothing that need concern her now. She gave the impression that marriage was an odd and tiresome condition and those suffering from it were to be pitied, even despised.

The plan was for Orly to collect Nora from Rottingdean and then drive her to London. They would share the second guest bedroom in Davy and Angela's house so that Orly wouldn't have to drive backwards and forwards to her own flat in the Old Brompton Road. Davy wasn't looking forward to having his sister-in-law under his roof; even though he had never consulted Orly professionally, he sensed that she regarded him, perhaps regarded everybody, as 'a case'. Sometimes, from the way she steepled her fingers and nodded her head while he was talking, he got the idea that she knew more about him than he knew about himself, and that what she knew was bad: that he was little more than an animal, a few basic responses buttoned into an Armani suit. Orly's knowing gaze seemed to reduce his most complex emotions to brute instinct. Angela, who agreed that Orly could be a bit intense, claimed that what she needed was 'a nice man', a need difficult to fulfil in Davy's view, since men who lived in London tended to be like Davy himself: predatory, of swaying loyalties, not to be trusted.

This Christmas presented a further problem: Davy was in no doubt that Angela had told her sister about his affair with Georgie Welliver. Orly's skilfully outlined and mascara'd eyes would, therefore, be more knowing than ever. Pinioned by them, he would have to put on a performance as the contented paterfamilias: attentive, devoted, faithful. The unfair thing was that he might reasonably be considered to *be* all these things. But, to Orly, being wasn't enough. Demonstration was required; an exhausting business when combined with elaborate meals and overexcited children. He looked out at the deepening snow and thought of Georgie's bed: cool, white and quiet, like snow itself. To be able to lay his head on that starched pillow again. . . .

Maud was kneeling on her chair, her hands clasped on his shoulder, pressing down on it to make him listen.

'What is it, lollypop?'

'Daddy, can me and Else have shrimps and ketchup and not any salad as a treat?' she wheedled.

'May they, angel?'

'Certainly,' Angela said. 'Everyone's let off the hook at Christmastime.' She beamed at him collusively to let him know that he, too, was let off the hook; all his sins shrivelled and dissolved in the warmth of her tranquil smile.

Surrounded by his wife and daughters, the little girls adorable in dark navy-blue dresses with cream smocking, he might have been posing for a picture called 'Family Happiness'. At the next table, a dark fleshy man, smoking a cigar, which crushed the corner of his lower lip, while absent-mindedly stroking the elbow of his companion, a very young strawberry blonde who was definitely not his wife, gave Davy a smirk that may have been sympathetic or envious.

He realized that Angela's eyes were fixed on Maud's plate. Maud was carefully easing each shrimp from its crisp lacquered shell and arranging the debris in a perfect half-circle around the edge of her plate. A sharp-eyed mimic, she was copying the way Georgie ate shrimps. It was as though Georgie herself were sitting between them, charmless in such a way that it made their own charm seem automatic and false, mocking their display of public joyfulness. Angela's smile became more resilient. 'A white Christmas will be bags of fun,' she said.

'Thank heavens that you got here yesterday,' Nora said to Orly, listening to the wind sucking at the windows. 'The motorway is impassable today, it seems. This is weather on a rather spectacular scale.'

Neither of them minded being marooned in Rottingdean over Christmas. They were self-sufficient women, rather at a loss in large gatherings and easily embarrassed by the strained jollity that was called for at this time of year. Orly brought in the case of wine which she had intended to give to Davy and they rummaged through Nora's freezer, pleased to find several Marks & Spencer recipe dishes.

'Just think,' Nora said, 'no stuffing, no giblets, no Lord-Mayor-in-chains. How I hated cooking lunch on Christmas Day. It was almost impossible trying to get everything ready at the same time. I remember that one year Ted, like a perfect fool, complained that the cranberry jelly was a bit too bland. If it hadn't been for you and Angela I should have run him through with the carving knife. No brandy butter, no crystallized fruit, no mince pies,' she continued happily. 'Let's stay in our dressing-gowns all day, have an omelette and a glass of wine for lunch, watch the video of *Terms of Endearment* and have a good moan about men.'

'Sounds reasonable to me,' Orly said.

*　　*　　*

'There's not much in the way of food, honeylove,' Evelyn called from the kitchen. 'I was going to do a last-minute shop at Sainsbury's on Christmas Eve. Isn't it romantic being snowed in like this? Don't get out of bed yet, I've got a surprise for you.'

She pranced into the bedroom wearing only a pair of high-heeled black patent boots and a string of tinsel wound around her body in a silvery spiral.

'Turkey, who needs it?' she yelled, flinging herself on top of Ted.

He did. Ted felt a sudden pang of longing for the Christmas lunch which Nora had served, year after year. He remembered the satiny gleam of the Regency dining table, the gold-rimmed goblets, the centre-piece of holly and Christmas roses. He remembered the solid feel of the carving knife in his hand as it bore down on the glistening skin of the turkey, the nutmeggy smell of bread sauce, the rich brown of giblet gravy, the Lord-Mayor-in-chains. Then he remembered Nora's bad-tempered exhaustion; hadn't there been one year when her hand, white-knuckled, had tightened alarmingly around the handle of the carving knife when he'd made some mild criticism? He remembered her ill-concealed disappointment at whatever present he had bought her. He had always failed to give her what she wanted, one way or another: a cookery book which she exchanged for a poetry anthology, a bright-blue silk shirt with full tightly-cuffed sleeves which she never wore. How much easier life was with Evelyn, who squealed with happiness at everything he did. He squeezed her tightly in his arms. 'Since the cupboard's bare, I'm going to have to eat *you*,' he growled, like the wolf in *Red Riding Hood*. He started to unwind the tinsel which was already shedding gritty strands on the sheets.

When the snow began to fall, Lavender was determined to get to London. They had to get away; at Hayden she and Simon were two doddery strangers in their own home, moving gingerly so as not to further disturb the atmosphere of muted fury that hung over the lavish fire-bright rooms.

Ellis and Eliza were hardly on speaking terms. Lavender knew this to be the case in spite of Eliza's studied politeness and Ellis's loud amiability – a sure sign that he was causing someone deep displeasure, and knew that he was. As for Simon, he had gone down a little in the last week or so, his graven profile had slackened. They both needed a jaunt. She went upstairs to pack.

When she next looked out of the window the garden had been blanked out with whiteness. She put on her boots and rushed to the back door, wanting to brush snow off the branches of her favourite shrubs and make sure that the koi pool in the Japanese garden was ice-free. Stinging snowflakes scratched and tore at her face, driving her back indoors before she had got to the end of the path.

Ellis and Georgie in padded coats and balaclava helmets were filling vacuum flasks with the mushroom soup that Georgie had made that afternoon. 'Sheep,' Ellis said. 'Blizzard from the east, always the worst.'

Dressed identically against the cold, Ellis and Georgie looked more companionable than Lavender had ever seen them; both exuding a fierce competence that made her feel wispy and inadequate. She started to make herself a cup of tea, but when Dinah Thomas came into the kitchen, her starched apron creaking like a sail, Lavender gratefully handed over the preparation, not trusting herself to perform the simple task of spooning tea into the pot.

Georgie and Ellis plunged into the blank landscape carrying torches and spades. Every so often, a smudge of darker white – the head of a trapped sheep – showed against the snow. Lying flat on the ground, they scrabbled with their gloved fingers to free the buried animals and then haul them onto the paths which the farm workers were cutting through the drifts. The snow was thickening. Pushing her spade downwards, Georgie estimated it at four feet deep. On she went, her feet sinking into soft whiteness, alert for the sound of muffled bleating. In front of her Ellis was yanking a terrified ewe along the cleared path to the yard. Lifting up her face to the falling snowflakes, Georgie felt something like fondness for him.

Jared had been going to have dinner with Eliza; afterwards, they had planned to draft a letter to the National Heritage Department, expressing the hope that the application to build holiday cottages on the Hayden Estate would face objections from every organization that cared for the preservation of the countryside. Their objective was to frustrate Georgie Welliver at every turn. 'She can't bear failure,' Eliza had said a few days ago. 'If she can't have what she wants, she'll clear off, just you see.' Her confident smile had pushed out her chin unattractively. She was not the ally that Jared would have chosen had another been available.

As though reading his thoughts, Eliza had gone on, 'Funny that we've joined forces. You're the last person I'd have thought would help me get Ellis out of Hayden. Ah, well, my enemy's enemy is my friend, and all that.'

Jared had blustered, untruthfully, that getting Ellis out of Hayden was not his intention. He wanted only Ellis's happiness which, he believed, would come about with Georgie Welliver's departure. It was entirely possible that Simon would make Ellis his heir, whether he was married or not; Eliza should understand that.

'Should I?' she had answered angrily. 'Maybe it's time for *you* to understand a few things. This is what would happen if Ellis decided that you were the one that he'd wanted all along: Mother and Pa would never speak to him again; inheriting Hayden would be out of the question; he'd probably have to resign from the boards of the Forestry Commission and the National Farmers' Union. It's something to think about, Jared.'

Jared's plump lower lip had trembled. 'Don't think that I haven't thought about it,' he had said. 'But don't you see that if Ellis were to make such sacrifices it would mean that he was really quite certain that he loved me?' He spoke as though the sacrifices had already been made; his fate and Ellis's already entwined. It made Eliza feel uncomfortable.

'So we're talking about love in a cottage, are we?' she had sneered.

'We are. A cottage with some rather fine eighteenth-century Irish delft and a really lovely toile by Brunschwig & Fils,' Jared told her, aware that she coveted both, and pleased to see her scowl jealously. But this evening he was in a more generous mood. He took down a plate that Eliza particularly admired – made by Henry Delamain in Dublin in the 1750s, decorated with landscapes by Peter Shee – and wrapped it up for her in shiny red paper.

He couldn't understand why the front door wouldn't budge, until it occurred to him to draw back a curtain. A whirling porridge of snow batted against the window. Even if he had managed to open it – no easy matter with the wind sweeping down from the hillside – and then climb out and shovel away the blocking drifts from the door, driving along the thin curling road would be impossible. Ecru, the Burmese kitten which Angela had given him as a house-warming present, shifted her paw from her sleeping place under the wood-burning stove. Jared drew the curtain again, smoothing its folds. It had been made up in the Brunschwig toile and then heavily interfaced and lined, keeping out the cold and the swishing sound of the wind. He lifted the telephone receiver and heard the continuous whine that meant the line was down. Ellis would not be able to contact him; the weather was playing into Georgie's hands. He wished every kind of bad luck on her.

'Well done, my dear old girl,' Ellis said, 'you were a tremendous help.' He took a perfectly ironed and folded tea towel from the kitchen shelf, shook it open, and began to dry Georgie's soaked hair, awkwardly rubbing her scalp.

She moved closer to his chest. His Viyella shirt smelled of hay and dogs and wood-ash, a soothing smell. It was morning and the sullen skies were clearing into storms of light. The entire flock was now safely gathered in; Georgie glowed with the ecstasy of achievement. 'Happy landings,' she murmured into Ellis's shirt. 'I mean, happy Christmas.'

When they went to bed, Georgie told herself that things were different. The night on the hillside, working together to save frightened foolish sheep, had surely brought them closer. Things must get better between them now; they could not go on scarcely able to tolerate the touch of each other's skin. But Ellis pushed his cold austere body against hers in his usual half-regretful way. There was something hateful about the way his long penis slid into her. How horrible that sex with him made her feel washed clean of pleasure, convinced that there was nothing left for her in the future. She ached for Davy Stearns, who had taken such a greedy delight in her flesh that when she arched herself in his warm arms life had seemed to unfurl around corners, full of hope. She would go through with this marriage because it would be the hardest thing for Davy to bear.

'So here we all are still,' Simon raised his glass emphatically. Their remaining at Hayden over Christmas had not caused any inconvenience. Georgie had been going to cook a young turkey with truffles in any event and the freezer would provide food for weeks to come, should they continue to be snowbound; it was stacked with plastic boxes, labelled and dated in Georgie's swift elegant handwriting: ' "Spring navarin",' Lavender read, on a furtive visit to the new pantry, where the freezer was housed. ' "Duck with bordelaise sauce", "iced apples", "Viennese cheese pancakes".' She had quietly shut the lid as she heard the creak of Dinah's overalls in the kitchen, feeling, as she often did these days, like an intruder in her own home.

'As always, the food is, you might say, superb,' Simon said, lowering his glass and forking up a mouthful of truffle stuffing.

'We've done ourselves rather better than we might have done in London. Which is not to say that Angela isn't an excellent cook,' he added, noticing Lavender press her lips together. She did not like to hear Angela disparaged, even though she found mealtimes at the Stearns's rather alarmingly informal, with the children allowed to climb onto Davy's lap and dip sugar lumps in his coffee.

'I see you now have a computer in the kitchen,' Lavender said to Georgie, changing the subject.

'It's an essential piece of equipment,' Georgie said. 'After every meal I can enter the menu, the date and to whom it was served, as well as any comments on the recipe.'

'But why should you want to do that?' Lavender asked hesitantly.

'Because it's bad form to serve the same food to the same people time after time,' Georgie said, knowing perfectly well that until she had got rid of Lolly Ward that was exactly what had happened.

Georgie is mad, Lavender thought miserably. It is insane to insist on such a degree of order, as though the world could be tamed down like carpet bedding: neat, immaculate with nothing left to chance. It could not; it was a rampant thing. Only a fanatic like Georgie would imagine that she could strip it of surprises.

Looking out of the window, Lavender saw that it had started to snow again, plushy flakes that fell heavily on the ground. Impossible to walk as far as the Japanese garden and check on the koi pool; she would stumble in the drifts. The koi must be left to their fate. Nothing gave her as much pleasure as that place of calm: its rain chain, stone lantern, Zen meditation garden, and the wooden bridge that crossed the water garden crookedly because evil spirits walk in a straight line. 'This weather won't do the Japanese garden much good,' she sighed. Georgie put a moist slice of Christmas pudding on a plate and set it in front of Lavender. 'Probably the best place for a Japanese garden is Japan,' she said.

*   *   *

130

'She's so crushing,' Lavender complained fretfully to Angela over the telephone as soon as the line had been repaired that evening. 'If I so much as mention the garden she gives me one of her disdainful stares, to let me know that, as far as she's concerned, I'm one of the idling rich. It's worse than that; she's begun to convince me that I'm nobody at all, that when I come into a room it stays empty, if you see what I mean.' She was close to tears.

'Don't take it to heart so,' Angela said. 'Remember that Georgie was up all night rescuing sheep. She's probably being so snappy and horrid because she's tired.'

'Not she. She stomped off to the office immediately after lunch to do some costings for the holiday cottages, working out which parts are exempt from VAT; a very festive occupation for Christmas Day.'

Angela could imagine how unimportant Lavender must feel in the face of Georgie's remorseless activity. It would be even harder for her when Simon died. Georgie would waste no time in sending Lavender packing. Angela was sure of that. She would find Lavender's presence unnecessary, a relic of an earlier, more indulgent time that had come to an end. Lavender would get the push. Just as the long-serving but unprofitable editors at the publishing company had done after Georgie's rise to power. The thought of Lavender weepily creating a new garden at the back of some Georgian rectory in Clyro made Angela want to groan with sympathy. That would be ridiculous. She must not criticize Georgie or encourage Lavender in the belief that Georgie was in any way unsuitable. Georgie must marry Ellis and stay busily involved at Hayden. On no account must Lavender's deepening hostility cause Georgie to break off her engagement and come back to London in a mood to make mischief.

'The weather forecast is looking a bit better,' she said consolingly. 'Why don't you and Simon come and stay over the New Year? We could go to the sales, and Elsie's longing to perform her solo version of *Riverdance* for you.'

'That sounds like a lovely idea,' Lavender said vaguely. She paused. 'Angela,' she said in a diffident whisper, 'of all the girls whom Ellis could have married, does it strike you as odd that he's chosen one who's, well, not what most men would think was particularly stunning?'

Take it easy, Angela told herself. Lavender doesn't know that Davy was in love with Georgie and may be still. Nor can she guess that she is insulting me horribly by pointing out that Georgie is a plain piece of work who no man in his right mind would look at twice, which happens to be my own opinion too. 'The word stunning always makes me think of Evelyn,' she said lightly. 'Daddy always refers to her as his stunner. She has this way of lifting one shoulder and baring her teeth at the same time.'

'How vampish,' Lavender said, interested.

'A good sort though,' Angela said. And it was true. Look at the way Evelyn had helped pull Elsie back to consciousness. Evelyn meant no harm. It had been Ted, or so he had sheepishly claimed to his daughters, who had insisted on leaving Nora and bringing his affair with Evelyn into the daylight; Ted who had had no stomach for the hotel rooms booked by the hour, furtive assignations and purpose-less lies that Nora had never believed. Georgie, Angela thought, *did* mean harm, although it wasn't yet clear who was to be the chief object of her snooty malevolence.

'A pocket Venus, that's what her type used to be called in my day,' Lavender said; she would not be budged from the subject of Georgie. 'I've never seen the appeal of short women. I should have thought it would be like having all your drinks from a mini bar.'

Angela was shocked when it dawned on her what Lavender meant by 'it'. How unlike her to be so crude; perhaps she was drunk. 'Try not to brood,' she advised.

'I shall,' Lavender said, 'although I can't help wishing that Jared had been a woman; I should have much preferred him as a daughter-in-law.' She gave a slurpy laugh. 'What an absurd notion; perhaps I'd better have a little lie-down. Thank you for listening to a rambling old woman, Angela.'

Jared had received a great many invitations over Christmas; from antiquarian booksellers, interior designers, practitioners of alternative medicine and romantic novelists, all of whom had been drawn to the Welsh borders by its beautiful, rather mystical mountain valleys and its supply of handsome stone houses. Expecting to be fed at buffet suppers and formal lunch parties, he had not laid in supplies. Reluctantly, he started to break into the treats he had been saving to share with Ellis on the dreamed-for day when Ellis would finally decide to follow his heart and come to live with him for ever. Jared opened a jar of caviar and offered a spoonful to Ecru. He drank a few glasses of a rare pale-gold vodka and felt the pleasing heat from the stove on the backs of his calves. He felt too mellow to worry about Georgie Welliver. There would be another chance and another one after that to wear her down. He would never give up; he had seen Ellis first. Jared went to bed early, Ecru curled against his spine, Ellis's stolen shirt under his cheek.

Davy watched a video of *Swan Lake* with Elsie and Maud. What he really wanted to do was shut himself in his study and put in a couple of hours on the computer, but it would have upset Angela. She took Christmas Day very seriously. Davy sighed. He felt that he had settled for a sad little happiness and had had no choice in the matter. He looked at the blue-white arms of the *corps de ballet* as they floated from one side of the stage to the other, and wished he weren't so bored.

'Mince pies,' Angela announced brightly, coming in with a tray. Her eyes, shining with joy, made him feel guilty. As always, she had indulged in an orgy of giving. She had spent hours making and decorating gingerbread ornaments to thread onto the Christmas tree and hadn't minded when Maud pulled them off and ate them in a couple of bites. She had given each of the girls a lifelike baby doll with a wardrobe of clothes that she had made herself. The dolls came with their own carved wooden cots for which Angela had made exquisite bedclothes, including patchwork quilts. She had stayed up for several nights making presents and Christmas ornaments and had neglected the house which had become frowsty and down-at-heel. From where Davy sat on the sofa, he could see feltings of dust on a window-sill, a rug with its corner bent over.

Elsie and Maud had been delighted with the dolls and cradles until they had unwrapped the Barbies sent by Ted and Evelyn. It was the Barbies who were propped on the sofa beside them now, improbable peroxide blondes wearing strapless satin ball dresses and tiny rhinestone necklaces. Angela's present to Davy had been a CD player, not quite as handsome as the one he had admired in Georgie's flat. Lost without Joyce, who had always chosen Angela's Christmas present for him, quite often when he was indulging in one of his lunchless lunchtimes, Davy had rushed distractedly down Bond Street, finally charging into Asprey and spending £5,000 on a solid-gold fountain-pen. He knew that he had no gift for giving. Although his life was spent choosing and distributing objects for complete strangers to buy, and despite his flair for assessing the market for personalized mugs and doorknobs that glowed in the dark, he could not make a connection between those he loved and particular pieces of merchandise. Angela had accepted the pen delightedly enough but, the moment she held it in her hand, Davy realized it had been an idiotic choice and that she would never use it. Its golden casing was too businesslike and intimidating for a home-centred woman like his wife. Jared had sent her a late nineteenth-century crystal wineglass etched with hearts and birds, Nora a hanging iron candlesconce for the garden. Davy felt reproached by both; they might have been designed especially for Angela. He felt that Jared and Nora loved Angela in a way that he couldn't, that they carried a vision of Angela in their heads constantly, and were able to

134

refer to it when shopping for presents. If only he could do the same, but the truth was that when he was away from her, Angela drifted out of his thoughts. Orly would have something to say about that if Davy were ever fool enough to confide in her.

Weighted down by remorse, Christmas lunch and the sense of being caged, Davy smiled at his wife and reached out for a mince pie which he did not want.

CHAPTER TEN

ORLY LIKED BEING ON TELEVISION. SHE liked being fussed over by make-up girls and assistant producers. She liked being recognized by the traffic wardens in Harley Street and the pharmacist at John Bell & Croyden. Most of all, she liked performing: racing along the tiered ranks of seats that made up the set of *Body and Soul*, microphone in hand, and engaging members of the audience in debates on some disturbing subjects – incest, AIDS, adultery. She was good at it too; comparisons were already being made with Oprah Winfrey, although Orly liked to think that her style of orchestrating public revelation was less fawning than Oprah's.

Sudden celebrity, she found, put a stop to the pity that her family and friends had felt towards her for some years because she was well over thirty and hadn't managed to find a husband. Stardom made her life enviable. Before, whenever she'd said – ruefully and with a slight twitch of her eyebrows – that she was wedded to her career, she'd been met with uneasy laughter. Now that this career had brought her fame and increased riches, it was suddenly understood that her job might be more fun and more fascinating than a marriage. Her single state wasn't the most interesting thing about her any more. What the interviewers from *Cosmopolitan* and *Marie Claire* most wanted to know was how much money she made. The answer was too much for Orly to admit to. She felt slightly ashamed of her enormous fee – money for old rope really, since you'd have to be a perfect fool (as Nora might put it) not to be able to get some really steamy stuff out of 'the vics' (short for victims: what the TV crew called *Body and Soul*'s audience). The vics had agreed to participate because they *wanted* to blurt and splurge and unbosom themselves all over the nation's living-rooms. All Orly had to do was ask a few dopey questions and jiggle her foot in her trademark gesture of concerned sympathy.

She had bought a Porsche Carrera and a small house in a pretty street behind Gloucester Road, both of which gave her a lot of pleasure. She began to think that money, if it couldn't buy you love, could certainly buy you happiness and, if you could be happy without love, wouldn't that be the best thing?

'Maybe,' Angela said in an unconvinced way when Orly explained all this, 'it's certainly uncomplicated, which is always a good thing. But don't you miss being the most important person in someone else's life and wouldn't you like to come first, and have someone come first with you?'

Orly wrinkled her nose. 'Not really. Being a sex therapist shows you the ugly side of commitment. The world's full of people crazily obsessing about other people who are just a waste of space. It's quite scary seeing so many couples striving to remain one when, believe me, Ange, they'd be better off being two.'

Angela pounced. 'So, if that's your view on hopeless marriages, couldn't you find it in you to forgive Daddy?'

'That's not the same thing at all. Daddy didn't even try to save his marriage to Ma; he threw it in the garbage.' She began to scratch the sole of her foot, her fingernails rasping unpleasantly. The truth was, although she would never admit it to Angela, that sometimes she thought how heavenly it must be to be loved by a man the way Ted loved Evelyn, finding her irresistibly and constantly delectable. Orly supposed that Evelyn put a great deal of effort into keeping her husband in a permanent state of rapture, an effort that she herself would find impossible to maintain – there was surely something undignified and ridiculous about working so hard to be adorable. Yet, Evelyn, with her bright messy hair and chaotic burblings, had it in her to be beloved. Orly envied her that. It must make you feel so womanly to have a man slobbering all over you. Orly sometimes felt that she had stopped being a woman years ago, perhaps she had never been one. She scratched her foot furiously, ripping her tights.

Angela said, 'Come with me to collect the girls from school and give Maudie a thrill. She loves having an aunt who's a television star.'

'Surely you don't let her watch the show?' Orly hated to think of Maud, that forceful and candid child, watching the vics, those weirdy losers, and hearing their terrible stories, many of them suspect, of violent spouses, bleak childhoods and futureless lives.

'Certainly not; I just cut out the magazine interviews with you. I can hardly bear to watch the programme myself; it's so upsetting seeing those poor people blubbing their souls out to you. Haven't they got any friends they can talk to?'

'Probably not. Friendship requires the social skills that the lonely lack because they don't have any friends to practise them on. Strangers are easier to talk to. Let's go in the Porsche; the girls haven't seen it yet.'

Maud and Elsie tumbled out of school wearing their winter uniform of pudding-basin hats and lumpy heavy capes.

'Wow, coolarama, coolarissima,' Maud said, when she saw the Porsche. 'This is yours, Orly? Get *out* of here.' She closed her eyes and arched her sturdy little body over the bonnet, her hands in their navy woollen gloves, splayed out at her sides, stroking the shiny metal.

'This is her latest bit of mimicry,' Angela whispered in Orly's ear. 'I can't remember whether it's supposed to be one of the super-models or Dolores in The Cranberries, anyway one of the glitzy babes she's been studying. It's a bit worrying; ever since Elsie's accident, Maud is always pretending to be somebody else.'

Mothers stowing children and satchels into estate cars, stopped to stare wonderingly at Orly. They recognized her as the energetic psycho-pundit on *Body and Soul*, a lunchtime programme that they watched while munching a lonely sandwich. She looked older than she did on television, but very expensive in her leather coat. They imagined that she had riotous affairs with famous television presenters and stayed in bed late on Sundays, if that was her fancy. One or two of the mothers tugged at their stretchy leggings, as much a weekday uniform as their daughters' ugly hats and capes. They looked wistfully at the Porsche as they snapped wriggly children into seat-belts and wondered how much money Orly Dimont earned.

Angela was nettled by their wistful stares. This was the first time that her younger sister was getting more attention than she was. Orly had always lived in her shadow; Angela was the beauty, the sought-after, the successfully married golden girl. Orly was noted for her scowls, her nervous energy and the spiky wit that was by no means universally admired. It was maddening to see her now, responding to the mothers' impressed gawps with a modest little grimace.

'Poor old you, it must be beastly having your privacy invaded like this, with everyone staring at you,' Angela said.

'I enjoy it,' Orly said, pulling away from the curb. 'Invasion of privacy is just another way of saying getting attention, and who could object to that?'

Maud, who had taken off her hat and was tilting back her head, imitating a model in a shampoo commercial, said, 'You are lucky being on television, Orly. Everyone knows who you are.'

'They just think they do, sweet pea,' Orly said.

People seldom came to Orly's consulting rooms on their own. They came in couples, shame-faced or outwardly composed, desperate to make each other happy or mutinously seeking assurance that the game was up, their marriage doomed, that it was time to move on. Packed with hate, blame, reproach; they came because they lacked the oxygen of love and felt that life itself was being denied them.

Odd then that the slightly built young woman, who Orly glimpsed in the waiting-room on her return from lunch, was by herself. Didn't she know that half the fun of sex therapy was being able to criticize your partner's technique – *his* thoughtlessness, *her* refusal to experiment – in front of a third party? Orly picked up the typed appointments sheet on her desk. She read, '2.30 p.m. Miss Georgina Welliver.'

Damn it, she thought, this is much too close to home, but I can't very well send her away now. She pressed the button on the intercom and asked her receptionist to show Miss Welliver in.

Heavens, her feet don't even reach the floor, she thought, when Georgie had settled into one of the chintzy armchairs, her legs dangling awkwardly. You'd be looking at her a long time before the word sexy might occur to you. She's lavishly got up but her make-up is all wrong, painted on top of her small kittenish face without being part of it. The bright cosmetics and dangling legs give her the look of a puppet. What a blow to Angela's pride this undersized girl must have been. Aloud, Orly said, 'Tell me about yourself, Georgina,' and moved to her favourite listening position, perched on the corner of her desk. She crossed her legs and began to jiggle her foot.

As Georgie began to talk in her quiet decisive voice, she pulled at her beige hair with both hands. She looked as though she were being blasted by great waves of disgust. 'The truth is I can't bear him to touch me,' she said. 'I can't bear the coldness of his bones through his skin. Even his penis is cold; wet and cold inside me like a dead eel.'

Orly thought, This is so sad. Jared, who longs for Ellis's body, is denied it. Georgie is made frigid by it, but forces herself to submit. 'You can hardly go on like this,' she said. 'Would it be helpful for you and your fiancé to see me together?'

Georgie shook her head violently. 'Certainly not. He mustn't suspect that anything is wrong. I thought you might be able to do something that would make *me* change. Vaginal exercises, or something,' she added vaguely.

'But is that what you really want?' Orly persisted. 'Why do you feel obliged to try and overcome your deep feelings of revulsion? Sexual incompatibility is a serious problem; you must know that.'

Georgie gave her a stony stare. 'It's not in my nature to admit defeat,' she said. 'I believe in bashing on.'

How tragically lonely she looks, Orly thought. Ellis has a real talent for making anyone involved with him feel totally isolated. The man is so triumphantly and cruelly unpossessed that nobody could ever feel at all central to his life. 'I *do* like to think of myself as some kind of exercise instructor,' she said, 'here to tone you up for lifelong maturity. But I don't feel qualified to give you the sort of help I think you need; I think you should perhaps consider seeing a psychiatrist.'

Orly's voice had been sympathetic, but Georgie almost shook with rage. She slid out of the enveloping armchair and snatched up her handbag. 'How dare you suggest that I'm mad,' she shouted; 'this marriage will bring me enormous advantages.'

Orly stared at the door which seemed to quiver after Georgie had gone through it, and then reached for her notepad. She wrote, 'Idea for a *Body and Soul* programme – women who marry men they find repugnant, and why.' It wouldn't be difficult finding people to participate; everyone wanted a chance to appear on television.

Her opinion of Davy Stearns, never high, sank lower. She'd never trusted his diligent attentiveness; he was too much the professional charmer, too aware of the effect that his sleepy-looking eyes and velvety voice had on women. Long before his affair with Georgie Welliver had come to light, Orly had noticed that he liked seeing women melt at his feet. Maybe that was Angela's fault. From the beginning Davy had been the one who was always in pursuit, Angela seeming to slip from his grasp, amused by his ardour and taking it, and happiness, for granted; the attitude of somebody who had long been used to men being in love with her.

Had Angela ignored Davy's need to be indispensable, Orly wondered. Was that why he'd fallen for Georgie, such a wretchedly yearning piece of work. Never underestimate the fragility of a man's ego, Orly thought. Even the Davy Stearns of this world, so handsome and clever and successful, have to be constantly assured that they matter. God, how pathetic.

The intercom buzzed; her next appointment was waiting. The beginning of January was always Orly's busiest time. Dissatisfied couples saw the new year as a chance to start over; even as they belted out 'Auld Lang Syne', pumping their arms up and down, they made the grim resolution to set their marriage to rights. Since she'd become a television star, Orly's professional advice was increasingly sought after; Maud wasn't the only one to believe that television gave everyone who appeared on it a seal of approval. 'Ask Mr and Mrs Consadine to come in,' she commanded the intercom, and prepared herself to listen sympathetically to the accusatory tones of those who thought that life owed them more than the marriages in which they were floundering.

It was only later, when she was driving home, that Orly realized how close she had come to betraying Angela. What had come over her: trying to persuade Georgie to leave Ellis, when Angela's marriage might not survive an unencumbered Georgie vengefully on the prowl? A mark of my professionalism, I suppose, Orly told herself; I was putting my patient's interests first. At least, I hope it was that, rather than some subconscious desire to drop Ange right in it; sibling rivalry is a messy business. Thank heavens, Georgie didn't listen to me. I'm going to forget to think about her from now on. This marriage to Ellis Peregory is her funeral.

Georgie had achieved what Angela had failed to do: cured him of his addiction to casual adultery. The woman sitting next to Davy on the plane to Tokyo was the type that he would once have seduced: showily dressed with a juicy mouth, panicky eyes and, from the way her hand flew to shield the top of her wineglass when the stewardesss made a move to fill it, someone who had fought off an alcohol problem. When her tray had been taken away, she propped her briefcase on her knees and began to flick through some computer printouts. Every so often, catching Davy's eye, she smiled at him, a nice dimpled smile that, less than a year ago, would have caused him to suggest a brandy. He could easily imagine her life; he had enjoyed – no, that wasn't the right word, indulged in was better – so many lunchtime liaisons with women like her. This one could be a fashion buyer, or a PR consultant, maybe even a civil engineer. He would lay a bet on it that she lived alone, or with a cat for company, in a flat decorated in a style that was a bit too perky.

Before he'd known Georgie, putting him next to a woman like this would have been like fire meeting straw. Professional women, models of self-confidence with their immaculate haircuts and quick smiles, but betraying by gnawed fingernails and darting eyes a wobbly hold on the world, had always been ready to fall in love with him. They had been so grateful for lunches at the Savoy, a few deliveries of red roses, some skilled and affectionate afternoon sex that, for a few hours, he could forget how excluded Angela made him feel by her absent-minded fondness. He had been moved by the familiar signs of lonely lives faced with courage: the single-cup cafetière with a bright-red lid, the portable television at the end of a double bed that was heaped with too many pillows, the fridge empty except for an eye-mask and a dish of minced chicken breasts for the indulged cat. He had been flattered by the women's hunger for him, even when, after a combination of guilt and boredom had led to a shabby parting, that hunger had shown itself disturbingly in the desperate telephone calls he had refused to answer. They were, as Georgie had called them, his indiscriminate enthusiasms. Because of her, his enthusiasm had waned; he had lost his appetite for the headlong rush into pleasure.

The woman sitting next to him, tapping her pen thoughtfully against her chin, didn't arouse him in the slightest. This was a strange kind of torment to be in; to feel, instead of pain, blunted and numbed. But it was torment all the same.

Outside the plane's windows, clouds were on the move. Georgie had been the real thing, he thought. Her legacy to him was this unforeseen fastidiousness, the feeling that anything less than the perfection of her small body was worth twelve times nothing.

The woman beside him turned her head. How that juicy mouth would once have excited him, sent him off on a quest for kisses. These days his kisses were all for Angela, who returned them distractedly, while her heart was elsewhere – with her adored little girls, or the friends who clamoured for her attention.

'We'll be landing soon,' the woman said, swiping a damson-coloured lipstick over her juicy mouth. Her voice had a lilt in it, its lightness trying to hide something downtrodden about her life, Davy was certain of that. He opened his wallet, a multi-pocketed affair, to check his Japanese currency. Held in a clear plastic compartment was a photograph of his wife and daughters, taken in the garden at Hayden. Angela was sitting on the grass with the little girls twining against her, Elsie's arms around her neck, Maud's head nuzzling her shoulder. Behind them, pale puffy roses twisted around a wrought-iron arch.

The woman next to him craned her neck to look at the photograph. 'My, what a beautiful family,' she said; 'you're a lucky guy.'

She flashed him a dimpled smile that meant, 'Who do you think you're kidding?'

Davy slid the wallet into his briefcase. He was doing his very best to give a credible performance of a devoted husband. That bitch with the mouth had no business to find his efforts so amusing.

'You know, my dearest, you're having a better time without Ellis than you could ever have with him,' Angela assured Jared. 'Maybe what you really needed all the time was a place you could call home. You've done wonders to this cottage.'

'Ellis is my home,' Jared said fervently. 'I only moved here to be near him, remember. This cottage is a means to an end.'

Angela gave him one of her looks which indicated that she intended to go on seeing him through a forgiving mist no matter how provoking his behaviour might be, and went on polishing the glasses.

Jared was giving a lunch party in her honour; she was staying with him for a few days while Davy was in Japan. Maud and Elsie were staying with Nora and Orly in Orly's new house. Orly had organized a tour of the television studios for them which Maud was looking forward to more than seeing Darcey Bussell and Jonathan Cope dance in *Giselle*, the treat that Angela had arranged to celebrate Davy's return.

'Have you invited Lavender to this lunch?' Angela asked. 'I feel rather bad about not having driven over to see her yet, but it's been so misty.'

'Not this time,' Jared said smoothly. 'Marius and Mignon Popple dined at Hayden last week and I think they can be relied upon for some major gossip. Lavender would cramp their style.'

'We've all taken Jared to our hearts,' a romantic novelist called Selina Chambers was telling Angela an hour later. 'Such a ravishing lad. He inspired me to create a hero with purply-black eyes instead of the usual ultramarine. I certainly hope he stays; a handsome extra man is every hostess's dream.'

Jared, who had overheard, smirked. 'Talking of entertaining,' he said, 'weren't Marius and Mignon witness to extraordinary goings-on at Hayden? Do tell.'

Marius, an antiquarian bookseller, a magnificently bearded man with a broken nose, wheezed gleefully into his wineglass. 'You tell them,' he suggested to his wife.

Mignon looked doubtful. 'I'm a bit tiddly,' she said. 'Well, all right, it is rather a good story. So, there was Georgie being the hostess from hell even more than usual. She had a kitchen timer slung around her neck on a cord, clashing nastily with Simon's mother's amethysts which we all thought should have gone to Eliza. So the moment it started going ping, ping, ping – the perfect conversation stopper – it was in to dinner with us, even though some people had only just arrived, on account of the fog.

'Very good little tomato tartlets we had to start with, but I don't see why they couldn't have stayed in a low oven for a few minutes longer and given us a chance to relax after a tricky drive.'

'Georgie has never been much of a one for relaxation,' Jared said cattily.

'Driven doesn't begin to describe her,' Marius agreed. 'The changes she's making to the estate . . . a very strenuous young woman, but without the vitality which might make her attractive.'

'Are you going to tell them or am I?' Mignon asked.

'Sorry, my passion-flower.'

'I always hate food that's so wonderful that you feel you have to keep on mentioning it, don't you,' Mignon mused. 'I liked it better in Lolly's day, when you could just push some dreadful sludge to the side of your plate without Lavender being the least bit offended, and make yourself a bacon sandwich when you got home. By the way, this boeuf Bourguignon is gorgeous, Jared.'

'Don't mention it,' Jared said, 'especially in front of Georgie. It was cooked by Dinah Thomas, her factotum. I persuaded her to do a spot of freelancing on the side.'

'Jared,' Angela said reprovingly.

'She needs the money, Angela-la-la. Georgie pays her a pitiful wage. Go on with the story, Mignon.'

'After the tomato thingys, we had quenelles of carp, so light, it was like eating fishy air, and then a saddle of venison. Everyone was yakking on about how amazing everything was and then Georgie said something about how everything on the table had come from the estate, and quite a bit of it from the garden. Lavender went the same colour as the tomato tartlets and rushed from the room with her napkin over her mouth. Simon followed her out, trying to look nonchalant.'

'Oh heavens,' Angela said, 'the quenelles. She cooked Lavender's koi. The beastly little bitch.'

Jared gave a delighted smile. 'So then what happened?' he asked, trying to sound only mildly curious, but giving a snicker of excitement that made Selina Chambers look at him thoughtfully. Angela thought that she'd probably revert to giving her heroes ultramarine eyes.

'Not a lot,' Mignon said. 'Georgie explained that Lavender had been a bit fretful lately because the weather had been too bad for her to get into the garden. I loathe the way Georgie talks about Lavender as though she's some shiftless unstable character whom she's trying to drag back from the brink of disaster. It's most unfair. Lavender was a magnificent woman until Georgie got her all rattled and confused. The evening ended quite early. One tends not to linger when Georgie's around and, besides, we all wanted to get home in case the fog got worse. Georgie could scarcely hide her relief. I dare say she was longing for us to be gone so that she could log the menu on to her computer, or whatever nonsense she gets up to.'

'Did Ellis say anything about Lavender being so upset?' Angela asked.

'Not a word. That chap hasn't an atom of feeling for anybody but himself.'

Angela had brought in a dish of goat's cheese, fresh figs, opened and warmed on the top of the wood-burning stove, and bunches of small black grapes.

Reaching for a fig, Mignon didn't notice Jared's frosty look when she criticized Ellis. 'If only *you* could be in charge of hospitality at Hayden, Jared,' she said. 'Look at us all now, elbows on the table, sprawling in our chairs, tearing our friends to pieces.' She stretched her arms above her head, interlacing her fingers and drawing attention to her large breasts, snug in a red mohair sweater. 'I needed this. After dinner with La Welliver, it's like being let out of school.'

The following day, Angela drove to Hayden by herself. Crusts of snow glittered on bare branches as she inched through the valley, chased by a high cold wind. Going in by the kitchen door, she found Lavender alone and moping.

'I heard about the koi,' Angela said, putting her arm around Lavender's shoulders. 'I'm more sorry than I can say.'

Lavender slid out of Angela's hug and led her to the window. Three men in wellingtons were trundling wheelbarrows towards the Japanese garden.

'I'm playing into her hands, I know,' Lavender said, 'but it's so wearisome disagreeing with her; easier just to give in.'

'But the rain chain and the meditation garden – your favourite spot in the entire universe,' Angela protested. She shouldn't be so surprised at this latest sign of Georgie's ruthlessness; slaughtering koi carp was no worse than the savage restructuring that she'd put into operation at the publishing company, but she hadn't expected her to behave so pitilessly towards Lavender, although, of course, that's what ruthless people did: destroy the weak before moving on to the strong. It was a dreadful thing to admit but Elsie's accident had been a blessing because it had strengthened her own hand. Had she not been able to reproach Davy for abandoning his child, she would have had nothing to put in the way of Georgie's terrifying determination; Georgie would have stripped her bare. Angela began to imagine herself and the little girls living in a pinched cramped way while Davy and Georgie led forceful high-powered lives, closing deals and being met at airports by company chauffeurs holding up signs chalked with their names. She closed her eyes in anguish, which Lavender mistook for pity.

'Buck up, dear girl, do,' she said buoyantly. 'The meditation garden has hardly kept anxiety at bay; probably not such a bad thing to be rid of it. Now, have I told you that Georgie's uncle, Harry Welliver, is coming here with his wife? He's making a speech to the Development Board for Rural Wales. It's quite a thrill; he was a hero of mine in the old days, even though Simon always said he was a traitor to his class.'

For a moment Lavender looked like her old self, flustered and girlish. Then Ellis came into the kitchen, gangly and slumped with tiredness. He'd been awake all night, keeping an eye on the lambing which had just begun. He gave Angela an absent smile of inattention, an insulting smile to give a beautiful woman. He made himself a mug of tea, clumsily splashing water and spilling sugar. 'I very much hope you will drop in for a drink while Georgie's uncle is here,' he said, and then more distantly, 'Jared too, naturally. You'd like that, wouldn't you, Mother?'

Without waiting for a reply, he carried his steaming mug out of the room.

Lavender and Simon, Zanna and Harry, a tall and handsome quartet, were standing self-consciously in front of the fire, as though posing for a group photograph. Jared sprang into the room and embraced Lavender, keeping his arm around her waist as Simon made the introductions.

Zanna Welliver was wearing a beautifully cut black dress – not at all suitable for the country; it would be covered in dog hairs in no time at all – and an amused expression. Her eyes flicked from the glass she was holding, engraved with the Peregory family crest, to Simon's slippers, embroidered with the same unrecognizable animal. Harry, listening to Ellis's views on headage, moved his hand to his mouth from time to time, as though trying to stifle a yelp of laughter.

Poor Lavender, Angela thought. It was obvious that her former hero was not impressed by her aristocratic gee-gaws. Lavender had had her hair done, especially for him, in a rather fluffy style, and it was in his honour that she had subdued her high colour with white face powder, which made her cheeks look soft and pouchy.

Georgie, bringing in a silver dish heaped with tiny vegetables that she had crumbed, deep-fried and speared with toothpicks, said crossly, 'Why is everyone standing up? There are plenty of chairs.'

Ellis sank down onto a sofa, his joints cracking with stiffness and fatigue as he stretched out his long legs. 'The lambing,' he apologized; 'aches and pains all over.' He rubbed the back of his neck, wincing as his fingers crunched down on sore muscles.

'You need a massage,' Jared said, his eyes never leaving Ellis's kneading hands.

'That's an excellent idea,' Ellis said. 'Can you recommend anyone? These valleys are stuffed with star-gazers and reflexologists and all kinds of touchy-feely healers of one kind or another; the sort of people you're always cultivating,' he accused Jared in a gruff teasing way that Angela thought was probably the nearest he could get to sounding loving.

Jared was almost vibrating with longing. His black eyes glowed as he watched Ellis rub the side of his jaw and then clutch his shoulder. He would have given his life to stroke Ellis's stooped shoulders, feel Ellis's flesh under his fingertips.

Georgie, too, was following the movements of Ellis's hand. When he had come to bed that night, very late, she had known that he must be tired to the bone. She should have smoothed his cheek, kissed his

151

eyelids, the way Davy kissed hers when she had been overworking. But she hadn't been able to bring herself to touch Ellis; there was something about his cold flesh that proclaimed its need to be left untouched by her. She had pretended to be asleep, hunched up on the far side of the bed, and Ellis had not tried to wake her.

Georgie began to pass around the canapés and then went back to the kitchen to get some more. Zanna followed her. 'What's wrong, Georgie?' she asked in the coarse low voice that Gomer had hated. 'Don't say nothing is, you'd be wasting my time.'

Georgie ignored her and poured a bowl of warm peanut sauce into a scooped-out red cabbage. She arranged small skewers of marinated grilled chicken pieces around the cabbage. Zanna, in one fast scuttling movement, seized the decorative tray of chicken kebabs and sauce, opened the back door and threw the tray out of it. She stood at the open door, looking out at the darkening garden, screwing up her eyes to watch a wedge of swans floating on the river.

'This is just what Gomer longed for, isn't it?' she said dreamily. 'Exactly the way he would have liked Utley to be, heirloom furniture polished half to death, money coming in, estate workers doffing their forelocks.' She closed the door, shutting out the sliding shadows of the trees on the grass.

'Gomer's dream, but don't expect me to believe it's yours.'

'Running Hayden will be a very interesting challenge,' Georgie said levelly.

'Marrying Ellis will be an even more interesting one, since waves of revulsion pour from you whenever he's in the same room. Can't you see that he's in love with that chap with the black eyes? All that massaging and stroking was for his benefit.'

'Love,' Georgie said, the word like chips of ice in her throat.

Zanna looked at her curiously. 'Then I was right,' she said, 'there's another man involved in this deplorable mess; the one *you're* in love with.'

CHAPTER ELEVEN

ELIZA WAS BEING UNCHARACTERIST-
ically amiable. She was often at Hayden these days, bringing
Marianne, dressed in clothes that her doting godparents had sent
her – canvas hats with rolled brims from Afghanistan and embroidered felt waistcoats (Jared); a velvet-collared coat and Viyella
dresses with deep bands of smocking (Angela).

Eliza tipped Marianne into the wooden play-pen in which Eliza
herself had once been furiously confined; you could see her teeth
marks on the bars. Marianne was a more placid child by far. She sat
dreamily in the middle of the play-pen, cooing happily to herself or
playing with her toys. More than all the bright plastic musical
telephones and activity boards, she liked the teddy bear that Jared
had given her. Jared had dressed him in his Garrick Club bow-tie
which Marianne had sucked to a rag.

Eliza was helping Georgie draw up a guest list for the wedding.

Georgie sat at the computer screen while Eliza scrabbled through the limp dog-eared pages of Lavender's address book, whose disordered entries had received one of Georgie's severe frowns.

The Peregorys, it appeared, were a complicated sprawling family whose minor branches were much given to remarriage and changes of address. 'Hmm,' Eliza said, squinting at a page of erratic crossings-out, 'my cousin Benedict has moved to Southampton with his ninny of a third wife. One doesn't like to think of him living in a town like that.' She rambled on while Georgie glared impatiently at the screen. 'That makes about two hundred and fifty people on our side,' Eliza decided at last. 'What about your lot, Georgie?' Georgie tapped a key and some names flickered onto the screen. 'Lord and Lady Welliver,' Eliza read, 'Howard and Aurora Sutch. Aren't they the couple who are always being profiled in the colour magazines? Something to do with shops, isn't it?'

'The fifth largest retail chain in the country,' Georgie said. 'Aurora is Zanna's daughter by her first marriage.'

'Ivan and Clemency Fadge,' Eliza read on. 'They're relations of Zanna's too, aren't they? But what about your own family, Georgie? Your mother could stay with us if you like. Hayden will be stuffed to the attics with Peregorys.'

Georgie clicked and tapped the list of names from the screen. 'That won't be necessary. My mother isn't up to travelling from South Africa.'

'Your brother and sister then. Surely they'd like to see you married?'

'We aren't close,' Georgie said in a voice that made it clear she wasn't going to discuss the matter further.

'Poor old Gilly,' Harry said, passing his sister-in-law's letter to his wife. 'She's dreadfully hurt that none of them have been invited to the wedding. Georgie is an unfeeling piece of work, she really is.'

Zanna read Gillian's letter with her lips pressed together. Gillian's brand of cheery martyrdom had always set her teeth on edge; the woman saw her whole life as a heroic struggle against great obstacles and made sure that everyone else saw it that way too. Now she had enthusiastically seized upon Georgie's heartlessness as another cross to bear. Gillian had written:

> Naturally, it's a disappointment that Georgie is too ashamed of her family to want us around on her big day, but then she has always been rather disagreeable and odd. Perhaps, my dear Harry, you would be very kind and send me some photographs of the wedding. Life isn't easy in South Africa in view of the great changes taking place all around us, but I'm sure that things will settle down eventually. Kate has just produced her third baby – another boy – and so I have moved in with her and Gerald to lend a hand. Kate still relies on her old mum, even though they have a nursemaid and quite a large household staff. How different from the days when Kate herself was small and I had to cope without any help at all, and without hot water, more often than not. Do you remember that hideous old boiler at Utley Manor? Sometimes I was close to tears when nothing would keep it going. Still, we managed to survive.

Zanna crumpled the letter in her bent hand and lobbed it into the waste-paper basket. 'Who could blame Georgie for not wanting her mother around,' she said. 'Gillian has made woundedness into a fine art. And Georgie was always her least-favourite child; I remember Gillian making cruel chirpy jokes about Georgie being moody and undersized. Gillian is one of those women who's addicted to failure. She adores Otto, the useless drunk, and Kate, the mindless suburban housewife. She can't feel at all comfortable with Georgie's achievements; not only does the girl become a brilliant publisher, but then she hooks a man who'll give her the run of his rolling acres. What a set-back for Gillian.' Zanna sighed irritably. 'How I wish Georgie wasn't going through with this, Harry. There is no romantic impulse at all about this wedding.'

'I can't imagine Georgie having anything as untidy as a romantic impulse.'

'That's where you're wrong. Just because she files her knickers doesn't mean she can file her heartstrings, and her heartstrings are all over the shop. I hate to see her pit herself against life in the same desperate way that Gomer did.'

'The way you talk about Gomer in that bad-blood-will-out way is just a trifle melodramatic, my darling,' Harry said mildly.

Marianne, sitting in the middle of the old wooden play-pen, lifted her arms up to Lavender, who picked her up. 'You're the only straightforward human being in the place,' she murmured into the baby's warm neck; 'the only one not putting on some kind of a front. No wonder you're so easy to love.' Marianne pointed to the window.

'Certainly we'll go out if that's what you'd like,' Lavender said. 'The periwinkles may have come into flower.'

She zipped Marianne into her snow suit and arranged her in her carrying sling so that she could look over Lavender's shoulder as they walked through the garden.

The weight of her grandchild against her body made Lavender feel better. She wished she could stay here for ever, breathing the hazy smell of snowdrops and the warm nutty smell of the baby's head. Marianne loved flowers as much as Lavender did, blinking with excitement as they approached the walls of the Edwardian wing which were covered in yellow jasmine and the paler yellow flowers of a late-flowering clematis.

'Clematis cirrhosa *balearica*,' Lavender told her. 'A swine to prune but worth the trouble.'

Inside the castle, someone had switched on the lights, turning dark windows into orange slabs. In the glassy overbright rooms, those who lived there were becoming increasingly murky. Simon and Ellis, Georgie and Eliza would be sitting down to tea, a meal like all meals at Hayden these days, marked by sly glances and silences, evasions and duplicity. 'Thank heavens for you, Marianne,' Lavender said fervently, making the baby look up at her with guileless eyes. 'Everyone else is going around like people in camouflage. I hardly know who they are any more and I can't trust any of them, not even Simon, who I used to love so much that I felt he was always inside my skin. Now I worry that I might not be able to grieve for him properly when he dies, and that breaks my heart.'

Walking reluctantly back to Hayden, Lavender could swear she heard, from inside the Edwardian wing, the wild laughter and crashing footsteps of young men who knew they were about to die.

Davy, finding his reserved seat on the Eurostar to Paris, saw that the woman with the juicy mouth, last seen on the plane to Tokyo, was sitting opposite him.

'What a piece of luck,' she said, 'the man with the pretty wife. This is my first time on Eurostar and I dreaded being landed with a bore.'

She was looking very sparky considering that it was seven in the morning. Davy told her so. She said that she was a morning person, which was a good thing, since she was able to give the baby his early-morning feed before going to the office.

Baby? Davy's left eyebrow shot up his forehead.

'My turn to flash the snappies,' the woman said. She took a folding black-leather photograph frame out of her briefcase. In one perspex-protected oval was a picture of a baby, only a few weeks old, with dark hair and long dark eyes. In the other, the woman herself was holding the baby, older now and with an alert interested smile. The woman was leaning back into the arms of a man who looked like a more finished version of the baby, with the same fine narrow features and an air of finding the world intensely fascinating.

'William and Tom Essens,' the woman said, flipping the frame shut. 'Tom's the baby.' She held out her hand. 'Hi, I'm Anna.'

How could he have been so wrong about her. She had been married since she was twenty. She lived in a big house in

Wimbledon which she and William had bought before the property boom. They had waited ten years to have a baby because Anna's career was going so well. She was the sales director of a company that arranged for wealthy tourists to stay in stately homes all over Europe. She had started as a secretary, but found she had a flair for finding properties – near a golf-course, with fishing rights – whose owners could be persuaded to open their doors to Japanese, German and, increasingly, Russian visitors. 'The alternative, often enough, would be for them to sell up,' Anna said. 'Instead, the wives cook and serve four-course meals and their husbands clean the shoes that the "paying guests" – what an oxymoron *that* is – leave outside their bedroom door.'

She saw Davy looking at her hand. 'That's right, I don't wear a wedding ring,' she said. 'Lawyers and accountants treated me like some kind of noodle when I did. They thought I should be at home pickling cabbages or something. Especially Frenchmen.'

'You travel a lot then?'

'Used to be part of the fun. But, since Tom was born . . . I don't know.' She looked tired suddenly and rubbed her forehead. 'To tell you the truth, I wouldn't mind packing it in, but it wouldn't be fair on William to send him out into the cruel world after all these years. Do you see what I mean?'

'Not really.'

'Well I was the one with ambition. We both knew that right from the start. So the deal was that I'd earn the money and William would do everything else. He's a wonderful cook, great handyman. He rewired the house, put in a new kitchen and bathroom, redesigned the garden, grows every vegetable we eat and now, of course, he looks after Tom.' She looked miserably out of the window as trees sprang towards it and then retreated.

Breakfast arrived. Anna tore off flaky shreds of croissant and loaded them with butter. She drank cup after cup of bitter black coffee.

'This is heaven on toast,' she said. 'William won't allow stuff like this in the house. If I never see another bowl of home-made muesli again as long as I live, it will be too soon. Would you think me a complete disgrace if I ordered a brandy? I've decided to come off my diet just while I'm in Paris.' She gave Davy a steady look which he took to mean that coming off her diet wasn't all she was going to do in Paris.

She had taken off her shoes and was picking up the last crumbs of buttery croissant from the plate with the moistened tip of her finger when she suddenly said, 'I shouldn't moan. I have a lot of girlfriends who come home to their cat and a boil-in-the-bag supper but . . .' she looked at Davy with pleading eyes, 'marriage is such a bummer because of the way you have to keep on making changes to yourself so that you can stay married. Or am I the only person in the world who sees it like that?'

The invitation in her eyes was so obvious that Davy heard himself ask her where she was staying like a man under hypnosis.

Anna's dimples flickered in her cheeks. 'My company keeps a flat in the Rue de Saintes Pères.' A pause. 'Be my guest.'

Davy took her hand in his and kept hold of it. Why not? he thought. Perhaps this is what I need; perhaps that beautiful mouth will make me forget that all I'm living with is a melancholy acceptance of the facts.

The flat on the Left Bank was stuffy and furnished in that peculiarly French way – bobbly silk tassels hanging from the handles of an enormous sideboard, bow-legged chairs placed in awkward groups around the edges of the sitting-room – that Davy had always thought was inspired by the decor of a well-appointed brothel.

Anna strolled through the rooms, opening shutters, kicking off her shoes, dropping her briefcase heavily on the ugly carpet.

Beneath the efficient dark-blue gaberdine suit, she wore under-wear of the kind that Davy associated with women like Evelyn

Dimont: an underwired bra and matching suspender belt both brand-new and – Davy was certain of this – bought for the trip to Paris in the hope of a pick-up. Poor William.

In bed, Anna was as responsive as a puppy. She clambered all over him, clasping, clutching; her fingers eager little claws. With his mouth on hers, Davy thought not of Georgie, but of Angela. As Anna ecstatically squeezed her eyes shut, he saw Angela's eyes, clear and kindly and, always at the moment he entered her, wide open and slightly amused.

He groaned and Anna's plump thighs tightened around his waist. It wasn't rapture that made him groan, but regret.

Philandering was pointless if it brought visions of his wife spreading out her large serene body with a tolerance that never failed to humiliate him. He wondered if he were being punished for all his adulteries; his punishment, never to be satisfied with the woman in his arms for regret over the woman in his head.

Anna's teeth nipped his shoulder, drawing blood. He made love to her skilfully, automatically, feigning an enthusiasm he didn't feel. He hoped she already had a dinner engagement.

'Don't be angry, but I'm booked for dinner,' she said.

'Me too,' he lied.

'You're not such a hedonist as you look,' she said.

'I'm sorry, Anna. I seem to have lost my taste for complications.'

'That's a shame. I should have liked being your complication.'

He kissed her on her beautiful mouth and let himself out.

'Oh, this is a major kind of day,' Jared said gleefully, shaking a copy of the *Western Mail* in one hand and an airmail letter in the other so that they crackled dramatically. He sat down next to Eliza on the terrace that he had built at the back of the cottage to catch the morning sun. From there they could see the life of the hillside: the glint of a brook moving over damp stones, a river of sheep making for a farm gate. It was the first warm day of spring and Eliza and Jared drank their coffee sitting on an elm seat with a curved ribby back. The sun brought out the biting smell of the narcissi which Jared had planted in studied drifts.

' "Planning permission has been refused for the proposed construction of a group of holiday cottages on the Hayden estate",' he read out. 'Dearie me . . . "not appropriate" . . . "quite out of keeping with the environment" . . . "pressure from the National Heritage Department" . . . "duty to protect and preserve our countryside" . . . what a supernacular rap on the knuckles for the she-devilette. And there's even more un-good news for Miss Hellspawn.' He gave the airmail letter another shake. 'When you told me she wasn't inviting her family to the wedding, I got a private detective in Cape Town to nose around. Much better than I hoped; her brother's been in prison. Drunken driving. And the third of his four wives wants to put him back behind bars for non-payment of alimony.'

'I can hardly believe it,' Eliza said, shaken. 'Ellis *dined* with him when he was in South Africa. He can't possibly have known that Otto had been to prison; he's terrified of scandal.'

'Don't I know it,' Jared said bitterly. He showed her a shiny black and white photograph of a man with dark deep-set eyes which looked challengingly out of a gypsyish face. 'Rather handsome, don't you think? Otto was definitely first in the queue when the good looks were being handed out at Welliver Towers. Only the scrapings left for poor Georgie.'

Eliza was fascinated by the photograph. She shielded it with her hands to keep off the sunlight and looked at the gypsy-like face for a long time. At last, she said, 'But you know, Ellis saw quite a bit of him; mentioned him in letters and so on. Said he planned to look up Otto's sister when he came home.' She was silent again, pushing at her large chin with her thumb and staring at the homeward-bound sheep on the mountainside without seeing them. 'I think we should bring Otto to England,' she said, in a hushed conspiratorial way.

161

It was Jared's turn to look unseeingly at the sheep flowing through the farm gate in a fleecy tide. 'That might be more than I am able to bear,' he said at last.

'No harder to bear than Ellis marrying Otto's sister, surely?'

Jared gave a tight brave smile. 'One never knows. That's part of the agony of loving Ellis; one never knows.'

'Chin up,' Eliza said. 'I'm off to Hayden, to drip with sympathy over the holiday-cottage scheme going belly up. I'll enjoy that. I read somewhere that people feel a cheerless satisfaction when others fail. Stuff that; I feel a very, very cheerful satisfaction when Georgie fails. Toodle-oo, my dear.'

When Eliza had gone, Jared sat for a long time gazing at the sunlit slopes of the hills, slipping one into another; then he went into the house and switched on the television to keep his mind off Otto Welliver's handsome face.

Orly Dimont was striding up a flight of wide, shallow steps, tossing the head of a microphone from hand to hand like a rock star in concert. She came to a halt in front of a middle-aged man with compassionate eyes who was mournfully perched on one of the tiers of low seating that furnished the set of *Body and Soul*, and flipped the microphone in his face.

'So tell us why you think the discovery of the so-called gay gene could get us all in trouble,' Orly commanded.

A strip of lettering scrolled across the screen beneath the man's striped shirt. It read: Dr Brittas Kamm, paediatrician. Dr Kamm, his eyes pools of worry, said that parents might seek an abortion if told that their unborn child might grow up to be a homosexual.

'And who could blame them?' boomed a voice from the other side of the studio.

Orly, swinging her microphone, leaped between the ranks of humiliatingly low seating to listen to a low-church clergyman who saw homosexuality as an abomination – 'yon evil incubus'.

Up and down the wide flight of stairs Orly skipped, catching words in her microphone; words that were prejudiced, anguished, angry, sourly amused. Orly's eyebrows glistened with interest as she fed the words into the microphone. She jiggled her foot and smiled encouragingly.

Jared watched Orly's programme in a disinterested way. He didn't think of himself as a homosexual since the only man he loved was Ellis. Nobody, apart from Ellis, had ever shunned him. On the contrary, nearly everyone he met warmed to him because he was good-looking, charming, and above all, very rich. He felt sure that were he to be introduced to the low-church clergyman, a thuggish-looking man with a lumpy face and thin purple lips, his elegant suits and pleasant manners would ensure that he was treated with respect, even with envy.

His difficulties were all to do with loving Ellis, loving a man he had never touched, although the scorching looks they gave each other were more passionate than any embrace. Denied Ellis's embraces, Jared had never been able to bring himself to touch anyone else. For years he had been celibate, a state that the lumpy-faced cleric must surely approve of.

Jared made himself study the photograph of Otto Welliver and realized that he was burning with jealousy. How strange, when he was not the least bit jealous of Georgie. Furious with her, yes; determined to get her away from Ellis and Hayden, yes, again; but not jealous. How could he be when ever since she had come to live at Hayden, Georgie had looked the picture of misery, uncomfortable in the expensive clothes that didn't suit her, her mouth pinched, her eyes smudgy and lost?

He had never been jealous of Georgie, Jared understood that now. He had never been jealous because he had never for one single moment believed that Ellis was in love with her. *Had* he believed that, he would like to think that in a spirit of pure nobility he would have let Ellis go, wished him every happiness with his thin drab bride. Was Ellis in love with Otto? The only way to find out was to bring Otto to Hayden and force a confrontation. Jared shivered although the room glittered with sunshine. He needed to discuss this risky venture with someone who could understand his feelings.

On the television screen, Orly was thanking the studio audience and reminding viewers at home to watch the next edition of *Body and Soul* at the same time next week. Jared clicked the remote, dissolving Orly's glossy eyebrows and fidgety pacings. It would never have occurred to him to talk about anything close to his body or soul with Orly Dimont. Few people did, except for the hundreds of complete strangers who turned up at the television studio and Orly's Harley Street consulting rooms. It didn't matter to them that Orly showed them no fondness; they took her lack of warmth as proof of her professionalism. But her friends found Orly too harsh a confidante; it was as though every secret they shared confirmed Orly in her dismal view of the world, a view she had held since the day her father ran off with Evelyn Coote. Her friends learned to keep their secrets to themselves, however unhappy they might be; they needed to feel that their personal misery was unfolding in a benevolent universe. Jared picked up the phone and dialled Angela's number.

By keeping a close watch on Georgie, Eliza had become a skilled computer operator. She skulked around Ellis's study when he and Georgie were working on the estate, and went through the farm's accounts. It hadn't taken Eliza very long to work out Ellis's password. First she had tapped out his birthday – 3APR56 – then the name of his dog – FAULDER – without gaining access. In a flash of inspiration, she had tried DAUMAN, and brought the screen flickering to life. Now she called up Ellis's address list and, within seconds, found out where Otto Welliver was living. Thirty-two Azalea Apartments. Eliza imagined a low-built housing complex, secure behind electronic gates; its blinding white walls smothered in fiery climbers which splashed orange, purple and crimson over the slabby stucco. The residents lurked inside: minor con men, divorced women, retired arms dealers, people on the way down, like Otto Welliver, aware of their own worthlessness in a new South Africa, too reliant on gin and bridge.

The voice that answered the telephone was bleary and suspicious, the voice of a man who had fallen asleep with his clothes on.

'We're in a rather delicate situation,' Eliza boomed in an excited insistent voice. 'I know that Georgie is not on good terms with her mother and sister and felt that she couldn't invite you and not them. But the fact is that she would love you to be here.'

'Unlikely. There's nothing in it for her.' Otto gave a derisive yawn.

'Needless to say, your fare and all your expenses would be met,' Eliza said. 'The ideal thing would be for you to get over as soon as you can, give us all a chance to get to know each other, see a bit of the countryside. It would be such a wonderful surprise for Georgie. Do say yes.'

Otto, dangling a hand over the edge of the bed, bumped his fingers on an empty gin bottle. It struck him that he owed money to most of his friends, as well as three weeks' wages to the maid who slept in the servants' quarters behind Azalea Apartments. He didn't think he would last long in his current job, managing a recording studio, because he'd been more or less permanently drunk for a long time now. He could hear attachment in Eliza Jones's honking voice, a desire to keep things the way they had always been: ancient houses, ancient fields, ancient customs. Otto Welliver, hung-over, broke and feeling sorry for himself, contemplated the aching boredom that Eliza and her kind represented.

'I'll see,' he said.

'I'll find out about flights,' Eliza said jubilantly.

'Will it not look rather odd for Maud and Elsie to be the only bridesmaids?' Lavender ventured cautiously. 'They are quite the most adorable little girls, but not related to us in any way, and there are so many Welliver cousins whose children should perhaps be considered. And the train is twenty feet long, you know, Georgie, my dear. I had six attendants to keep it clear of the floor and I do believe that Simon's mother had ten.'

'I shan't be wearing the train,' Georgie said.

'But it's been in the family for more than three hundred years. Every Peregory bride has been married in it.'

'That explains why it looks like an old floorcloth. You're just like my father, Lavender, hanging on to every bit of tat for no reason at all except for the fact that it's always been hung on to.'

Lavender gave up. The Peregory train was an exquisite length of Valenciennes lace which had the Peregory crest worked into the design. Lavender loved its gauzy shimmer, the soft drift of it as it floated above the stone floor of the church, carefully borne aloft by numerous bridal attendants. Even sturdy, booming Eliza had become a beauty on her wedding day, as the train billowed out from the waist of her wild silk dress, shielding her hefty hips.

'I hate old things,' Georgie said, in the mood for a fight.

'Very well then,' Lavender said, struggling to retain the air of bland self-assurance that she knew Georgie found infuriating.

'Now that's what I call a really sweet gesture,' Angela said in a dangerous voice. 'Georgie wants our two little cup-cakes to be her bridesmaids – her only bridesmaids, in fact,' she added, glancing again at Georgie's neatly typed letter. 'What a treat that will be for you, my darlings.' Maud and Elsie clambered onto her lap to see the proof of this surprising invitation, and Angela clamped her arms around them and began to kiss them fiercely.

She had hoped that Davy would see her professed enthusiasm for this grisly idea of Georgie's as the very model of civilized behaviour but, when she looked at him over the top of Elsie's silky hair, his face had gone quite white. He pushed away his plate of poached eggs on toast.

Jared, who was spending a long weekend in London with the Stearns's, gave Angela a betrayed look. 'If I thought for one moment that the wedding was going to take place, I'd take enormous exception to the children of my very best friend traipsing down the aisle behind Miss Hellspawn,' he said.

'Maud, Elsie, go and finish your breakfast in the play-room; you can watch cartoons,' Angela said, putting bowls of muesli and glasses of orange juice on a tray. She sailed out of the room with it, followed by the obedient Elsie. Maud, sensing some excitement in the air, dragged her feet until Jared swung her onto his shoulders and galloped into the play-room, tossing his head and neighing.

When Angela and Jared were back in the kitchen, Davy asked, 'What the hell are you talking about, Jared?'

'Didn't Angela tell you? Otto is coming to England.'

'Jared has this novelettish idea that Ellis has a thing about Georgie's brother,' Angela said.

'Well none of us really believes that Ellis has a thing about Georgie, do we? I mean, this isn't Jane Eyre we're living in,' Jared said crossly.

Davy poured himself some more coffee. It was Jared's favourite kind, Brasileiro, which Angela served only when he was staying with them. She always made an extra effort for Jared: the breakfast table was set with linen napkins and daffodils in a cream lustre jug and Angela's home-made muesli had been tipped from its usual plastic box into a wooden bowl from the Shaker Shop. Looking at the hard raisins and chunks of dried apricots stirred into dusty-looking oatflakes made Davy think of Anna Essens's buttery fingers stuffing croissants into her juicy mouth. He smiled.

'Smile if you must,' Jared said, 'but I mean business. The she-devilette must go. At the very least Otto's visit will disconcert her, and she reacts badly to being disconcerted.'

Angela's eyes were flickering worriedly. Davy understood at that moment that she hadn't told Jared about his affair with Georgie. He was touched by her loyalty. Hadn't she always claimed that Jared was like a special kind of girlfriend, the one who helps you choose your clothes, the one you moan to when someone casually breaks your heart? He wanted to kiss away the frown on Angela's broad forehead, make it become as calm as marble. He wanted to tell her, his loyal, brave, golden girl, that Jared's determination to get Georgie out of Hayden was idiotic and must fail. Except that a part of him, the part that still ached for Georgie Welliver's small breasts and thin wrists, wanted Jared's plan to succeed. This is what his longing for Georgie had come to – a silent collaboration with Jared Dauman, that ridiculous fantasist who never knew when it was time to hand in his chips, that pretentious lunatic who'd locked himself into an obsession and swallowed the key. Deeply ashamed of himself, Davy kept his eyes on the slice of toast he was spreading with marmalade.

'But if Ellis turns out to be in love with Otto, I can't see where that leaves you, Jared,' he remarked languidly, as though the whole subject bored him to tears.

'With Ellis, after Otto's taken him for a very fast ride and gone back to South Africa and all his past and future wives,' Jared said decidedly. 'There I shall be, the soul of sympathy, ready to pick up the broken pieces of our lives. Poor Ellis; when it comes to dealing with his own emotions, he's a hopeless case.'

It takes one to know one, Davy thought but remained silent. Jared was right; Ellis was a hopeless case, and not only emotionally. Georgie should not, could not marry him. Hadn't she noticed the disdainful way Ellis tipped back his head whenever she mentioned her childhood, which was something she needed to talk about – it was her way of scraping it out of her mind – although she did go on a bit about her father's looniness and how unhappy she'd been. She must be just as unhappy now, full of misery and fury; much of it, Davy was certain, directed at him. Why would she want his children as her bridesmaids except to wound him as she had been wounded?

At a time like this she needed to be watched over and comforted in ways which were beyond Ellis. Even so, this plan of Jared's was ludicrous.

As though he had read his thoughts, Jared said, 'You've got to be obsessed with what you want, you know.'

Davy and Angela stared at him with appalled attention. 'Jared,' Angela said, 'it's my dearest wish that, one day, you will settle for someone other than Ellis.'

'Not on, Angela-la-la. I'm incapable of the ordinary, I'm afraid; it's so tedious doing things that you know you can do.'

Maud came into the room wearing Elsie's white leotard and the flesh-coloured nightdress that Evelyn had given to Angela. On her head was a haphazard wreath of wilted snowdrops and hairgrips.

'I'm a bridesmaid called Giselle,' she announced. She stalked around the room, elbows wide, feet turned out, her eyes fearful and glittery. 'A mad bridesmaid,' she explained.

'Move over, Darcey Bussell,' Jared said. 'Maudie, you are supernacular. You look as nutty as pecan pie.'

'I can be your Giselle-bridesmaid too, if you like,' Maud offered.

'Tragically, I don't appear to be getting married.'

Maud pulled at the leotard which cut into her thighs; she was fatter than Elsie. 'It doesn't have to be now,' she said. 'My Giselle costume is stretchy.'

When Jared had gone out shopping to buy a topiary wire frame for Lavender who wanted to make Marianne an ivy cat in a pot, Davy said awkwardly to Angela, 'This isn't easy for any of us.' He made a movement towards her, as though to take her in his arms, but Angela went on folding napkins, stacking cups on a tray. She gave him a forgiving smile which pressed down on him like an unbearable weight.

'We'll all feel a lot better once this wedding is over,' she said, and began to load the dishwasher.

CHAPTER TWELVE

'GEORGIE, DO GO INTO THE GARDEN, you'll never guess who's there,' Eliza said to Georgie. In so far as such a hefty woman could look roguish, Eliza did; her large chin quivered with excitement.

'Oh well, all right,' Georgie said. 'If it's Ben Cantalupo, I want to know why it's taking him so long to resubmit plans for the cottages.' As she rounded the side of the castle, on grass furred by the morning's rain, she saw a familiar figure leaning against an oak tree, cupping his hand around the cigarette he was trying to light in the gusty wind.

'Otto,' Georgie called furiously.

He ambled towards her, smiling sheepishly, raising his shoulders against the wind. He was dressed far too flimsily for the cold spring day, in a thin black suit with cuffed trousers and a white T-shirt. His wild hair was slicked back from his forehead and had a sticky shine.

'You look like the manager of an untalented pop group,' Georgie said in greeting.

Ignoring her rudeness, Otto kissed her on both cheeks. 'You look great, little sister, healthy as a trout,' he lied. He thought that Georgie, who'd always been a nondescript mousy girl, looked worse than he'd ever seen her, with dull skin and hair the colour of parched earth. She looked like the ghost of a dead soul. He flipped his cigarette butt into Lavender's clipped box hedge and waved his hand around the budding trees and the smokily blue mountains in the distance. 'Funny thing about the countryside,' he said, 'how it manages to be so beautiful and so balls-achingly boring at the same time. That's also true of quite a lot of women when you come to think about it.'

'You're the expert,' Georgie said angrily. She'd never understood why women tumbled into love with her unreliable brother. Couldn't they see what a phoney he was? The way he shoved his stupid wraparound sunglasses onto the top of his head so that he could stare into their eyes. Hadn't they noticed that what Otto wanted was love without real life attached? Evidently not. Otto careered from woman to eager woman, leaving outrage and chaos behind him. His last wife, Melissa, in a state of cold fury, was about to take him to court for non-payment of alimony, although she earned more money than he did these days. She still hadn't forgiven him for throwing up in her gold kid evening boots, and leaving her to find out.

It seemed hardly any time at all since Gillian had sent Georgie a wedding photograph of Otto and Melissa holding a knife over a tiered cake which was iced with their intertwined initials and the words 'Totally Always'.

What a feckless idler Otto is, Georgie thought, as her brother lit another cigarette, squinting lazily at the mist steaming from the hills.

What a tyrannical tiresome bitch Georgie is, Otto thought, watching her look frowningly around the garden, daring a weed

172

to show itself. She reminded him of their father, although she wouldn't have thanked him for the comparison. He'd been amazed when he'd heard that she'd landed Ellis Peregory. Ellis had seemed rather a decent chap when Otto had met him in Cape Town; he'd taken Otto to good restaurants and had always insisted on paying. At the end of his visit, Ellis had pressed a cheque for £500 into Otto's hand and mumbled something about knowing that the music business was going through a difficult time, while his extraordinary ears glowed like red-hot coals. An edgy guy, though. When Otto had put an arm around Ellis's shoulder to thank him, Ellis had nearly jumped out of his skin and his ears had burned even brighter.

Ellis came into view, emerging from a patch of woodland, looking more at ease than he had in South Africa, wearing a waxed jacket and tweed cap, his sheepdog obediently to heel. Otto thought that he looked like the lord of all he surveyed, and probably was. Perhaps Ellis felt awkward only in places he didn't own.

Otto strolled towards Ellis who, at the sight of him, stood stock-still, his ears reddening. Watching Ellis in the scrutinizing way she had, Georgie's first thought was that it wasn't fair on her or on Jared for Ellis to look at Otto in that besotted way; he was being unfaithful to both of them.

'Hi, Ellis, good to see you again,' Otto called as he got nearer. Otto wouldn't have a clue about what was going on, Georgie realized. He was an idiot and always had been. Stumping ferociously across the grass, she caught up with her brother.

It was Georgie who propelled them indoors. Ellis seemed oblivious of the sudden drizzle, or of anything except Otto's presence. In the drawing-room, Otto stood in front of the fire – he'd forgotten how those westerly winds struck at your very bones – while Ellis sat stiffly in a chair at the far side of the room.

'What a bit of luck that you're still out of prison,' Georgie said conversationally.

'Georgie, give it a rest.' Otto was embarrassed for Ellis's sake rather than his own.

Georgie raised her eyebrows. 'Doesn't Ellis know about your spell inside?' She settled herself in a chair next to Ellis and touched him lightly on the arm, staking possession. 'It was rather a scream because of the way that Mother carried on. She just didn't understand why her precious darling boy had to go to jail when all he'd done was run over a black. She had half a mind to bring us all back to England but Otto had just got engaged to Jinty, or was it Lila?'

'Celia,' Otto mumbled.

'That's right. Celia. Sometimes I forget which order your wives came in; they all look so much alike. Otto likes the nightclub singer type,' she explained to Ellis: 'turquoise sequins and matching eyeshadow.'

'I hadn't realized you'd been married,' Ellis said. He was hunched in his chair, defensively hugging his knees.

'Never for very long,' Georgie said, tightening her grip on Ellis's arm. 'Four divorces. Poor mother. Sometimes she doesn't dare show her face at the bridge club.'

There was no mistaking the message she was sending Ellis. She was warning him of the dangers that lurked in the world. Everywhere, people were waiting to lure him into a life of debauchery. He must resist their lures or risk losing Hayden. Georgie had so arranged matters that, in Simon's eyes, she had become the emblem of respectability; only by becoming her husband could Ellis come into his inheritance. There was no point in wishing things were otherwise; his fate was sealed.

'Please excuse me,' Ellis said. 'I have an appointment at one of the farms.'

'I should never have come,' Otto complained, in a wounded way, when Ellis had left the room, 'but Eliza persuaded me that you wanted me to.'

'Why on earth should I want a thing like that?' Georgie said.

'Why would I want you at Hayden when one of the reasons I left South Africa was to get away from you and your drinking and your car crashes and Mother always making excuses for your behaviour because you were her favourite? You really must be a prize chump, Otto, if you thought I was going to provide a welcome in the hillside.'

Her grey eyes swept over his shoddy crumpled suit and the yellowed tips of his fingers, which trembled slightly as he lit another cigarette. Her dislike of him seemed to batter the air in front of his face. He should never have come. Easier to face Melissa and her crew of vengeful lawyers than his sister's snapping eyes.

'Clever of Eliza to have smoked you out of the woodwork,' Georgie observed. 'I should have known she was still against me; all of them are.'

She fished out a cheque-book and pen from the leather pouch which housed her mobile phone and which she carried everywhere. 'I'll pay you to scram; I want you out of Eliza's spare bedroom by tomorrow.'

'I'm not staying with Eliza. A chap called Jared Dauman picked me up at the airport and we rather hit it off.'

Georgie began to laugh mirthlessly. 'If Jared knew what was going on, he wouldn't be giving you houseroom.'

'Now I've really lost the plot,' Otto said miserably, 'but then, as you say, I'm a chump.' He looked thoughtfully at the cheque Georgie had given him: an impressive sum, more than he'd got from Ellis. 'May as well spend a few days in London,' he said; 'see the sights.'

'I want you to swear to me that you won't try to get in touch with Ellis.'

'What would be the point after you've told him about my wicked ways? He'd tell me to go to hell.'

'You really *are* a prize chump if that's what you think,' Georgie said. 'Now get lost; you remind me of failure.'

* * *

'Should I laugh or cry?' Jared asked Angela during one of their daily telephone conversations. 'Otto's going down to London to look at some recording equipment, or so he says. And he insisted on repaying Eliza for his air fare. I think he's guessed we're up to something and doesn't want any part of it. He's one of those not very bright people who shine with innocence. Makes me feel a bit tarnished, to tell the truth.'

'Crikey,' Angela said, 'shining with innocence after four marriages; that takes some doing.'

'What I'd really like is for you to put him up, if that's all right, Angela-la-la. Frankly, I feel rather responsible for him; wouldn't want the poor chap to be at a loose end.'

'Doesn't sound like the type who'd be at a loose end for long,' Angela said. 'Of course he can stay. Bye now.'

'Kissy, kissy.' Jared pressed little popping kisses into the receiver before putting it down.

'Four wives,' Nora said faintly. 'Orly, my darling girl, your happiness is my dearest wish, but are you sure that this is a good idea?'

'Quite certain of it. Whatever Otto does can't possibly be as bad as what I imagine him to be capable of doing,' Orly said cheerfully. She had decided to marry Otto Welliver the very same evening that she had met him at the Stearns's house exactly one week ago. His slicked-back hair and gypsy eyes, his narrow black suit and the way he almost threw himself across the dinner table to light her cigarette made her feel that he was her manifest destiny.

Until she met Otto, whenever Orly had thought about marriage, it had been with a sinking heart. In her mind, she catalogued all the men she knew and found every one of them uninspiring; the psychiatrists with pens clinking in their inside breast pockets, the television producers who bounced on their heels as they talked. None of them seemed worthy of the hard work of daily living which was what marriage was.

Otto was more flawed than any of them; she knew that. He was rich in flaws, so irredeemable that she would never be tempted to try to redeem him.

'He is so absolutely sublime,' she said.

Nora thought that her younger daughter had never looked better. Success, as it so often does, had improved her appearance no end, giving her a fluid and shapely prettiness. Her legs, in pale glossy tights, looked as though they had been lightly and devotedly polished. Love had something to do with it too. What Nora thought was that Orly saw Otto Welliver as the solution to Ted's unforgivable betrayal of her (Orly had never seen her father's leaving home as a betrayal of *Nora*). Now she was marrying the most unsuitable man in the world, knowingly, with her eyes wide open, to stop herself from having expectations which might not be fulfilled.

'Otto is your Evelyn Coote,' Nora said. 'Maybe all of us need an Evelyn Coote at some point in our lives.'

'Oh, Otto's far worse than Evelyn,' Orly said. 'According to him, he's only one drink away from imprisonment.'

Nora smiled gamely. 'If he's your heart's desire . . .' she said and raised her glass.

'Don't worry, Ma. We've got a pre-nuptial agreement; what's mine stays mine. In theory, at least. The fact is, I enjoy watching Otto splash about in the unfailing fountain of my *Body and Soul* fees. He's better at spending money than I am.'

'It's Jared I feel sorry for,' Nora said, hurriedly changing the subject; she didn't want to hear any more about Otto's spending habits. 'Everybody's pairing up like the end of a Shakespeare comedy and Jared's left out in the cold. The least that Ellis might have done would have been to have asked Jared to be his best man.'

Orly sniggered. 'I agree. It would have been most appropriate.'

'It would have been the *civilized* thing to do,' Nora said reprovingly.

'A consolation prize for the years of heartbreak that Jared endured, failing to become Ellis's lover?'

'Since you put it like that, yes.'

'You're a tolerant old stick, Ma.'

Nora coloured with pleasure. 'Just as well that I am if I'm to be Otto's mother-in-law. Four wives,' she marvelled again. 'Four wives.'

Not for the first time, Orly was tempted to tell Nora about Davy's affair with Georgie, just to see how far her mother's tolerance would stretch. Nora adored Davy; sometimes Orly felt that she loved him more than she loved her own daughters. In Nora's eyes, Davy was the dedicated and generous provider, the devoted father. How tempting to provide another picture of Davy: the lightsome adulterer, who would almost certainly have run off with Georgie Welliver, who Nora regarded as a frightful, heartless girl, had it not been for Elsie falling off a breakwater.

Orly resisted the temptation. Nora needed Davy Stearns to be everything that Ted Dimont had turned out not to be. It would break Nora's heart to find out that Angela was married to a man who had been unfaithful to her. Nora needed to believe in the possibility of the perfect marriage and looked to Angela and Davy to provide a demonstration of one. That was the reason Nora pretended to like Angela's wholesome indigestible casseroles, why she boasted about Angela's energetic chauffeuring of Maud and Elsie to ballet classes and museums and swimming-pools, even though Nora herself lived on snack food and often stayed in bed all day. How lucky I am to be the second-born, Orly thought. Because Angela is so perfect, I'm allowed to make mistakes.

'Do you think we should let Maudie be a Giselle-bridesmaid at our wedding?' she asked, tucking her arm affectionately in Nora's as they scuttled along the windy promenade back to Nora's house.

'Oh, she stopped being Darcey Bussell three days ago,' Nora said. 'Her latest impersonation is of you, Orly. She races up and down the stairs, trailing an extension cord and chucking it from hand to hand. We thought she was being Cher at Las Vegas until she stopped in front of the newel post and asked how it felt the first time it saw its husband wearing a dress. Angela never lets her watch *Body and Soul* at home, but she saw it at a schoolfriend's house. She seems to think it's some kind of dramatization and all the people are actors. Sometimes I wonder myself.' Nora hooked her arm more firmly into Orly's. 'Do you think it's anything to worry about, Maudie always pretending to be someone else?'

'No I don't,' Orly said. 'I know what you're driving at, Mother. You think that Maud blames herself for Elsie's fall and her impersonations are a way of escaping from herself.'

'Yes, I do. Although Elsie's accident was my fault. I was a perfect fool to close my eyes.'

'Everything's turned out just fine. And don't lose any sleep over Maudie; she's just trying on personalities for size. A textbook case of finding the outer child.'

'What tosh you do talk,' Nora said.

Georgie saw the photograph of her brother, Otto, and Orly Dimont in Dinah Thomas's *Daily Mirror* before Otto had got around to telling her his news. The *Mirror* photographer had posed the newly engaged couple in the deserted studio of *Body and Soul*, in front of the tiers of uncomfortably low seating. Orly's arms were around Otto's neck; Otto's arms were around Orly's waist. They both wore expressions of blissful lust and looked as much a part of each other as to be breathing the same breath. The caption beneath the photograph described Orly as TV's sex pundit and Otto as a rock music entrepreneur.

Georgie thought about her unsuccessful consultation with Orly and the desperation that had brought her to a sex therapist. At the time she had been almost crazy with shame because she could not bear the slimy touch of Ellis's flesh against her own. Things were much easier now. She had pulled herself together without Orly Dimont's help or anyone else's. She had conquered her feelings of revulsion, and, indeed, all her other feelings. She had managed to deaden all her responses, so that she scarcely felt alive any more. This made it much easier to live with Ellis and the lies that they told each other and the world.

'You know who *she* is, don't you?' Dinah Thomas had shuffled quietly into the kitchen and was pointing to the photograph with a fat pink finger. 'She's the sister of that Angela who stays here sometimes; the one who likes gardening.'

Georgie was appalled. To think that she had revealed her sexual problems to none other than Davy Stearns's sister-in-law. She wondered if Orly knew about her affair with Davy, if Orly had told Angela about her unsatisfactory sex life with Ellis. Did sex therapists have to observe the same rules of confidentiality as qualified doctors? Georgie didn't have the least idea. Her pale face grew paler.

Dinah, engrossed in the story of Orly's engagement, didn't notice. 'It says here that he's had four wives. Four wives. It's her I'm surprised at. She's brilliant on telly; they say she earns almost as much as Cilla. You'd think she'd be able to take her pick. Welliver his name is, same as yours.'

'By no means an unusual name,' Georgie said. 'If you've finished reading the paper, Dinah, we'd better bash on with the game soup for the freezer.'

Dinah looked up and saw that Georgie's face was drained of colour. 'You look done in,' she said. 'I can manage by myself. Go back to bed for a bit.'

Georgie spent as little time as possible in Ellis's bedroom. She hated the heavy brown curtains, the colour of dead mice, the rows of photographs in cheap plastic frames, the sagging bed which, however many times she turned the mattress and changed the sheets, seemed to envelop her in choking dust. Ellis had refused to let her buy a new bed or change the curtains. She put on her coat and walked round the back of the castle to the Edwardian wing. Her coat wrapped around her, she huddled in a massive armchair, shrouded in mildewed canvas. She brooded miserably on the moment that she had yelled at Orly Dimont, insisting that marriage to Ellis Peregory would bring her enormous advantages.

She should not have lost control like that. She should not be filled with black dread now, just because she'd seen a photograph of Orly and her brother, Otto, looking so buoyantly and joyously in love. Hadn't she always known that after Davy Stearns left her nobody would ever love her again? Hadn't she agreed to this marriage to Ellis with no expectation of passion or desire? Love was not among the enormous advantages that she would gain. But land, position, wealth, these were not to be despised. Since childhood, Georgie had recognized that the world was divided into winners and losers and that everyone made themselves into one or the other. By working out exactly what she wanted and concentrating on that and nothing else, Georgie had shaped herself into a winner. The secret of her success was very simple; it had required only single-minded effort and concentration. Georgie had worked harder than anyone else she knew. A social life had been out of the question, but that had never mattered. She didn't get on with other people. She had no charm and knew it. Sometimes life had been lonely, but a new manuscript to assess, a new imprint to develop, would take her mind off her aloneness.

Her career had soared, but she had never been able to shake off the feeling that one day things would go wrong for her, as they had gone wrong for Gomer. In a few months, Davy had wiped away her fear of failure. He had loved her into a state of serene self-confidence and happy courage; he had made everything in her life seem right. The sound of his key in the lock undid all the damage of her blighted childhood.

Georgie sank deeper into the musty folds of the sheeted armchair.

It had not occurred to her before that sex gave life its meaning, good or bad. Making love to Davy had put her in step with the world; making love to Ellis had turned her existence into the loneliest business on earth.

She was not going to mope; that would be a sign of giving in. She was going to bash on and turn Hayden into the most efficient estate in the country. If only she didn't feel so weighed down with loss; it was an effort to shift her thin body out of the mouldering armchair in which she was crouched. Once she had found the strength to move, she stopped for a moment at the top of the chipped marble steps and looked out at the darkening hillsides. Simon had entrusted her with their care; the sheep flitting over a ditch, magpies gathering in the lambing fields, a herdsman walking home with the stiff careful walk of the arthritic.

'You're a safe pair of hands,' Simon had told her, looking at her carefully out of hooded eyes. 'You know what I mean.'

And Georgie had known.

CHAPTER THIRTEEN

'COME ON, ELSE, IT'S MAKE YOUR MIND up time.' Davy was playing scrabble with Elsie with less than his usual patience. At the other end of the room, at a lamplit table, Angela was sewing tucks around the hem of Maud's bridesmaid's dress; her bright clattery mood was getting on Davy's nerves. Georgie's wedding was two weeks away.

'B–A–S–H.' Elsie set the letters down with her delicate fingers. 'Double letter score, double word score,' she pointed out and began to wind her hair around her fingers, always a sign that she was tired. She closed her mouth over a yawn, but Angela heard it over the rustle of the organdie she was stitching.

'Bedtime, I think, my gorgeous one,' she said.

'Just let me finish the game,' Elsie wheedled half-heartedly. Maudie, sitting under the table, pasting photographs of Orly, which she had cut from magazines, into a scrapbook, kept very quiet.

'Tomorrow,' Davy said. He hoisted Elsie on one shoulder and bent at the knees so that Maudie could climb on the other. 'Duck,' he yelled, charging at the door, enjoying the little girls' squeals as they clung to him. He wouldn't be able to do this much longer; his shoulders felt as though they were being ground to powder.

Left alone in the room, Angela hummed 'The Folks Who Live On The Hill' as she eased a bell-shaped sleeve into the dove-grey organdie. The colour had been Georgie's choice. Angela thought it a bit austere and the stiff thin fabric reminded her of nuns' headdresses. Angela was looking forward to Georgie's wedding for all sorts of reasons. It would mean the end of uncertainty, especially for Simon. If anyone needed and deserved eternal rest it was him. The last time Angela had seen him, a week ago, she had marvelled at his frailty; his light wispy fingers and jerky walk, the exhaustion in his hooded eyes, brought about by his own tenacity. He refused to die until the marriage was solemnized and he could sign the will that left Hayden to his son. After that, he would give himself permission to stop living.

Even with the wedding only weeks away, Simon's eyes were watchful whenever Ellis was around, as though he still expected his son to trick him in some way. It would be just like Ellis to announce a change of plan at the last minute, his voice aloof and disconnected, a sulphurous smile on his lips. There was a meanness of spirit in Ellis that made him enjoy seeing other people beleaguered and fumbling.

Lavender would be devastated by Simon's death at first, but Angela was certain that she would soon feel strong enough to plan the rest of her life, and would even enjoy it. At the moment she was living in a miserable limbo, feeling betrayed by Simon and threatened by Georgie. She hadn't even got around to ordering new roses; a very bad sign. As for Jared and Eliza, those two obsessive plotters, well, they would have to face the facts at last, understand that Ellis was married and Hayden belonged to him. In time they would see that this wasn't the end of the world. Angela had no fears for them. It was in her nature to expect things to go well for herself and those close to her.

All in all, this wedding would put an end to a lot of messy unfinished business. Tomorrow, she would go to Harrods and buy a new hat. Perhaps Jared would come with her if she told him that she needed a new hat in any event, even if the wedding were to be called off at the last minute, as he still ridiculously insisted that it would be. They could have lunch at the Hyde Park Hotel afterwards. Lamplight shone on the blond hairs that edged the rounded curves of her arms, haloing them. The effect was pleasing. Angela smiled and hummed and finished the grey organdie sleeve.

Jared, who now stayed with the Stearns more frequently than Davy would have wished, came in after a day in town. 'How are you, angel?' he asked fondly.

'Never better,' Angela beamed. She looked more than serene; she looked smug.

Jared plucked the organdie out of her hand and tossed it to the far end of the table. 'Don't waste your time making bridesmaids' dresses. I've just had a consultation with Morgane Landemare.'

'Jared, this is what life is not about,' Angela said sternly, tidying up her sewing things. 'The banns have been read.' She could see that Jared was excited about something; his black eyes glittered and danced. She relented. 'Oh go on then,' she said. 'Whop me with it. What's occurring? as Maud would say.'

'Angel, I know you think I'm one crystal short of a chandelier where Ellis is concerned, but I feel in my bones that this wedding isn't going to happen. I know it isn't, and so does Morgane.' He reached for Angela's hand and gripped it tightly. 'She read the cards for me. Sudden death came up every time. Simon's.'

'I could have told you Simon was dying just by looking at him, anyone could. It's extraordinary that he's lived this long, kept alive by his own obstinacy. He's determined to see Ellis safely wedded, with the emphasis on safely.'

'Tragically, he won't live to see the day. Neither will anyone else, as there isn't going to be a day.'

'I don't follow you.'

'Simon has only himself to blame. He refuses to sign his will until he's witnessed the marriage. So, if he dies before the wedding, his will won't have been signed and Ellis won't automatically inherit Hayden. Getting married will be neither here nor there, so what's the betting he'll tell the she-devilette to pack up her three different kinds of saffron and her horrible new frocks and go? And there you have it.'

'But Georgie's been a tremendous help in running the estate. Ellis might well think that she's indispensable.'

Jared sniffed. 'I grant you that Miss Hellspawn is more useful than decorative. But that hardly makes her irresistible. The only reason Ellis had for marrying her was that it forced Simon's hand and secured Hayden. But no will means no Hayden and no point in retaining Georgie's services. It's not as though he thirsts for her. I mean can you imagine anyone thirsting for Georgie?'

Angela pulled her hand out of his. Whenever Georgie was criticized, she felt wounded. A stupid reaction. She hoped that after the wedding she would stop thinking about how close she came to losing her husband to a girl who, it was generally agreed, was plain and pinched. It was no reflection on her that Davy had fallen in love with Georgie Welliver; it was a regrettable lack of taste on his part for which she wasn't responsible. Hadn't Orly said that it had nothing to do with *her*? Well then.

She was glad when Otto and Orly arrived, giggling over the absurdity of their marriage, which had taken place secretly in a small town in Dorset with two road sweepers as witnesses. The reason for the secrecy was the unpredictable behaviour of Orly's fans. She had been worried that one of the nutters who wrote her obscene love-letters and worse, were convinced that Orly welcomed them, might find out where the wedding was taking place, turn up and pull a knife on Otto.

In Dorset, the register office had been in a building made of joined-together portakabins. On the registrar's table, a computer stood next to a fleshy display of gladioli and tulips. The registrar, a young woman in a suit that looked like an air stewardess's uniform and with a flight attendant's bland welcoming smile, failed to recognize Orly, which Orly pretended to be relieved about. The wedding ring was Orly's old ring of interlocking circles of different coloured golds, which Otto took off her finger and then put on again. That had been two days ago.

Tonight, Orly and Otto were dressed in narrow black suits over white T-shirts and Doc Martens. Clothes apart, they had begun to look like each other in the way that married couples sometimes do, but not usually so immediately. Jared, with an uneasy glance at Otto, told them about Morgane Landemare's prediction of Simon's imminent death.

'Nah,' Orly said. 'I don't think so. If people are keyed up for some big event in their lives, the chances are that they'll live to see it. *Then* they die. Will-power's a wonderful thing.'

'Morgane was certain of it,' Jared said. 'Everything pointed to an immediate death.'

Orly saw Angela shudder and said in an argumentative way, 'Morgane is just the latest in a long line of dodgy mystics who have rightly predicted that it won't take them long to prise you apart from the contents of your wallet.' She hoped that this would get Jared going and distract Angela from thinking about the possibility of Georgie Welliver being on the loose again. It did. Jared began a loud defence of astrologers, clairvoyants, graphologists and an elderly man who had once swung a crystal in front of Jared's handsome white forehead and advised him to start the day by hopping fifty times on the left foot and then fifty times on the right.

Otto wondered if they had all gone mad. Orly had told him that Georgie and Jared had had a major falling-out over some cottages she had wanted to build at Hayden, but that hardly seemed a reason for Jared to want Simon Peregory to die. Was there something he'd missed? During all the years in South Africa, he'd forgotten that people in England were so quietly, politely treacherous. Eliza Jones, whom Otto hadn't taken to at all, was a typical example: outwardly gushing but hoarding secrets. Ellis, too, wasn't on the level. There had definitely been something furtive about the hunch of his shoulders when he'd been listening to Georgie spill the beans that embarrassing day at Hayden Castle.

Furtiveness was the one thing you could never accuse Georgie of, the little bitch. A scorching honesty burst out of her, uncomfortable and disturbing. You could always count on her to say the wrong thing at the wrong time. But that day, her honesty had been more deliberate, more calculating. She'd been downright malicious, which was unusual for her. She cared so little for other people that she couldn't be bothered to hurt them. But she'd hurt Otto, telling Ellis about his time in prison and his reckless marriages. Ellis was someone whose respect he wouldn't have minded having. What Otto couldn't understand was what was in it for Georgie – telling the man she was about to marry sordid stuff about her big bad brother. She'd never have done it though if there hadn't been some advantage to be gained, Otto was certain of that. Getting on in life was all Georgie ever thought about, which made her both boring and terrifying.

Orly, sitting close to Otto on the sofa, their black-clad thighs touching, butted him gently on the shoulder and he pressed the back of her neck with his fingertips, which he'd found out was something she enjoyed. Orly was as outspoken as Georgie, although, unlike her, she didn't use the truth as an offensive weapon. She used honesty as a way of setting herself out on display, so that you could be sure of what you were getting; a very generous impulse. Nora and Angela had the same air of candour, you could see it in their clear blue eyes that were as open as water. Otto thought that all three of them were smashing women. He hadn't minded when Nora had told him that she was putting small brass plates on the back of every piece of furniture that she was leaving Orly in her will. The plates were engraved with the words: 'A gift to Orly Dimont from her mother.'

'You see, dear,' Nora had explained to him, 'when I heard about the four wives, I was expecting you to be a lecherous clown; it seemed only sensible to make sure that you wouldn't be able to walk off with the half-moon table and the Victorian hatstand that Orly has loved all her life. But now that I've got to know you, I can see that you would never take anything you weren't entitled to. In fact, I'm beginning to think that all those marriages of yours were the mark of some perverse kind of integrity.'

Orly was equally forthright. She had a way of telling him exactly what she was thinking that set Otto reeling. This was particularly true when it came to sex, to which she attached the greatest importance. 'It's what life is all about,' she maintained. 'I couldn't do my job properly if I thought otherwise. Really, nothing else matters, certainly not companionship. I can't remember anyone ever coming to my consulting-rooms in a really wretched state because their marriages lacked companionship. It was the lack of sex that they couldn't tolerate. I've known that for a long time, ever since my father ran off with Evelyn Coote, the sexpot of the South Downs.'

'I find you much more attractive,' Otto consoled her.

'Of course you do. It's only geriatric idiots like Pa who get bamboozled by ankle chains and cleavages.'

Otto had blushed. His previous wives had all looked rather like Evelyn Coote, with lots of tumbling hair and ridiculous shoes. The difference was that Evelyn didn't take herself seriously; she saw herself as a good joke. It seemed to Otto that Evelyn could hardly stifle her giggles as buttons popped off her blouses and her skirts snaked up her thighs while, all the time, Ted gazed at her in awed delight. You could almost hear the blood thumping through his veins in mad flurries of desire.

'Now can't you see that I'm right?' Orly would question him

sharply after they had made love for hours on end. 'Much as we'd all like to think that love is about sustained feelings of protectiveness, it isn't; it's about appetite.'

'Are you saying that there's no difference between someone like you and someone like Evelyn after all then?' Otto had asked her once.

'Of course there is,' Orly had told him sharply. 'Evelyn genuinely likes men, whereas I don't; I just like you.'

Otto worked his fingertips gently into the back of his wife's neck, a gesture that made Angela look at him rather wistfully.

Davy had heard Jared come in and then, some time afterwards, Orly and Otto. He felt harassed and invaded by the constant stream of visitors. Stretched out on the top of Elsie's bed, he shut his eyes and imagined he could hear the muted roar of lions, the sound floating across the London sky, murmurous as bees in lavender.

Jabbering noises from downstairs seeped through the floor-boards. Davy could hear Angela's sunny voice, the sound of which, Lavender had once said, made the clouds blow away. Jared was telling her something; he sounded jumpy. Orly was cackling with glee over something Otto had said. Otto was nothing like the dumb ox that Georgie had described to him; he was a thoroughly pleasant man, particularly thoughtful where Nora was concerned, showing an interest when she told him about the lectures she attended at Sussex University, even buying her a packet of plastic folders in wine-gum colours to keep her notes in. Otto had the charmer's gift of being able to spring to intimacy in a moment. Perhaps that was why Georgie didn't get on with him, rather than his calamitous personal life. Georgie always found charm suspect. Yet they were not all that different, Otto and Georgie; there was something not quite grown-up about either of them, a startled look in their eyes that made Davy think that perhaps becoming an adult had taken them unawares. It could be that neither of them had expected to survive their rotten childhood. It was this childish quality that was the most attractive thing about them both. Davy remembered how the sight of Georgie wearing a riding jacket that would fit a twelve-year-old had made him drive her out to a ruined priory and kiss her until both their mouths had burned. Weeks later, when he had lifted her in the air, she had flung out her arms for balance like a child. 'Happy landings,' they had both shrieked as he had lowered her to the ground. He hadn't been quite grown-up then either. He had never been so happy in his life.

Maud was pushing his eyelids open. 'Elsie's gone to sleep,' she said, 'but you can read *me* a story if you like.'

At her insistence, he read *The Snow Goose*, reluctantly, because he thought the themes of wartime and loss were too serious.

When he had finished, Maud said, 'Watch over me until I'm asleep so that the snow goose won't come in and peck my hair.'

'I always do,' Davy said. 'Watching over you is my job.'

CHAPTER FOURTEEN

'SIMON'S SPIRIT IS REMARKABLE,' DR Kirkland said. His soft rumbling voice failed to reassure. Simon had come down with a chill; he shivered and sweated and his hooded eyes were hollow and dry in his sickly face. Even so, Lavender had a difficult time of it trying to keep him in bed. He wanted to summon his tailor to alter his morning coat to fit his shrunken body. He wanted to see a copy of the new directives on set-aside. Most of all, he wanted to consult with his solicitor on the signing and witnessing of his will.

The will; it was keeping his family in a state of excited exhaustion. Dr Kirkland accepted Georgie's invitation to stay to lunch reluctantly; it would be an unrelaxing occasion. Georgie, especially, looked as though she might snap in two at any moment; too thin, too lonely, her mouth a hard red stitch in her small face, her grey eyes blank as though she'd locked herself into a fortress of solitude. Smartening herself up had been a mistake; he'd found her rather appealingly waif-like when she'd gone around in shapeless ash-coloured clothes and no make-up.

Lamely trying to make conversation, he said to her, 'You'll be starting a family soon, I suppose. Makes economic sense on a farm to breed your own labour.' A heavy-footed remark, he knew, but surely not so offensive to merit the look Georgie gave him, as though she wanted to shake him warmly by the throat.

The atmosphere between Georgie and Lavender was thorny. Weddings were always a strain, and the uncertainty of Simon's health could only make matters worse, although, in his opinion, Simon wasn't quite ready to peg out. 'He has a wonderful spirit,' Dr Kirkland repeated to Lavender, taking her into lunch, appreciatively sniffing the air in the dining-room which smelled deliciously spicy. Georgie had made a lamb curry, his favourite dish. Lunch with the Peregorys might turn out to be rather pleasant after all.

Once she had let him fuss her into her seat, Lavender turned away from him and stared out of the window, watching the wind whir through the budding trees. She had not been up to see Simon before lunch and felt guilty that she hadn't but, really, it was impossible to feel that this dying old man had anything to do with her. The Simon that used to be, tall and commanding, tossing his head as though he ruled the world, his face always slightly bronzed, even in winter, as though he carried the sun under his skin, that was the Simon she loved, and he had already died. She sighed.

Her son-in-law, Warner Jones, shyly put his hand over hers. He chewed his teeth for a while and then said, 'It's an awkward thing to talk about, Lavender, but I want you to know that we, well, should there be any difficulties about you staying on at Hayden after, you know, afterwards, we'd want you to come and live with us.'

He made sure that she had all the accompaniments that Georgie had prepared: chutneys and sliced bananas and cucumber chopped into yoghurt. 'It doesn't do any harm to think about the future,' he mumbled shyly. 'Eliza's had a word with Ben Cantalupo about converting the old stone store at the back of the house into a little place for you. All private and snug, but you'd always know that we were near.'

Lavender was horrified. She saw how easy it would be for her, when Simon died, to become almost a ghost. If she moved into this proposed snug conversion, she would be effaced. Eliza would use her as a babysitter and otherwise ignore her. She had seen other old women, living with married sons and daughters in one or two of the farm cottages, squawking for attention, which was never forthcoming. She did not want to be one of them. The person she most wanted to be like was Nora; independent of her children, yet lovingly close to them. How Lavender envied the way that Nora, Angela and Orly linked arms when they went for a walk, chatting to each other in an unguarded way. Ellis and Eliza would never do that. Since they were children, it seemed to Lavender, they had refused to reveal themselves, mockingly challenging her to tear down their defences, which she had never been able to do. At the moment, both Ellis and Eliza were affecting a monstrous gaiety which was quite out of place. Ellis was pouring wine with abandon while Eliza commented enthusiastically on the success of the curry, and the beauty of the almond tree, outside the window, which was magnificently rocking its blossom. Lavender knew perfectly well that they were both calculating the most probable date of their father's death. Eliza would want him to die immediately, his will unsigned, leaving a question mark over the inheritance. Ellis would prefer him to hang on for a bit longer, that is, unless Simon could be persuaded to make Hayden over to him before the wedding. And what about Georgie? She was her usual silent scrutinizing self, no doubt despising the noisy show of unconcern that Eliza and Ellis were putting on. The drama that Simon was making about his will didn't seem to touch her. From the moment she had Ellis's engagement ring on her finger, she had behaved as though Hayden already belonged to her, its possession part of a deal she had made, although Lavender was unclear about its terms. Although she said little during lunch, her every gesture was proprietorial: the way she signalled to Dinah to clear the table, the way she rubbed her thumb over the crested handle of a spoon. It made Lavender want to be a long way away.

She thought she might move to London. She could join the Friends of the V & A, invite Nora to stay and go with her to matinées, design a small town garden and, of course, be near Angela. Why not? Wherever she lived she would lie next to an empty pillow, that couldn't be helped, but she would be more independent in London. That her independence might annoy Eliza made it more desirable. She squeezed Warner's hand. 'It's so very sweet of you to want to take care of me,' she said, 'but it's really too soon to make any plans.'

When Dr Kirkland had left and Georgie and Ellis were in the office, going over the VAT returns, Ellis said, 'Mother seems a bit low. Maybe we should invite the Stearns up for the weekend, if Father is up to it; somehow Angela always manages to cheer up Mother, get her clicking on all cylinders.'

'Good idea,' Georgie said, careful not to express either surprise or annoyance, 'we can have a bridesmaids' rehearsal.'

This was Ellis's way of telling her that she was out of favour with Lavender, not that she needed to be told. Lavender couldn't stand her ruthless efficiency in running the estate, but then Lavender had never chosen to be responsible for anything except her bloody garden. She was a useless fluttery sort of woman; no wonder she was so fond of Angela Stearns who, like Lavender, was shielded from the world by money and charm, unlike Georgie herself, whose well-being had often been precarious. Thinking of Angela brought Davy to mind. She hoped that he would squirm when he watched his daughters follow her down the aisle. The whole point in having them as bridesmaids was to make him miserable. If there were any justice in the world her wedding day would be even worse for him than it was going to be for her.

Ellis was looking at her curiously and she realized that she'd been clawing at her hair and must look quite demented. Ever since she had revealed Otto's scandal-filled past to him, Ellis had been more remote than ever. He was angry with her for exposing him to things he had rather not known about; his anger showing itself in oblique criticism, his every word laced with contempt. That couldn't be helped. The important thing had been to get Otto away from Hayden before he could wreak his customary havoc.

'Your hair could do with a bit of attention,' Ellis said. 'By the way, old thing, mind your back where Eliza's concerned. When she gushes like an idiot she's at her most dangerous.'

'I am surprised, naturally, that you are so enthusiastic about this marriage when it's causing poor Lavender such distress,' Nora said to Angela rather reprovingly. 'The latest horror story from Hayden is that the cleaning women from the village are threatening to leave because Georgie makes them iron the dusters and then put them back in the cleaning cupboard in a particular order. The girl is clearly berserk. The only thing that keeps Lavender going is making quite absurd plans for what she's going to do when Simon dies. The silly woman has no idea of the amount of time mourning takes. She's under the impression that she'll be able to sail off to fascinating lectures at the V & A before the body is cold.'

'You're the inspiration there, Ma,' Angela said. 'Lavender was full of admiration for the way you rebuilt your life when Daddy left.'

'That was a quite different state of affairs, and you know it. If I had cracked up, it would have made the ex-hub even vainer than he is already. I wanted to show him that he was completely dispensable which, mercifully, he has turned out to be.' Nora gave a satisfied glance at her kitchen, in which they were sitting, with its views of the rubbery grey waves scuttling towards the cliffs, and its lack of all but the most basic equipment, since she hardly ever cooked. 'Lavender will be able to weep and howl as much as she wants,' Nora said. 'Widow's perks. I should have preferred to have been a widow; it's tidier somehow. Does that shock you, darling?'

'No,' Angela said. 'I can see the attraction; everyone oozing sympathy and being impressed however you behave. If you're in floods you're magnificently grief-stricken, and if you're dry-eyed you're being tremendously brave.'

'That's it exactly,' Nora cried. 'Whereas, if you're an abandoned wife there's always a suggestion that it might be your own fault. At least, that's how most of my friends made me feel. It caused a certain coolness at the time.'

'Perhaps they envied you,' Angela said, quick to soothe her mother's hurts. 'You do have a way of making staying in bed all day and living off ready-to-eat rubbish sound like bliss.'

'Self-indulgence is my self-indulgence,' Nora said with a modest wiggle of her shoulders. 'But it wouldn't do at all for Lavender. She'll need to have a long period of grieving after such a devoted marriage. That's what it really was; a charming romance that went on for fifty years.'

'Not altogether,' Angela said doubtfully. 'She and Simon aren't getting on too well at the moment. Lavender resents the way that Georgie has won him round.'

'He must be the first man she has been able to manipulate; a more charmless young woman you could never hope to meet. Now don't give me one of your reproving looks, Angela; even Otto agrees, her own brother. I fully understand what Lavender must be going through. She so longed for Ellis to marry someone like you, or so she tells me at least twice a week. Although I should have had something to say if you'd chosen a husband as evasive and patronizing as Ellis Peregory.'

'Out of the question, I agree, Ma. Jared would have been very put out.'

'Well, I wonder,' Nora mused. 'If he can't have Ellis himself, he might prefer him to be married to someone he approves of, someone who'd be willing to share.'

'Mother, your opinions are too daring for a woman of your advanced years; drinking with all those university students has gone to your head.'

Nora coloured. 'I didn't mean share in *that* sense,' she said. 'What Jared really pines for is to be included. That's why Ellis is so detestable; at the first sign of intimacy, he shoos people away. So many men are like that. Not Davy; he's more than superb. Lucky old you.'

'Lucky old me,' Angela echoed cheerily.

Nora said, 'Even though you're my own daughter, I can't help feeling jealous when I see Davy go with you to choose curtain material or put the children to bed. Imagine Ellis doing either of those things, or the ex-hub for that matter. If I'd ever waved a swatch of fabric in front of Ted, he'd have seen it as a threat to his masculinity, like a perfect fool.'

'What are Orly and Otto up to right now?' Angela asked. She hated it when Nora pointed out Ted's shortcomings, although it was perfectly true that Ted had never read her a bedtime story or cut her toast into fingers the way that Davy did for Elsie and Maud. But, even so, she and Orly had worshipped Ted when they were children; they had squealed with delight when he had chased them out of the room so that he could read the *Economist* in peace. Nora had said the word 'masculinity' in a sneering way, but Ted's manliness was what his daughters had loved best about him. He represented a different rougher world, a world of offices and powerful cars and intense Saturday morning golf. Orly had been inconsolable when, at the age of five, she had suddenly understood that she wouldn't be able to marry Ted when she grew up. Angela could remember taking her little sister in her arms and promising her that one day she would meet someone just as nice as Pa, only half believing it herself.

'Otto and Orly have gone to Jasper Conran's showroom to

199

discuss her wardrobe for the next *Body and Soul* series,' Nora interrupted Angela's train of thought. 'Otto very much wanted to be involved,' she said. She was delighted at the way Otto was turning out.

'Otto's masculinity must be solid as a rock,' Angela said.

'I hope you like northern Italian food; it's become rather our thing,' Orly said. She had discovered an easy way to entertain which was to have a local restaurant deliver the food and transfer it to her own pottery dishes, ready to serve. Otto had suggested that an even easier way would be to take their guests to the restaurant so that they wouldn't have to clear up afterwards, but Orly insisted that when people got married, they entertained at home.

This evening, their guests were Ted and Evelyn Dimont. It was the first time they had set foot in Orly's Kensington house; the first time they had met Otto Welliver. Everyone was on edge.

Orly looked nervy and stylish in one of her new black trouser suits. She was very carefully made-up with smoky wings of eye-shadow and pale, rather powdery lips. Her hair was slicked back tightly against her scalp. Ted and Evelyn looked at her doubtfully. Evelyn was wearing a short, tight white dress and high-heeled patent boots that reached her knees. Her hair was a messy cascade of auburn curls and a heavy gold chain swung between her breasts, emphasizing them. Her appearance was so exaggeratedly sluttish that, once again, Otto became convinced that it was all for Ted's benefit, proof of Evelyn's generous spirit.

Orly banged down plates of courgette flowers stuffed with ricotta cheese and a basket of garlic pizza bread. 'This is yummy,' Evelyn said, smiling encouragingly at Ted who didn't like eating things he hadn't eaten before.

Ted bit cautiously into the squelchy creamy filling, not much caring for it. He felt uncomfortable in Orly's pretty but rather poky house which she had filled with pieces of furniture that had once belonged to himself and Nora. The table they were sitting at, he had bought years ago, at an antique shop in The Lanes, in Brighton, intrigued by the way it could be extended with extra leaves clamped on with brass brackets. Photographs in oval silver frames stood on every surface, a frame by frame pictorial exhibition of the way the Dimonts used to be before he'd smashed up his family. On the mantelpiece was a picture of Ted and Nora taken at the time of their engagement; Nora's candid eyes squinted against the sun, her mouth a beam of pure happiness. Also on display were photographs of their wedding, of a rather terrified-looking Ted holding a very small Orly uncertainly in his arms, of the four of them on the beach at Brighton. Angela, aged fifteen, was wearing a pink and white checked bikini, looking knowingly luscious, while Orly, a bony twelve-year-old with big hands and feet, looked sadly at the camera, already resigned to being the little sister of a beauty.

Among the most recent photographs was one of Nora with Elsie and Maud, taken in the kitchen of the Stearns's house. The little girls were making a cake – the table was covered with bowls and wooden spoons and those ancient dented enamel tins that Angela kept flour and sugar in. Nora was smiling at her granddaughters in just the same way she had smiled in her engagement picture, taken almost forty years earlier; a smile that suggested that she was complete, that all her dreams had come true and that she wanted for nothing. It was a smile that made Ted feel as though he had been shunted onto the sidelines. There was not one single photograph of Evelyn. He minded that a lot, although Evelyn wouldn't be at all bothered, water off a duck's back. She was giggling at Otto, sprawled in the fiddle-backed chair that had once been Nora's, kicking her legs in the air. For a fraction of a second, Ted saw his wife through Orly's critical unforgiving eyes: the thrusting breasts, the greasy pink lipstick, the greedy way she slurped her wine. Then Evelyn slowly crossed her glorious legs and he felt hot with desire. She was his stunner, his love of loves. He inched his chair nearer to hers. 'Hi, dreamboat,' Evelyn whispered. Taking the coffee-cup that Orly handed her, she managed to spill some on her white dress and, inspecting the damage, let it ride up her thighs.

Ted knew why Orly had invited him here. It was to show him that she could take marriage as lightly as he did. A vengeful sparkle in her eyes, she joked about Otto's four divorces, the business failures, his fondness for gambling, all the while giving Otto soft thumps on the arm as though to reassure herself that her rascally husband was real. She was deliberately presenting Otto in the worst possible light for Ted's benefit. Any mistake you can make, Orly was signalling to him, I can make a worse one. Like father, like daughter. Aren't we a pair? The truth was that neither of them had taken a wrong turn. He was happier with Evelyn than he had ever been; she lived fully for him in a way that Nora hadn't been able to do, or, perhaps, hadn't wanted to. Independence had been important to Nora; she had made a point of taking long solitary walks and had sometimes refused to go with him to the golf club's dinner-dance. Once, after the girls had left home, he had suggested to Nora that he might come home for lunch occasionally, provide a bit of company for her in the middle of the day. 'That doesn't fit in with my plans,' Nora had said, although, as far as he knew, she had no plans.

Evelyn was a clinger, and he loved her for it. She never wanted to be by herself or with anyone other than him. She made him feel gloriously indispensable. Orly was just as happy with Otto as he was with Evelyn, Ted could tell by the conspiratorial glances that they flicked at each other. When Orly was mischievously elaborating on Otto's past, Otto had smiled resignedly, indulging her. What struck Ted was that they seemed so maty and close; they even looked alike in their dark narrowly-tailored suits, like temporarily trained gypsies. He raised his brandy glass to his daughter who lifted her own. 'A toast,' she said. 'Here's to us and those like us. Damn few.' She drained her glass, her eyes never leaving Ted's face.

Evelyn thought that Orly's house was a dreary little dump; you'd have thought with the money she was said to be earning for *Body and Soul*, she could have bought herself a new place, purpose-built with a garage; they'd had a heck of a time trying to find somewhere to park. The inside of the house could have been made out of dust: grey walls, grey velvet-covered button-back sofas, greyish paint, wearing thin on the doors.

'Smashing place you've got,' she said.

'It cost a fortune to get the paintwork properly distressed,' Orly said, and to verdigris the cast iron so that it looked on the verge of crumbling away.'

Evelyn was puzzled. Why should anyone want to do that, to make their house look old and decaying? In the council house in Shoreham where Evelyn had been brought up, her parents had half killed themselves, trying to keep everything in perfect nick. They spent whole weekends choosing high-gloss paints at Texas Home Care and then applying a wet-looking shine to the cheap skirtings. The house was bright with scatter cushions, silk flowers and Formica worktops with glittery gold flecks in them. Evelyn tried to achieve the same cheerful effect in her own home but she didn't have her mother's determination to keep everything spotless. Her untrained Yorkshire terrier had chewed the once vibrant chair coverings in the lounge and there were scorched brown rings on the kitchen units where Evelyn had hurriedly put down a saucepan as she rushed into the hall to greet Ted with big smacking kisses, although he'd only been out of the house for an hour or two. When Ted's golf-club friends came round, Evelyn whipped around the house, tidying up. Days later, Ted would find the dog's lead in the fridge, one of Evelyn's spike-heeled shoes on top of a wobbling pile of plates in a cupboard. Our house might be a bit of a tip at times, Evelyn thought, but at least you can see what you're eating, which you can't do here. Orly's dining-room was narrow and dusky, the only light from a candelabra on the table, made of some greenish-silvery metal with a twisted stem, clotted with honey-coloured candle wax. Poor Ted, he'd hardly eaten anything. Maybe they'd pull into the Happy Eater on the way back to Brighton, if he weren't too tired; have a nice big fry-up. The candlelight aged Ted; it splotched sharp shadows on his face, made the hand resting on the table fleshless and sinewy.

'You getting excited about your sister's wedding?' Evelyn asked Otto. 'Elsie and Maud showed us their bridesmaids' dresses. Grey, like your walls here. Funny colour for kids, made them look like a pair of little nuns.'

'We haven't been invited,' Orly said, not sounding upset. 'Georgie thinks that Otto is an absolute disgrace.'

'Georgie is a shade intolerant,' Otto said. He refilled the brandy glasses.

As Orly was helping Ted on with his coat, she whispered, 'Well, what do you think of him?'

Ted realized suddenly that she wanted him to be concerned about her. Perhaps that was what she had wanted all along, and he never had been. Orly was so much like her mother: private and strong-willed; he'd assumed that she would be able to cope with any upset. It was Angela he'd worried about when he'd left home, his soft-hearted angel girl. He'd been afraid that Nora might lean on her too much, take advantage of her compassionate nature. He'd been wrong there. Nora was much too proud to rely on other people, even her own loving daughter. She'd pulled herself together and gone out and got herself a life, made out that everything had worked out for the best. It was Orly he should have been thinking about. Instead he'd hurt her deeply by implying that she'd be able to deal with being hurt. Ted put his hands gently on each side of Orly's sleek head and kissed her brow.

'I think Otto is a decent guy but, even if I didn't, it wouldn't matter. What matters is that you're crazily in love with him. People might tell you that basing your life on romance is folly, and they might be right; it's only a bit less stupid than basing your life on something else. I've

204

waited a long time for you to understand that, Orly, and now I think you do. You look lit up from the inside.'

Evelyn drove the car back to Brighton. She had taken off her knickers and kept Ted's hand clamped between her thighs. They decided not to stop at the Happy Eater as they were in a hurry to get to bed.

CHAPTER FIFTEEN

NOTHING COULD BE TRUSTED, NOT even the weather. The heat in the soil that Lavender crumbled in her fingers was a trick, tempting her to start planting out, although her gardening diary showed that the last likely frost date was still a week away. At any moment, the thin blue sky might be cracked open by freezing winds. More reliably, Lavender felt the grumbling twinges in her joints that usually meant rain was coming, whatever the weather forecast might say about it remaining fine and dry.

'Divine day,' Eliza trilled, joining her mother beside the borders of the Edwardian wing.

'Won't last,' Lavender said, busy with twine and bamboo supports. 'Rain by tomorrow, and a lot of it.'

'I hardly think so, Mother. The BBC Weather Centre is optimistic.' Eliza threw back her heavy shoulders and pointed her large chin towards the sun.

'I'm usually right about the weather if nothing else,' Lavender said huffily and went into the house to change out of her grass-smeared trousers before the Stearns arrived.

Ellis stood at the front door, steepling his fingers and inclining his head over them by way of greeting. If there were a more irritating gesture, Davy couldn't think of one.

'Mother will be very bucked that you've arrived so early,' Ellis said in a sinister confident way that was as detestable as his steepled fingers.

A thin skull-like smile flashed onto his face and was dismissed. His hospitality exhausted, Ellis strolled off, his impressive ears translucent in the sunshine.

The Stearns had been put in the old nursery suite, their favourite rooms at Hayden, light and timber-ceilinged with arched windows. The nurseries smelled of warm clean towels and freshly bathed babies, although the last baby to have been bathed in front of the small fire was Anabel, who had recently celebrated her thirtieth birthday.

Davy stretched out on the bed and stared unseeingly at the wooden ceiling, trying not to dwell on Ellis's mean slice of a smile. Angela moved gracefully about the room, hanging up the grey bridesmaids' dresses in a big oak wardrobe, humming something under her breath which Davy could just recognize as 'The Folks Who Live On The Hill'. Elsie clambered onto the bed and nuzzled her head under Davy's chin. She started to suck her two middle fingers. How unreal this all was; as shaky as a dream. Davy felt that he was sleepwalking through the roles of husband and father. Automatically, his body made the required gestures: his hand squeezed Angela's shoulder, tucked Elsie's pale hair behind her ear, while his mind wheeled free, imagining another existence in which he was loving Georgie, was thick as thieves with her in a way that Ellis never could be. With Georgie, he had been almost mad with happiness, wild with love. Desire. Desire. Desire. It was the only thing.

He could never leave Elsie again, even though, at this moment, he felt so detached from his daughter that she might have been a stranger's child. In his heart he was as irresponsible as his buccaneering brother-in-law, Otto Welliver. The only difference between them was that Otto had the guts to walk out when the time was right. There was something shining and reckless about Otto. Davy felt a sick flutter of shame. He clutched Elsie tightly in his arms, heard her heartbeat knock against his chest. Maud, excluded, began to pace up and down, steepling her fingers, her lips clamped over her teeth in a perfect imitation of Ellis's icy smile. It was disturbing the way her stocky little body mimicked Ellis's stringy limbs and rigid shoulders, the stiff-hipped gait of his, brought on by walking for hours in damp fields.

'That's enough of that now, Maudie,' Angela warned. 'It's annoying Daddy; he's tired after such an early start.' It had been Davy's idea to carry the little girls out to the car in sleeping-bags and set off at first light. He was sleeping badly these days, ready for the day to begin at five in the morning. Quite often that was the time he got up, a lonely wakeful man in a house of sleeping females.

'Guess who I am then,' Maud demanded.

'A church going for a walk?' Davy suggested.

Maud's hair slapped against her cheeks as she shook her head and began to pace the carpet again.

'I'm not telling you again,' Angela said. 'Take that horrid smile off your face right now.'

'I know who it's supposed to be,' Elsie said. 'Ellis Peregory. I can do him too.'

She slid off the bed and copied Maud, pressing the tips of her fingers together and looking over her steepled hands, grimacing horribly.

'If you don't stop that at once we're going straight home,' Davy said, in such a cold voice that Elsie looked tearful and Maud rearranged her face into its normal expression.

'Let's go out for a bit,' Angela said; 'see how the lambing's getting along, and I think Lavender said something about a new foal.'

Georgie, hidden behind the ugly brown velvet curtains of the room she shared with Ellis, watched them walk across the shining grass. Angela's hand rested familiarly on Davy's rump as they headed towards the farm. From time to time, he gave his wife's hair a gentle tug. Georgie knew every bone, every knuckle of the hand that pulled Angela's blond hair, drew itself down her spine and finally settled around her waist. Georgie shut her eyes, remembering the warmth of that hand. When it had touched her own body, tenderly mapping it, she had felt an ease in her bones, felt herself become as fluid and elastic as a kitten. The little girls were skipping ahead. Georgie saw Elsie stop, spread her arms and then race back towards her father, who lifted her high above his head and then set her carefully back on the ground. She crumpled the edge of the curtain in her fist and didn't hear Ellis come into the room until she felt his breath on the back of her neck.

'You'll bring the curtain down, gripping it like that,' he said.

'I hate these curtains.'

'You've made it perfectly clear that you hate this room,' Ellis said. 'I've been thinking, dear girl, why not move to something you like better, that you can put your own stamp on? The old nursery suite, for instance, it's hardly ever used.'

Georgie's face was grey with defeat. 'I thought . . .' she began.

'Oh surely not,' Ellis said. 'There'll be no need for this idiotic pretence after Father's death. We shall each of us be able to lead our own lives. Neither of us has a talent for sharing, as I'm sure you have discovered.' He noticed how beaten down she looked and spoke more kindly. 'You're a bad colour today; you should go riding with Eliza, make the most of the sunshine?'

Georgie felt that she was sliding off the face of the earth. She straightened her shoulders and managed to say, 'That sounds like a good idea,' quite calmly.

Angela decided that Lavender needed a break: from Simon's demands, from Georgie's scheming, from Ellis's cagey smiles. She drove her into Hay to have lunch with Jared at the Bon Gout café.

'What bliss to be out on a spree,' Lavender said. She stretched her arms and gave a girlish bounce on the car seat. Sunlight flashed through the beech trees like quicksilver as the car rocked over the cattle grid at the end of the drive. Once she had hated leaving Hayden, worried that she might miss a flower's blooming, the turning of a leaf. But now the rattle of metal as they bumped onto the road lifted her spirits. Hayden had become a place of schemes and plots, resided over by a taciturn wraith called Georgie Welliver. Lavender leaned back, watching Angela's capable hands on the steering-wheel. Angela was so brimful of her own serene presence; she was as good as bread. How unlike Georgie, whose deadened soul and callous indifference to life sucked you down like wet clay.

When they drew up in front of the Bon Gout café, Lavender got out of the car as eagerly as a child. 'Soggy chips and dried-up chops are what I want,' she said. 'I'm sick to death of delicious food.'

Jared was already waiting for them, sitting at the window table and turning his best profile to the middle-aged women reviving themselves with tea and cheese on toast after their Saturday morning shop.

'Getting all keyed up for the big day?' he greeted Lavender, his voice heavy with mockery. 'Are you up to *here* with veils and vicars?'

'Not in the least,' Lavender said. 'Georgie insists on doing everything herself. She has told me more than once that all I have to do is wear beige and shut up.'

'Such a charmer,' Jared said.

Angela gave him a warning look. He was quite capable of upsetting Lavender by telling her about Morgan Landemare's batty predictions.

'So,' Jared said, ignoring the look, 'has there been any more evidence of Georgie going mad in an interesting way?'

'It's more that she's dauntingly odd,' Lavender said. 'Did I tell you about the diagrams she drew showing the way she wanted the dusters to be ironed and folded?'

Jared shook his head although he had heard the story several times. It showed Georgie in the worst possible light, so he liked to hear it repeated. He raised an eyebrow encouragingly.

How childish they are, Angela thought, and how amazed they would be to learn the full extent of Georgie's sins. Stealing other women's husbands was rather more serious than being fussy about dusters. She had half a mind to spill the beans. They would be chastened to learn that she too had been humiliated by Georgie Welliver and had behaved with silent fortitude. Lavender and Jared would surely admire the dignified way that she had coped with Davy's betrayal and realize how silly and obsessive their own rantings were.

No, she couldn't do it. She couldn't expose Davy to their disapproval. She needed him to be held in high esteem so that they could both go on being The Stearns: good-looking, intelligent, successful, enviable. How much braver Orly was. Orly didn't give a damn what the world thought of Otto; it was enough that *she* thought the world of him. Since childhood, people had assumed that Angela was the self-confident one and that Orly was thinner-skinned and savagely critical of herself and others. The truth was that Orly had the confidence to be difficult; she simply didn't mind whether people liked her or not. Angela recalled a very young Orly, scarcely out of her teens, coming back from an unsuccessful supper party. She had been put next to a self-opinionated undergraduate who had ignored her for most of the evening. 'Sod it, Ange,' Orly had said, 'I'm quite pretty and fairly interesting and very clever, so if he didn't find that enough, that's his problem, don't you think?' And she had gone unworriedly to bed.

No man had ever ignored Angela but, if one had, she would have blamed herself. No, that wasn't true; she would have relentlessly charmed him into adoring her, even if he were repellent. 'Damn you, Ange, you always do the right thing,' Orly had yelled at her after Ted had walked out on Nora, and Angela had refused to reproach him for it. But if you did the wrong thing, made people feel uncomfortable and resentful, they might stop loving you. Orly, who'd let Ted know in no uncertain terms that she thought him a despicable jerk, never took that into account.

'We ought to be getting along soon,' Lavender said, finishing the last soggy chip on her plate. 'The heavens are about to open.' She held up her hands so that they could see that her thumb joints, shiny as worn satin, had bent inwards.

'I think we've time for apple pie and coffee before the deluge,' Jared said indulgently, looking out of the window at the hard blue sky.

'Have it your own way, but don't blame me if the road back is slippery. As far as I'm concerned I could stay here until the second coming. I thought Angela might be wanting to get back to the children, that's all.'

'Davy's looking after them; they'll be fine.'

'Yes, of course. He's so absolutely devoted; they can't possibly come to any harm.'

Jared signalled for the bill. He decided that they would leave after all; he had no wish to stay here listening to Lavender laud Davy to the skies while Angela simpered rather vulgarly, as though Davy's devotion to his children was the result of a training course that she'd put him through. Come to think about it, that *was* the way Davy looked: trained in dutifulness. Not a shred of spontaneity in him. Jared gave a bored yawn. 'Sorry,' he said, 'it's the thought of this wedding; it's making me quite dizzy with excitement.'

'Jared's in a strange mood,' Lavender said when they were in the car. 'Whenever he mentions the wedding he does it in a very sarcastic way, as though it existed only in our imaginations and couldn't possibly happen in real life. It is going to happen, Angela, isn't it? Or is there something I don't know about?'

'Of course it's going to happen, Lavender. Jared just likes to make a big intrigue out of everything. Listen, did you hear that rumble of thunder? Your thumbs were right about the weather, as usual.'

When the rain started, Otto and Orly decided to spend the rest of the day in bed. They would give each other massages, drink a decent bottle of wine and roll sleepily on top of each other whenever they felt like it.

'Now isn't this nicer than being at Hayden?' Orly asked, rubbing warmed oil into Otto's thighs. Otto had begun to brood about his exclusion from Georgie's life, especially when he'd found out that the Stearns had been invited to Hayden that very weekend.

'Anyway,' Orly went on, 'Angela's only going there to prove for the umpteenth time how civilized and tolerant she is.' As the wedding got nearer, Orly found herself becoming irritated by Angela's permanently smug mood. Anyone would think that Georgie's marriage was part of some divine plan that God had devised as a personal favour to Angela, a reward for her good behaviour.

'Turn over,' she ordered.

'Everybody agrees that Angela is remarkably civilized and tolerant,' Otto said, obediently lying on his back. 'Who does she need to prove it to?'

'Herself, I suppose. She goes to endless trouble to meet her own superhuman standards. What I've never told you, Otto, is that Davy fucked your sister.'

Otto sat up, knocking the bottle of scented oil out of Orly's hand. 'But why on earth would Davy . . . ?' he left the question unfinished and smacked his head down on the pillow.

'Why would he bother going out for a hamburger when he's got steak at home? That's what you mean, isn't it? That really got to

214

Angela too. She kept on saying she could understand him falling for someone more gorgeous than herself – not that Angela believes that someone more gorgeous than she is walks the earth. The way I see it is that Davy sensed that Georgie had enormous needs. Very cute of him when she goes to great lengths to present herself as a cold ambitious shrew. My brother-in-law isn't stupid where women are concerned. I wouldn't be surprised if there were others before Georgie, although I don't think there've been any since. Georgie can give herself that satisfaction.'

'You're jealous of Angela,' Otto marvelled. He thought that Orly was so wonderful, he couldn't understand why she should be jealous of Angela, whose life was far less interesting than her own.

'Used to be,' Orly admitted. 'Not any more, not since I've got you. I mean, who cares if Angela was handed out the bosom and the blond hair, if I got the sex life, right?'

Later, after she'd proved that she'd got the sex life, she said, 'Angela's probably having a great time at Hayden. Being nobly forgiving is what she does best. Poor Georgie, it can't be much fun being at the receiving end of Angela's noble spirit.'

'Angela should have told Davy to go to hell,' Otto said, 'that's what you would have done.'

'I'd certainly have done Georgie over,' Orly said, 'but we're talking about Angela Stearns here. She thinks it's beautiful to be good.'

Davy watched Marianne's ball bobbling along the kitchen floor. He and Warner Jones and their three daughters had been instructed by Eliza to fend for themselves at lunchtime; everybody else, except for Simon, who was being served something light in his room, had things to do. Dinah Thomas had left out a honey-baked ham and a bowl of cold ratatouille.

Warner sniffed the ratatouille, put it in the larder and made a big pile of ham sandwiches. From the pockets of his quilted parka he took out several cans of lager, a tube of English mustard and some packets of crisps. He winked at Davy. 'Nice to have a rest from all the swank sometimes,' he said, waving a sandwich in the general direction of the gardens and then stretching his mouth wide open to take a big bite out of it. 'Bit of a snobatorium, this place. Built for people who start at the top and stay there, if you know what I mean.'

Elsie had found the small willow basket that Dinah used to collect the eggs. She wanted to put some sandwiches in it so that she and Maud and Marianne could have a picnic in the shrubbery.

'Not too far now, weather's going to break,' Warner said, opening the kitchen door for them. Marianne, holding Maud and Elsie's hands, toddled between them, planting her feet decisively on the path like a careful drunk. Warner tossed Davy another can of lager and scratched his chest luxuriously. 'Between you and me,' he said, pushing his solid round head closer to Davy's, 'I'm pleased as Punch about this wedding; gets me off the hook. Eliza's still pretty stirred up, goes without saying.' He lifted his shoulders to indicate that Eliza being stirred up was nothing unusual. 'I don't like Hayden,' he went on, extraordinarily confiding after a few lagers. 'Has it ever struck you that every bloody piece of furniture in the place looks like a stage prop?'

'Not in here,' Davy said. 'This kitchen is as functional as a flight-deck.'

'Yeah,' Warner said. 'So is the woman who had it installed. Not the decorative type.' He screwed up his eyes and looked out of the window. 'Better haul the kids back inside; rain's about to hit.'

Davy stepped outside, about to call the children. In the distance he could see Eliza and Georgie walking towards the stables, Georgie wearing the heathery riding jacket that she'd owned since childhood. He couldn't see the expression on her face but, from the set of her shoulders, guessed it to be bitterly unforgiving of herself and him and the entire world. How much lager had he drunk? Enough to put him, like Warner, in a confessional mood. He wanted to call Warner over, point to the tiny furious figure stomping along the pathway and say that he loved her more than life itself, that her very unyieldingness made Angela's tolerance seem lazy and undisciplined.

Warner joined him in the doorway of his own accord and put a hand heavily on Davy's shoulder. 'Eliza's looking frisky,' he observed, watching the bulky figure of his wife looming animatedly over Georgie. 'Has it ever occurred to you, old son, that what marriage means for chaps like us is learning not to come first? Or is that being unfair?'

'I've often thought the same thing myself,' Davy said, relieved to see the three children crawl out of the shrubbery and amble towards the house.

Warner gave one of his disconcerting winks. 'Trouble is, there's never quite enough happiness to go round, is there?'

The liver-coloured thoroughbred flicked his lightly skinned head from side to side, all fire-eyed defiance. When he reared, as though trying to plunge upwards, into the sky, Eliza noticed that Georgie flinched.

'This boy's been known to hot up,' Eliza said. 'I'd better ride him.' She didn't hide the condescension in her voice, although she knew it would rile Georgie, who would guess that Eliza had noticed that she was afraid.

'Ellis gave him to *me*,' Georgie said. She mounted and rode off. Eliza stood and watched her until the stallion was just a waxy glisten on the hillside.

Eliza was still saddling up her own mare when a rainstorm started to jangle the branches of the beech trees. She stabled the mare and made for the house in thickening rain.

In an instant the track had turned to greasy mud. Georgie refused to turn back. It would look like a defeat and she was someone who had known too many repeated defeats. The stallion bucked like a piece of twisting metal in the wind. When a snapping branch sent him crazily lurching downhill, Georgie made no effort to restrain

217

him. Her whole life had led up to this moment of wind and rain and terror. Death was nothing.

Dinah Thomas spooned the uneaten ratatouille into a plastic container, labelled and dated it and opened the door of the vast freezer. There wasn't an inch of room. Every rack held similar containers, labelled in Georgie's plain clear hand on the labels she had designed herself and printed on her computer, displaying contents, number of servings, date of cooking and date by which the dish should be eaten. Yesterday the freezer had been half empty; Georgie must have been up half the night, preparing, cooking and stacking. Dinah pulled one of the racks forward and read the labels on the boxes: lemon chicken, *blanquette de veau*, toffee pudding, all the bland nursery dishes that were Simon's favourites. Why in the world had Georgie prepared so many treats for the old man? Anyone would think that she was planning on going away, which was nonsense with the wedding only days away.

Dinah closed the freezer door, shuffled back to the kitchen table and began to eat the ratatouille straight from the container with a teaspoon. She could only think properly when she was eating, and she had some thinking to do. She felt for Georgie so much that it was like being her. That was something she'd never admit to a living soul. People would laugh at the notion of a fat, slow-witted woman thinking that she could get inside the head of someone as small and skinny and fast-moving as Georgie, but it was true. She and Georgie were both alone in the world; Dinah because of her size, Georgie because of her wilful refusal to fit in. She wouldn't take part in chit-chat and compliments; she spoke her mind, didn't ponce about. It made the rest of them feel uncomfortable. That's why they were out to get her. Dinah couldn't have said exactly how the Peregorys and their kind were out to get Georgie Welliver, but she could tell that something was going on. Especially when that Jared

Dauman was hanging around. Then you could really cut the atmosphere with a knife.

Dinah hadn't been sorry to see Angela Stearns turn up that morning. Not that she liked Angela; she, more than anyone, reminded Dinah that she was an isolated misfit. She had this way of letting you know that she, Angela, hummed in tune with the world and you didn't. She smiled at you with all her big perfect teeth while her eyes softened with a pity that you could have done without. But Angela calmed things down, took Lavender off for a drive, prattled away at mealtimes, saying how perfectly lovely everything was – the food, the flowers, the promise of warmer weather – making Simon laugh, humouring Eliza.

Life would be easier for Georgie if she could only be like Angela and make mindless small talk, suck up to people a bit. But Georgie wasn't interested in an easy life, only in setting herself tasks and getting them done with maximum efficiency. However early Dinah got up, she'd find Georgie already at work, sitting at her computer or making a start on the day's menus.

The freezer. Why had Georgie made all that food? Dinah suddenly let the teaspoon clatter onto the table. They needed all the freezer-space for the champagne sorbets they were making for the wedding reception. How could Georgie have forgotten that when she never forgot anything? Dinah was so agitated that it was some time before she heard the thud of rain on the kitchen window. She grabbed a laundry basket and ran heavily to the washing lines where, earlier on that sunny morning, she'd hung out her big shield-like aprons.

As she tugged the last apron from the line, she saw Georgie's horse, riderless, its reins trailing, its sides sticky with mud, picking its way towards the stables. She started screaming Ellis's name before she had even reached the house. Rain fell on the abandoned laundry basket; in moments the starched aprons were a sodden pulp.

*   *   *

Ellis was in his office when Dinah lumbered in without knocking, her lips purple from the effort of running, quite incoherent and stabbing at the window with her thick finger. 'Georgie,' she wheezed at last. 'Fallen.'

Ellis raced down the hall and out of the back door. The thoroughbred was standing moodily under the shelter of a beech tree; its saddle blackened by rain, its ribcage trembling. 'Very well, Dinah,' Ellis called back to her. 'Go and sit down. Get yourself a brandy. I'll deal with it.'

The soaked saddle suggested that the horse had been riderless for some time. What had happened to Georgie? How irresponsible of her not to have turned back when the weather changed; she'd been riding long enough to know how slippery the mossy tracks became when rain fell after a dry spell; even the sheep sometimes lost their footing then. It was infuriating that Eliza had been the one with enough sense to cut short her ride. Ellis had seen her on his way to the office through the half-open door of their mother's little sitting-room. Eliza's feet were on the low table where Lavender kept the seed catalogues, disarranging the stacks. Had Georgie been thrown? Ellis tried to think of her sprawled on the bright acid-green mosses with a twisted ankle, a broken leg. Or even worse. With the realization that Georgie might be dead, Ellis gripped the door handle for a moment, no longer than that, needing its support.

Georgie had been more than usually sullen that morning; he thought of her white knuckles kneading the bedroom curtain as she looked out of the window at the sunny grass which she seemed not to see. And her shocked face when he'd suggested that they keep separate rooms. He had not expected that. He had assumed that they were both colluding in a charade, conspirators in a scheme to acquire Hayden by putting on a show of a marriage for Simon's benefit. He had not supposed that stating the obvious to Georgie would give her so much pain. Had distress made her abandon her usual caution and sent her out riding on a murderous path?

Almost convinced now that Georgie was dead, Ellis felt a mixture of relief and annoyance: relief at not having to live with her, annoyance because her death might lose him Hayden. The circumstances of her death were unpleasant and inconvenient. Simon would almost certainly blame him for buying her the wretched horse, which Ellis had not even intended to do until he'd overheard Warner say that Eliza was interested in the beast. Thwarting his sister's plans had always been one of his keenest satisfactions; Ellis had immediately put in an offer for the liver-coloured stallion.

Eliza had reacted with predictable anger when he told her he'd given the horse to Georgie. 'This boy wasn't designed for shrimps,' she had snapped. 'He needs a grown woman, even if you don't.' Ellis's answer had been a tight restrained sigh, calculated to make Eliza seethe. Perhaps he'd been a shade impetuous; that panicky flicking of the tail should have made him hesitate before paying over the odds. Ellis was as annoyed with himself as with Georgie; he had acted on impulse, something he hardly ever did, and there would be hell to pay.

Taking his time, Ellis put on his boots and waxed jacket. He was halfway out of the house again when he turned back to the office he shared with his fiancée. Her grey cardigan hung over the back of a chair. Ellis folded it neatly and put it in the waste-paper basket. Then he whistled for his dog and set out in the rain to find Georgie's body.

'What a journey,' Lavender said as they turned into the drive. 'And now look, the sun's out again. It's as though the tempest never raged.'

It was true. Although, as they passed the stables, they saw rainwater running in quilted streams over the cobbles, the clouds were edged with dazzling platinum and the brick walls of the outbuildings flickered with sharp blue-grey shadows. The earth was warming up again; on the lawn a robin cocked his head, listening for worms.

'The house is very quiet,' Lavender said. 'I wonder if Simon . . .'
She raced for the stairs, Angela rushing after her, her car keys in her hand.

Simon was sitting in the bedside chair in his tartan dressing-gown which was rimmed with a silky braid that swooped into curlicues on the edges of its cuffs. He was glaring at Eliza, who was standing in front of the fire looking strangely shrunken and scared, holding on to her elbows.

'There's been a bit of a commotion here,' Eliza said. Her loud excited voice was jumpy; her tongue flicked over her lips.

'It's all wrong,' Simon groaned. 'Bloody bad show. Sheer injustice. I was meant to go first. *Her* wedding followed by *my* funeral. Devil of a mess now.'

Angela finally grasped the situation. Georgie was dead. Had she wanted this? Yes, she had. No, she hadn't. Had she? She would think about it later.

'How did it happen?' she asked.

'Riding accident,' Eliza said. 'Silly girl *would* go out on Radical. I tried to warn her.'

A cold gnawing silence fell. Angela was certain that Eliza had had a hand in Georgie's death. She knew that she would never mention this to any of the Peregorys and that none of them would ever mention their own suspicions to her. It would be too embarrassing.

She thought of the people who took part in *Body and Soul*, people to whom secrets of any kind were an intolerable burden. The things they confessed to chilled Angela's blood: they slept with their mothers-in-law, beat up their wives, gambled away their houses. Sick, self-indulgent blabbers was Angela's opinion of them, but it occurred to her now that their misdemeanours were limited to what could reasonably be confessed into Orly's ravenous microphone. They would never connive in a murder because that was one of the few crimes you could not confess to on prime-time television. We are far worse than they are, Angela thought. We confess to nothing.

We set up ripples of chatter and jokes and gossip on top of dark loathsome deeds which sink down into our unconscious. The manner of Georgie's death was one of these unmentionable deeds. Quite soon they would all pretend to have forgotten her.

Around Simon's chair was a scattered pile of mottled-grey box files. He gestured to them brokenly. 'Have to start again now,' he said. 'The will was already drafted. Georgie was to get half the estate.'

Eliza gave a horrified hiss. Simon fixed her with a cold stare. 'If Ellis proved *unreliable*,' he explained, 'she would have been able to buy him out.' He tossed his head in the old imperious manner. 'Hard to talk about her in the past tense. Could do with a drink.'

Angela went to fetch him a brandy. She decided to take up the silver tray with the decanter on it and four brandy snifters. She needed the distraction of pouring brandy into glasses to keep her mind off Georgie's broken-necked body.

As darkness fell, the rest of the family began to return to Hayden. Warner brought Elsie and Maud back from the farm, where he'd taken them to see the new black piglets, and handed them over to a weepy Dinah Thomas. Ellis came back from the hospital where Georgie had been pronounced dead on arrival, looking so aloof that Angela thought it would be a mockery to try to offer him any words of solace. It struck her that nobody had told Jared that Georgie was dead and she went into Lavender's sitting-room to phone him.

'What serious horridness,' Jared said. 'Of course, I wanted to put a stop to the wedding, but I seem to have stopped it too much. The most I asked was for her to pick up her nasty frocks and go back to London. How is Ellis taking it?'

'He went straight to his study. I think he's arranging the funeral.'

'I'll drive over first thing tomorrow morning to see what I can do to help.'

'I thought you would,' Angela said. 'Bye now.'

It was quite late before she realized that Davy had not come back from wherever he had been during the afternoon. She was very tired;

Maud and Elsie had been overexcited, clamouring to be allowed to go to the stables and assure the poor horse that he was not to blame for Georgie's death, which Angela had refused to allow. She had had to read them six Babar books before they went to sleep. She dozed in the squashy bed in the old nursery suite, waiting for Davy.

Nobody heard his terrible cries from the empty stable where he had hidden himself, his eyes squeezed shut, hot tears squirting from their corners. He flung his head back against a wooden post and let his jaw hang open in clumsy grief, like a wolf's. When, at last, he walked back to the house, he had pulled himself together. Only the grey shadows around his lips betrayed his desolation.

'No,' Angela said wearily to her children. You may not go to the funeral and you certainly may not wear your bridesmaids' dresses to it. And no means no.'

Elsie began to blink rapidly, the prelude to floods of heartbreaking tears, while Maud took a deep breath, ready to argue.

'Why not let them wear their bridesmaids' dresses; they would look charmingly sombre passing round the sandwiches when people come back here after the funeral,' Jared suggested. Seeing the betrayed expression on Angela's face, he added apologetically, 'Just a thought.'

'Well, the dresses *are* grey,' Angela conceded. 'But do behave yourselves, my little cream puffs, tomorrow will be a very sad day for us all.'

'Ells isn't sad,' Maud said.

'Ellis is being very brave and hiding his feelings, so as not to upset other people,' Angela said.

Jared, following her lead, put on a serious expression and said, 'Dignified behaviour is a very big thing with Ellis, always has been.'

'May we pick Dinah some flowers?' Elsie asked, bored with the turn the conversation had taken. 'She's been crying in the kitchen for ages.'

'I'll come and show you what you're allowed to pick,' Jared said, 'and then we'll get Dinah busy making vol-au-vents for after the funeral, take her mind off things.'

Already, Jared was squaring his shoulders, taking charge. Before long, Angela thought worriedly, he'd be rearranging the furniture, deciding which vegetables were to be served at dinner, making himself more at home at Hayden than he had a right to. Jared was getting soft and fleshy; the skin on his cheeks was shiny and pampered-looking. He looked as though he'd been preserved from real life for too long, and the truth was that he had. While he'd been waiting for Ellis to return his stupid obsessive love, he'd lost his crispness and dash. What a waste, Angela thought, as much of a waste as Georgie's death.

Orly and Otto arrived at Hayden the day before Georgie's funeral. Gillian had decided not to make the long journey from South Africa because one of Kate's children had an ear infection and Kate needed Gillian's help, or so Gillian said. Otto doubted that his flustered disorderly mother would be of much assistance in a sickroom.

Orly sat on the squashy bed in the nursery suite, swinging her legs and watching Angela try on a selection of black tunic jackets that Orly had brought down from London. Angela was the only woman Orly knew who didn't possess any black clothes of her own, something that Orly thought a bit unsophisticated of her.

'For heaven's sake, Ange, leave it unbuttoned,' Orly said bad-temperedly. The sight of Angela's magnificent breasts straining against the severe black wool stirred old jealousies.

'Yes. You're quite right. You're so lucky to be so slender,' Angela said, with a genuine sweetness of heart that increased Orly's bad temper.

'From what I've heard, Eliza doesn't come out of this smelling like pot-pourri,' Orly said, scowling.

'Is that what Otto thinks?'

'Nope. Otto's like you; he thinks well of practically everyone. He's dripping with gratitude because Simon insists that Georgie is buried in the Peregory plot.'

'That is a worry. It will be so awkward if Ellis were to marry someone else.'

'Ha. Fat chance,' Orly said. 'Jared will keep a closer eye on him now. It was very clever of him to get Lavender on his side.'

Angela pressed her hands to her temples. 'Lordy,' she said. 'Has Eliza been more fiendishly clever than I would ever have given her credit for? Did she nudge Georgie towards her death thinking that it would send Ellis scuttling back to Jared, which would incur Simon's disfavour all over again, and perhaps persuade him to leave her Hayden after all? This can't be real life; it's like an episode of *Dallas*.'

'There's certainly a touch of tawdry epic about it,' Orly agreed, 'but things often get a bit stagey when large amounts of dosh are at stake.'

'But what next?' Angela breathed out each word slowly as she found herself stumbling among plots and counterplots. 'If Eliza tries to put Ellis in bad odour, won't he start hinting that she's implicated in Georgie's death?'

'Not he. Not Mr Calculated Restraint. Ellis is a master of serpentine subtlety. He'll just quietly give Eliza to understand that he has something to use as evidence against her should he ever want to.'

Angela plopped down on the bed next to her sister and rubbed her eyes.

'How peaceful London will seem after this,' she said.

'Don't bank on it. Lavender and Jared will be on the telephone hourly, draining you dry. You're their guardian Angela.'

'They're my friends,' Angela protested. 'They need me.'

'They need a damn good psychiatrist. But they're much too lofty for that, and why should they pay for professional help when they can take up your time for free?'

'You can be very cold-hearted, Orly.'

'Let's just say I have a highly developed sense of self-preservation.'

'Selfish beast.'

'Soppy bleeding heart.'

They started to tickle each other quite viciously, the way they had done when they were children, and soon fell into a state of squawks and giggles.

Jared gave Otto a determinedly radiant smile and led him towards a front pew. He was pleased with Otto who, by marrying Orly, had shown a desirable independence where Ellis was concerned. Now, by appearing at Georgie's funeral, looking suitably saddened, he was living proof that Georgie had a family of her own, and that the Peregorys were not entitled to claim her as one of their belongings.

Jared's mood brightened further when he saw Lord and Lady Welliver enter the church. They were the very picture of mourning relatives: Zanna startlingly pale and Harry stooped inside a large ancient overcoat. Jared almost danced down the aisle as he ushered them into seats beside Otto.

Zanna huddled inside her fur-collared coat. She hated this church which smelled of damp stone and slow decay; it seemed a terrible place to mourn someone as young as Georgie who had been so furiously alive. The cold was painfully stiffening her arthritic hands. Without turning his head towards her, Harry reached out and put her hands in the linty pocket of his coat and moved his thin haunches closer to hers.

Zanna's curious eyes swept over the congregation. Jared, taking charge of the seating arrangements, cavorting down the aisle as though placing guests at a dinner table, angered her deeply. He looked altogether too dapper for the occasion. Zanna swivelled her neck away from his odious spruceness.

Her attention was caught by a man in his thirties sitting on the opposite side of the church next to that glowing blonde who'd been at Hayden when Zanna had last visited; the evening when she'd guessed that Georgie was in love with somebody whose name wasn't Ellis Peregory and was getting married out of desperation and spite. The man opposite was decidedly attractive, Zanna thought; passionate mouth and slightly slanted eyes. But what a terrible steady look in them, and his hands were shaking. Zanna pushed her pocketed hand sharply against Harry's leg. When he had bent towards her, she whispered, 'He's here. I was right. I've found the man who Georgie was in love with and I can see that he loved her too. Oh, my dear, this is a blessing in a way. Such a comfort that Georgie knew what love was; something that Ellis would never have been able to show her.' She gave Davy another sharp stare. 'Full of romantic melancholy, although his wife hasn't noticed. She is very occupied in being gloriously serene.'

'Do shut up, my heart,' Harry murmured, 'Ellis is about to deliver a eulogy.'

Ellis's voice fell on their ears like cold rain, each word chopped off separately. 'I am enormously grateful for everything Georgie did to improve our life at Hayden, and enormously proud to have known her. I know that my entire family' – here, he looked pointedly at Simon who was painfully arching his neck – 'will honour her memory for the rest of our lives.'

Kneeling in prayer but not praying, Davy whispered into the hands that covered his face, 'Georgie, you took the whole of my heart, so that not one single piece of it was held back.' Loving without detachment, that was what he had had with Georgie, and what he had thrown away. How unenlivening his life was now; he had never felt so burdened by it.

It was a dull morning with swollen dirty clouds; beyond the churchyard, the river looked heavy and darkly creased. Spring had melted back into winter. Lavender, irked by Simon's dragging weight on her arm and by his mouth that hung open with the effort of walking to the graveyard, began to fret about the likelihood of late frosts.

This was the worst part: the thud of earth on wood. Davy stood as far from the lowered coffin as he decently could, but could not get out of earshot of the rattle and bounce of the clods being thrown onto it. In his head, he heard Georgie's voice, full of delight, saying, 'Happy landings' as he lowered her carefully to the floor.

CHAPTER SIXTEEN

IT WAS HIGH SUMMER BEFORE ANGELA visited Hayden again. Davy had gone to a trade fair in Dusseldorf and Nora was happy to stay in Fulham over a long weekend, taking the children to the summer sales, armed determinedly with lists, but ready to be swayed from purchases of bath sheets and school knickers should her granddaughters so much as pause before a Liberty print pincushion in the shape of a mouse or a glass jar of sugar-pink bath salts.

Changes had taken place at the castle. The big leather wing chair in which Georgie had liked to hide herself away had been replaced by one of a pair of low armchairs covered in velvet, the colour of a duck's egg, and fringed with silk cord. There was a profusion of cushions on sofas and a new fireside rug in the drawing-room. French windows were swathed in white voile wound around wrought-iron poles and the flower arrangements looked frenzied.

Everything seemed to be in a different place. It was clear that Jared had been at work.

Lavender, following Angela's glance as she took in the altered furnishings, gave an embarrassed sigh. 'Simon disapproves,' she said, 'but Ellis won't put a stop to it. Jared is spending his own money on all these changes; he is the soul of generosity.'

'So what do you think, angel?' Jared had come in from the garden, looking fit and streamlined in white jeans, his black eyes gleaming with happiness.

'Very fresh and light,' Angela said tactfully. As soon as they were alone, she would warn him that he was going about things the wrong way, jumping in too fast. His overexclusive love for Ellis made him blind to Lavender's fidgety embarrassment and Simon's muted fury, both of which, Angela felt certain, would provide Ellis with no end of malicious enjoyment. Spending money on Hayden wouldn't buy poor Jared Ellis's affection. There was a sadistic streak in Ellis which made him relish the emotional discomfort of others. It was a mistake for Jared to look so obviously joyful; Ellis had always preferred him to be in a state of morbid constancy.

When Lavender had gone upstairs to sit with Simon, Jared made them both vodka martinis. 'It could all be so screamingly perfect from now on,' he said. 'I think the Peregorys are finally beginning to accept the fact that I'm here to stay. Lavender's made no objection to my keeping my own napkin-ring in the breakfast-room.' He blushed slightly and, at the same moment, they heard a car hiss to a stop beside the front steps, followed by the clatter of Ellis's footsteps going to meet it.

'Someone on estate business, I suppose,' Jared said. 'There are no other guests this weekend; we wanted a cosy time.' He was refilling their glasses when Ellis came in carrying a small leather knapsack, and ushering in a young woman who was obviously the knapsack's owner. She was slightly built with straight hair that was the light golden colour of weak tea.

'This is Claire Bedam,' Ellis said. 'A surprise for Mother. She has no idea that I've invited Claire to stay the weekend.'

Angela thought that there was nobody Lavender would have greater pleasure meeting than Claire Bedam, who was the gardening correspondent of *Country Nature* magazine, to which Lavender was a devoted subscriber, and a leading expert on peonies. Angela felt pretty excited at meeting a professional gardener herself, although this small prim-looking young woman was not at all what she had expected Claire Bedam to look like. From her robust articles, Angela had imagined her to be tall and flamboyant, a wearer of outlandish straw hats. She stood up and held out her hand. 'Lavender will be thrilled to the spine, and so am I,' she said; 'we are both unshakeable devotees.'

'I've put Claire in the old nursery suite,' Ellis said; 'it has the best view of the borders.' Angela was put out; she liked to think that she had first claim on those charming rooms, and did not feel nearly as comfortable in the first-floor guest bedroom with its Napoleonic *lit bateau* and too many silk-shaded Chinese lamps where she had been installed, no doubt on Ellis's instructions. Ellis held open the door for Claire Bedam to pass into the hallway. As she did so, he put an arm lightly around her shoulder, casually proprietorial.

It's as though Georgie has never been, Angela thought. Every trace of her removed, even her favourite chair, and another decoy woman installed with indecent haste. All she could feel at this outcome was guilty relief, small drifts of joy that she couldn't help revelling in. Georgie, who had tried to wreak havoc, had left them much as they had been before.

'I was going to ask Dinah to make her rather special passion-fruit sorbet,' Jared said bitterly. 'I don't think I'll bother now.'

Angela put a hand on his knee. 'Why don't you come back to London with me?' she suggested gently. It was a suggestion she had made many times over the years, whenever Jared had been particularly badly treated by Ellis. And Jared brightened as he always did when he heard the loving concern in Angela's voice, which managed to indicate that he was vital to her well-being and that her life would be a colourless affair were it not for the intoxicating whiff of drama he brought to it.

Well now,' Lavender said. 'Tell me, what do you think of her?'

'Perfectly decent woman,' Angela said, 'although she sounds more earthy, somehow, on the printed page.'

'I could tell Simon liked her,' Lavender confided girlishly, beginning to plant the dwarf irises which she and Angela had spent the morning dividing.

'Who knows?' she murmured, and her eyes grew dreamy.

Angela smiled at her. 'Who knows, indeed,' she agreed. Although we damn well ought to know the pattern by now, she thought. Decoy women who come and go; Jared who is determined to lurk around for ever, pining for Ellis who will give him the cold shoulder unless Simon sets him free to follow his heart by making it plain that he's leaving Hayden to Eliza. But following his heart was not something you could ever imagine Ellis doing, whatever the circumstances. He had no heart to follow.

Angela had kept an eye on Claire Bedam over dinner the evening before. Claire, still wearing the limp flower-splashed cotton dress that she had travelled in, had looked languorously amused by them all: their formal clothes, Jared's glowering sulkiness, Lavender's breathless anecdotes about her gardening experiences, Simon's grave courtliness. He had made an effort to come down for dinner, too weak to eat more than a few mouthfuls, but looking at Claire intently from under his hooded eyelids. Ellis had been noisily solicitous, behaving as though their enjoyment of the food and wine provided was of the utmost concern to him. He was playing games; they all were. Claire swung a cool glance over them. She looked as though she were trying to store up the memory of the way they looked and talked and ate so that she could tell somebody about it later, the way she might describe a play.

This morning, after she had finished writing an article on grey foliage plants, Claire had promised to let Lavender take her on a tour of the garden.

'I'm so excited, I don't think I can manage a boiled egg,' Lavender had said at breakfast, within Jared's hearing. Treacherous Lavender, lolloping after Claire like a puppy, the loyalty she owed to Jared quite forgotten. No matter that he had befriended her when she had felt the world turn against her, betrayed by Simon, disliked and patronized by Ellis and Eliza, whose behaviour had been detestable. It had already slipped from her memory that Jared had made her laugh by ridiculing her tormentor, Georgie Welliver, by waspishly nicknaming her Miss Hellspawn and the she-devilette, stripping Georgie of her malevolent power, making her dwindle into a harmless fusspot. All that was water under the bridge. It was true that Lavender had grown quite fond of Jared, but not as fond as she was of social approval. The relays of decoy women whom Ellis invited to Hayden were more acceptable than Jared could ever hope to be, for they allowed Lavender to entertain wistful hopes of a Peregory dynasty reaching through all the future centuries. It had been nothing short of brutal the way she had left her breakfast uneaten while she babbled scattily about whether it would be presumptuous on her part to ask Claire's opinion of peat substitutes. Angela had felt quite ashamed of her.

'When I've finished the corner bed, I'm going off for a picnic with Jared,' Angela said; 'you'll be able to have Claire all to yourself.' She rinsed her hands under the outdoor tap and shook them dry, such a subtle gesture of disapproval that Lavender didn't notice it as such and gave her a dreamy wave.

Claire dutifully admired the garden, suggested a few architectural plants for the terraces and wondered to herself why the imposingly large vegetable garden had been allowed to get so neglected when everything else was so well cared for.

She wished she hadn't let Ellis persuade her into making this visit. Other people's gardens didn't interest her. She wanted more than anything to be in her own three acres in Berkshire, dividing the Mrs Sinkins pinks with her friend Patti, grit under their fingernails; then, in the evening, sharing a scented bath in their jointly owned cottage. It was too lush here; the waving grasslands sickeningly abundant compared to her own sour chalky lawn. The Peregorys and their friends were similarly too opulent and creamy. That woman, Angela, couldn't open her mouth without rich burbling laughter coming out of it along with her blandly amusing conversation. Overly luscious she was with her downy arms and crowded bosom. Claire thought longingly of Patti's knobbly elbows and flat chest. She had been stupid to come to Hayden Castle. She'd been introduced to Ellis at a drinks party at the Royal Geographical Society, following a lecture on soil erosion by a famous environmentalist, and had accepted Ellis's invitation because of his commanding manner and because she had been flustered by the grandness of her surroundings and too many dry sherries. The way he'd talked about the gardens at Hayden had led her to believe that they might provide her with material for an article but, really, they were just the usual kind of rich woman's pleasure garden, borders spilling onto old brick paths, shrubs massing together, their flowers plump and waxy. Claire preferred stark outlines and the impression that a wilderness had been tamed only by great and concentrated effort.

'I think, if you don't mind,' she said to Lavender, 'I'll push off straight after lunch. I'm giving a lecture at the RHS next week and I stupidly left my notes at home.'

'You'll visit us again though?' Lavender pleaded.

'Of course,' Claire lied, 'I wouldn't miss seeing the dahlias for anything.'

'Isn't this bliss?' Angela said. They had brought a picnic to the ruined priory where she had once come with Davy and the children on a day like this one, the grass flecked with light and birds wheeling slowly in an opal sky.

'Utterly perfect,' Jared said tragically.

'Jared, don't let it get to you; don't let yourself be dashed down by Ellis's mischief. Show a bit of grit.'

'You're right, angel. As long as he's thinking about ways to annoy me, it means that he's still thinking about me. I should hang on to that.'

Angela began to pack up what was left of the goat's cheese, venison paté and wine into the lined wicker basket that Dinah Thomas had filled for them. It had compartments that held silver forks and ivory-handled knives. Davy would have said that it looked like something out of a pantomime. On the day of their family picnic, they had brought burned sausages, crisps and orange squash in a much-folded plastic bag grudgingly provided by Lolly Ward.

Angela felt the future stretch ahead of her, no different from the present, comfortable but with the risk of being tedious. 'Jared,' she said tentatively, 'would you ever consider consulting someone like Orly professionally?'

'To cure me of this pathetic obsession, is that what you mean? I don't think so. I don't want to be cured. I just want someone who's always there for me while I endure the hell of loving Ellis. A sympathetic witness is what I suppose I mean. Someone like Orly wouldn't do at all. I'm much better off with you.'

CHAPTER SEVENTEEN

DURING HER TWO PREGNANCIES, Angela had been golden and glowing, from the first appearance of a neat little bump just below her waist to the moment when the babies were born. She went into labour luminous and rapt, concentrating on her breathing and smilingly refusing offers of epidurals.

Things were different for Orly. She seemed to have become pregnant all over; her neck fattened, so did her ankles. When Nora arrived with a suitcase full of Angela's bright soft maternity dresses, Orly raged because they were too tight under her podgy arms. Even though Otto swore that he loved her new rumpy curves, running his hands over her body as though she were an expensive sports car and whispering into her ear, 'Too much of you is never enough,' Orly didn't believe him. She felt sick, she looked like a tub of lard and her forehead was covered in pimples. Orly's self-confidence drained away; she was convinced she was unattractive, second-best. Worse, her producers had decided to postpone a second series of *Body and Soul*. The television screen demanded that Orly race up and down flights of steps, svelte as a whippet, her long legs flashing, swinging her microphone from hand to hand like a rock star. Nobody would want to watch a lumbering mother-to-be encourage a studio audience to disclose its misdemeanours; it would be a real downer, the producers said, staring rudely at the pimples on Orly's forehead.

Her jealousy of Angela resurfaced. It wasn't fair that Angela was always radiant, sweet-tempered, filling the world with her goodwill. Orly stumped sulkily about her pretty house, under-occupied but too listless to make a start on writing the tie-in book for the *Body and Soul* series which she was contracted to do, or to take much of an interest in her Harley Street practice.

'Most of the punters only come to see me as part of some ritual humiliation they're inflicting on each other,' she snapped at Nora who was putting Angela's dresses back in the suitcase. 'Everything about sex therapy is a charade.'

'That's not true, Orly,' Nora said. 'You have a very helpful approach to people's problems, brisk, but with a sympathetic curiosity – isn't that what *The Times* television reviewer wrote?'

'*Guardian*, but they have to write *something* don't they?' She tossed a blue muslin smock into the case, creasing it. 'What a laugh, not being able to fit into Angela's clothes when it's always been the other way round. I swear to God, I'll never be jealous of her big tits again, as long as I live. Bosoms are always getting in the way, an absolute magnet for crumbs and dribbles of toothpaste. If mine don't go away after the baby, I'm having a breast reduction.'

Orly's sudden moods of low self-esteem rattled Nora. She felt that Orly's doubts about her own womanliness were her fault; she was to blame because she had given birth to Angela, with whom Orly had always been – *would* always be – unfavourably compared. In her heart of hearts, Nora loved Orly best, but had never told her so as good mothers did not have favourites. And so Orly had gone through a miserable childhood and adolescence, sometimes disparaging her own considerable gifts and talents, sometimes overbearingly self-confident, scorning the world's opinion of her. Once she had overheard a neighbour in Brighton say to Nora, 'Your girls are so delightful. Angela's going to be a real heartbreaker in a couple of years and Orly is such an interesting little thing.'

Nora had been anguished on Orly's behalf. Interesting had never counted for much. It was Angela with her bland sunny smiles whom men had loved. Until Otto, that is. Nora very much hoped that Otto was on his way home from the recording studio where he now worked.

Hoping to divert Orly's attention from her bloated body, Nora said, 'I'm worried about Davy. Don't you think he looks dreadful; reedy would be the word, wouldn't it? He's lost all that sleek vitality. When I rang the other day, he answered the phone, saying his name, "Davy Stearns" as though he were tired of the sound of it.'

Orly *had* noticed a change in Davy. His thick strong hair had begun to recede, showing pointy triangles of white skin above his brow, which made him look like a sad demon. There was something dry and shredded about him; there were dingy shadows at the corner of his mouth. 'He's been working too hard, Ma, that's all it is,' she said. 'Davy's never been good at knowing when to stop.'

Orly had gone with Angela to see Davy's new offices, a suite of rooms overlooking Regent's Park. He had chosen desks and filing cabinets in a glaring white lacquered finish – an odd choice, Orly had thought; they were already getting grimy. He had upgraded his computer system; now he had voice mail and a machine that zapped messages from his screen to those of other workaholic entrepreneurs all over the world. 'Very impressive,' Orly had said, and Davy had smiled and said, 'The best thing about working here is that you can hear the lions; it's not far from the zoo.'

'Davy's spent squillions on his new offices,' Orly told her mother.

'He can hardly bear to draw himself away from the Internet at the end of the day. If Ange wants him home earlier, she'll have to get on-line and all that nerdy stuff.'

'It's no laughing matter,' Nora said stiffly. 'Davy's always been a wonderful provider, but I don't think this is about work.'

Orly always got touchy when Davy was praised. In the low sad state that pregnancy had reduced her to, she found Nora's admiration of Davy unendurable. 'You're right, Ma,' she said bitterly. 'It is more than work. The fact is Davy is in a sort of mourning.'

She was going too far; she knew that, but the need to undermine Angela through Davy was irresistible. At that moment, she hated her sister for her delicate air of self-satisfaction, for being so good-humoured when she, Orly, felt dull and sour.

'Something I've never told you, Mother, is that Davy had a scorching affair with Georgie Welliver.'

Nora went on folding Angela's maternity dresses and putting them in the suitcase. 'That doesn't surprise me,' she said.

Orly nearly fell off the sofa. 'But you've always held up Davy and Angela as the perfect married couple.' She heard her own voice, hard and accusing, and wished more than anything that she could call her words back again.

'I try my best to be a supportive mother,' Nora said. 'It's quite hard going at times.'

'But you agreed with Lavender that Georgie Welliver was ghastly; we all thought that. Don't you find it amazing that Davy fell in love with her?'

'Not in the least. Georgie would have treated Davy as an event. He was probably the first man who paid her any attention; she would have put him right at the centre of her life, no doubt about it. Davy likes to feel crucial to people, more than he lets on.' She gave Orly a sharp look. 'I don't remember you ever mentioning that you met Georgie; I thought Otto kept well clear of her.'

Orly rubbed her thickening ankle. 'It was before I knew Otto,' she said. 'Strangely enough, Georgie came to my consulting rooms. She didn't know that I was Angela's sister. The affair with Davy was over by then, anyway.'

She looked down at the carpet. Nora would think that she had acted improperly; the decent thing would have been to have arranged for Georgie to see another therapist. Curiosity to meet the woman who had come close to wrecking Angela's marriage had got the better of her. To her relief, Nora didn't seem to be angry.

'Now that does surprise me,' Nora said. 'Such a determined girl. When she sang "I Know Where I'm Going" that evening at Hayden, I thought it a very appropriate choice. Can't imagine her needing to confide in anyone else. What was the problem?'

'Who, not what. Ellis.'

Nora shivered. 'Oh, the pity of it,' she murmured.

'Mother, don't be soft. The she-devilette, as Jared called her, went into the whole Ellis business with her eyes open. She found him sexually repellent, but was prepared to marry him to get her mitts on Hayden Castle, the mercenary little bitch.'

'You're missing the point, my dear,' Nora said. 'This would have been about Davy, having to prove to him that she didn't need him, that, as far as her happiness was concerned, he was of no consequence. That's something I understand very well.'

'You'd better understand something else, Ma. If Elsie hadn't fallen off that breakwater, Davy might have run off with Georgie. So stop blaming yourself for the accident; it saved Angela's marriage. She says so herself.'

Nora let the lid of the suitcase drop out of her hands. 'Angela knew?' she asked weakly, her eyes clouded by pain. Her poor brave Angela. No wonder that her smiles had become too wide, her manner exaggeratedly warm. To suspect that a woman like Georgie had almost taken her husband away from her would have been the worst kind of hell. At least, Nora thought, Evelyn Coote was younger and better-looking than I was. When Ted left me for her, he tipped us

243

all into a cliché: middle-aged man trades in lifetime partner for a younger model. Hackneyed situations are easier to handle because you know that loads of other wives are in the same boat as you are. But man leaves beautiful blonde wife for small, plain, charmless mistress, what a horrible novelty value that would have had.

She thought back to that weekend at Hayden: Davy playing the piano, his long-lidded eyes half shut, deceptively relaxed, while Georgie sang in her unexpectedly rich voice. The song she sang had been a message to Angela that she was out to get Davy. Nora could see that now. Angela and Georgie, they were well matched for grit, those two. Look at the way Angela had applauded Georgie's song, so enthusiastically that her bracelet, the pretty enamelled one that Davy had given her, had bounced up and down her arm.

'I wonder why Angela never breathed a word,' Orly said. Both she and Angela imagined that the other had a closer relationship with their mother, more confiding and affectionate than their own.

'Angela would never tell me anything that might reflect badly on her,' Nora said.

'But Ange has been more than usually super-angelic over this,' Orly said. 'I was watching out for that bug-eyed brittle look that some wives get when they stand by their man, but she's been as serene as ever. She always manages to give the impression that she's walking firmly on air.'

'Even so,' Nora said, 'when people know that your husband is having an affair, they can't resist speculating whether you are at fault in some way. Believe me, I speak from blistering experience.'

Orly rubbed her ankle more frantically and avoided Nora's candid eyes. It was true; when Angela had told her about Davy's unfaithfulness, she had wondered, for a moment, if Angela had been partly to blame. She had dismissed the thought immediately, angry with herself for paying lip-service to the old saw that men were adulterous because their wives were unloving. The truth was that the bastards had affairs because that was their idea of fun. As a sex therapist, she spent countless hours coaching tense married couples in sexual techniques that were supposed to make them feel like lovers again. She showed them videos of different positions, demonstrated with an array of vibrators how to get their bodies talking, ignoring the truth of the matter which was that the man wanted to make love to a woman who wasn't his wife.

Orly slid heavily off the sofa and knelt beside Nora on the floor, beside the neatly packed suitcase. 'Everyone thought Pa was barmy to leave you for Evelyn,' she said loyally.

'No they didn't. They put it down to sex, and they were right. They would have done the same if Davy had run off with Georgie. How dreadful that would have been for Angela.'

Nora stood up, suddenly looking like a crushed trembly old woman, the way she had done when Elsie had been in hospital, half expected to die. Orly felt thoroughly ashamed of herself. She had betrayed Angela and made Nora miserable: a bad afternoon's work.

'I shouldn't have told you,' she said. 'It's just that I'm feeling so grumpy.'

'No, you shouldn't have,' Nora agreed. 'Now I'm going to have to do something about it and I'm much too selfish to relish interfering in other people's lives.'

'You're making too much of this. Things will be back to normal soon; apparently Ellis is already on the track of suitable decoy women to play the usual game of charades.'

'Davy won't be back to normal,' Nora said. 'He's so distanced and bleak. It's as though he's forgotten how to make things happen, like a sleepwalker wading through a bad dream. The frightening thing is that Georgie can do more harm dead than alive. Davy's such a romantic; he might spend the rest of his life grieving for the lost love beside whom his living wife can't hope to compete.'

'Not being the ethereal type,' Orly suggested.

'Much worse than that. Angela doesn't understand that she must put Davy above everything, she's never understood that. Without him, she is absolutely nothing.'

As Orly gaped at her in disbelief, the front door slammed and they could hear Otto walk noisily through the hall whistling 'Pretty Woman'. When he came into the room, Orly tumbled into his arms and he began to rub her back, his chin propped on her shoulder, winking conspiratorially at his mother-in-law,

'It's good to be home, babe,' Otto murmured into Orly's neck. 'I'm that fond of you, I need you more than I need a drink.'

He can already read Orly like a map, Nora marvelled; he knows how much she craves reassurance, and a year ago he hadn't even met her. It saddened her a little to know that she was too old to read someone like a map. You needed youth and patience for that, to be as close as skin with the one you loved.

'Stay to supper, Nora,' Otto wheedled. 'I shall make my renowned courgette flowers stuffed with ricotta cheese.'

And although Nora knew that he would slink into another room and order all the food from Cosa Nostra, she happily agreed to stay and drive back to Rottingdean the next morning. It was such a comfort that at least one of her daughters had a very satisfactory marriage.

Angela and Nora sat on hard chairs in a stifling church hall in Knightsbridge watching Elsie's ballet class give an end of term performance of *Night Time In The Woods*. Elsie, dressed as a moonbeam with a gauzy yellow sash draped over her white leotard, wasn't dancing well. Her frondy arms waved listlessly to the thumping piano music, although her eyes were glittery with nerves. She was not enjoying herself at all and Nora knew that the child's unhappiness had something to do with Davy.

'Wasn't that adorable?' Angela enthused, when the children had taken their final bow. She clambered nimbly over people's knees to be the first to congratulate the woman whose daughter had danced the leading role of Queen of the Forest. Nora stood aside awkwardly, wishing Angela would stop gushing. She smothers everyone in devotion except for Davy, she thought sourly. Where he's concerned, the adoration has to be all on his side.

They emerged from the church hall into a baking London afternoon. Their nostrils clogged with the smell of hot petrol and dusty geraniums and the inside of Angela's car enveloped them in a tinny heat. Even Maud, usually so tireless and sturdy, looked wan when they collected her from school. Only Angela seemed untouched by the weather. She was wearing her bright-blue linen dress which rustled crisply around her bare legs and her hair looked cool and slippery. 'Soon be home, my cream puffs,' she said, driving through the parched streets and, for once, Nora found her complacent contentment grating.

The telephone was ringing as they walked through the door. It was Lavender: Dr Kirkland had just told her that Simon had only days to live. 'Of course, I'll come up,' Angela assured her. 'It's not a problem. I'm sure Ma will stay and look after the girls.'

That is by no means certain, Nora murmured to herself as she walked through the house into the garden. She would have liked nothing better than to stay with Maud and Elsie, and there were no other demands on her time, but that wasn't the point. Angela should be where Davy was. If she continued to flit about, an always available source of tea and sympathy, Davy would leave her. He would find another Georgie Welliver, an unsought-after woman who could make him feel crucial to her very survival. That was something Angela had never made him feel. She had never allowed him to encroach on the stainless surface of her life or to have any inconvenient needs of his own.

Nora sat down on a chipped stone bench, knowing that she must insist that Angela devote herself to her husband. It seemed an odd thing, now, that *she* had never considered devoting herself to Ted when he had first become infatuated with Evelyn Coote. She had known what was going on, of course she had, and even now, was sure that she could have won him back had she put her mind to it. But, at the time, the effort needed to save her marriage had seemed too great. The idea of regarding Ted, such a vain silly man, as a trophy to be fought for and won had seemed distasteful and rather indecent.

But I am not Angela, Nora told herself, and Davy is not Ted. I am able to accept the stigma of divorce, which Angela would not be able to do. Her notion of herself is based on her unquestionable excellence as a wife and mother.

She would have to confront Angela very forcefully about this; she must not sound vague and reluctant. Nora cast her eyes doubtfully over the garden, which was not looking its best. Border plants flopped onto the thirsty lawn; a single rose, an overbright burning-red flower, exploded against a wall. Nora closed her eyes to shield them from its lurid petals. She did not know the name of this rose, but felt that it should have been called Evelyn Coote.

That weekend at Hayden, when the talk had turned to gardening, and Georgie had scowled, Nora had said to her, 'I gather that horticulture holds little interest for you,' trying to show Georgie, in a subtle way, that she had noticed her bad manners and disapproved of them. To her surprise Georgie had been quite expansive on the subject. 'I don't like things that are never finished,' she had said. 'In a garden, however well you plan things, chance always plays a hand: birds drop seeds, there's an outbreak of honey fungus, you never know where you are. It's impossible to be in complete control.' And she had given Angela and Lavender an almost yearning look as they sat together beside the fire, arguing about the best way to propagate hydrangeas.

No, Nora thought, shifting on the stone bench so that the red rose was out of her sight, Georgie could never have understood a gardener's happy acceptance of the unplanned. Georgie had to know exactly where she was going, which was why she had been such an excellent cook. She would have been comforted by the precision of recipes: how much to weigh, how long to bake, so that, in the end, you achieved what the recipe had led you to expect. Gardens didn't have end results; they meandered on, season after season. Angela was able to accept that because she would assume that whatever thrived or failed, it would turn out to her advantage, like everything else in life.

Angela. Nora's heart sank at confronting her. She had never been able to tell Angela the truth. When Ted had walked out, Nora hadn't dared to present herself to her elder daughter as someone who had failed. Angela would have been frightened by a display of emotional nakedness and would have disguised her fear with more tender sympathy than Nora would have been able to handle. So, for Angela's sake, Nora had built herself a new life and had not indulged in a moment's self-pity. She had succeeded in giving the impression of always doing exactly what she wanted to do. Funny how Angela, without being in the least aware of it, forced her entire family to collude in the lie that life was more or less perfect all the time.

Nora slapped at a mosquito on her wrist harder than she needed to. How conciliatory and cowardly she had been. What a hideous pretence they all lived, and Davy was the latest victim of it. Angela was ruthlessly ignoring the signs of heartbreak that were visible in his drooping mouth and exhausted eyes, because to acknowledge its cause – his enduring love for Georgie – would be to acknowledge that her marriage was not altogether blissful.

The sunlight falling on the grass hardened and grew cold. Birds were creaking into flight towards the mottled sky. An evening breeze prickled Nora's bare arms, making her shudder, her courage at a low ebb. Once her daughters had grown up, she had found it hard to speak her mind to them. She found herself censoring the words in her mouth, afraid of saying something that might give them cause to dislike her. They were so judgemental, so much better at everything than she was and, without meaning to, letting her know that they were. Fearing their disapproval, Nora went to humiliating lengths to avoid awkwardness, and despised herself for doing so.

'Mother,' Angela called from the kitchen window, 'what would you like for supper?'

'A salad will be enough,' Nora called back.

'I'll make some fishcakes,' Angela decided. Nora resigned herself to a bout of Angela's haphazard cooking, of whirring blenders and flour on the table and something heavy and rather indigestible at the end of it all. She went into the house to give a hand, feeling on edge.

'We won't wait for Davy,' Angela said. 'He rang to say he has to wait at the office for a very important fax from Tokyo, which will let him know if the Japanese are ready to roll with his Elvis Presley refrigerator magnets that sing "Love Me Tender" when you open the fridge door.' She shook her head, smiling at the ridiculous capers of other people, and then started to pound boiled potatoes with a battered tin potato masher.

The telephone rang again. Angela answered it, sitting on the edge of the kitchen table which was covered with the usual debris of breadcrumbs, some pots of fuchsia cuttings and the jars of lemon curd that Angela had made that morning.

This is not charming, Nora thought, tearing lettuce leaves into a bowl. It is slapdash and showing-off slapdash at that. Lavender had complained bitterly to Nora about Georgie Welliver's obsessive tidiness; her immaculate kitchen where dishcloths had to be stacked in the cupboards in a particular way. Could Georgie's neatness have been alluring to Davy? It was possible, Nora thought, noticing that most of the breadcrumbs, displaced by Angela's swishing skirt, had fallen onto the floor.

'Sit tight, old pal,' Angela was saying, obviously to Jared, Nora had no doubt of that. 'I'll be there as soon as I possibly can.'

Angela put the phone down and turned to Nora with excited eyes. 'Well, this is fascinating,' she said. 'Jared has been barred from Hayden. He's dreadfully cut up.'

'That's Jared's problem, not yours,' Nora said.

'Ma, Jared needs me. Could I refuse him?'

'Yes you could. You have problems of your own.'

Angela smiled at her sweetly; her blue eyes were so untroubled, they might have been blind.

Nora refused to be deterred by this show of blithe unconcern. 'You must stop this,' she demanded.

'Stop what, Mother?'

'Offering the promise of salvation to everyone except the man you're married to. If you want to be a rescuer, forget Lavender and Jared, forget all of us. Salvage Davy; he badly needs saving.'

Angela stared at her. 'I didn't want you to know,' she said, then put her head down on the messy table and cried her heart out.

'That's better,' Nora said; 'that's excellent.' She tugged at the kitchen-towel roll and put several sheets on the table beside Angela's head, and then poured them both large gins.

The cheery knocking of ice against glass made Angela sit up and mop the tears from her cheeks. She managed another smile, more wary than the last one had been. Nora handed her a fizzing glass. 'I should never have called you Angela,' she said. 'I was asking for trouble; all those connotations of ministering angels, angel in the house and so on. You didn't stand a chance.'

'The first time I met Davy,' Angela said, 'he played "You May Not Be An Angel" for me on the piano.'

'Ah, but he was wrong. You are an angel, definitely a supernatural being above the common fray. You've no idea, darling, how annoying that is for the rest of us. The unwearying solicitude of someone who denies that she has any problems herself can leave a poisonous after-taste.'

'Is that how Orly feels about me?' Angela asked, beginning to cry again. 'Is that why she told you about Georgie Welliver?'

'No. She's having a rotten pregnancy, made worse because you didn't. It was a moment's viciousness, instantly regretted.'

251

Angela was all concern. 'Poor love. I'd better give her a ring.'

'No. No. No,' Nora shouted. 'The last thing Orly needs is your magnificent forgiveness. She would shrivel. How many more times do I have to say this: it's Davy who needs you.'

'I can hardly raise Georgie from the dead for him,' Angela said, 'although I know that it's the only thing he wants.'

'I don't think so,' Nora said. 'What he wants is for you to understand that he is grieving for Georgie.' She leaned across the table and gave Angela's shoulder a harsh little shake. 'Go on,' she urged. 'Go where you've never been. Console Davy for loving another woman.'

Maud strutted into the kitchen. She had stuffed a cushion inside her knickers and was wearing one of Angela's maternity dresses which Orly had rejected. Its hem dragged among the crumbs on the floor.

'Look at me,' she said, 'I'm having a baby.'

'I'm all eyes, my duck,' Nora said.

Angela sat on the stairs in the dark. The telephone rang twice. Jared? Lavender? But she stayed where she was, leaning her head on the banister rail, her feet awkwardly tucked under her. She had told herself that she had behaved in a brave civilized way, never referring to Davy's affair with Georgie, never reproaching him for it. But she saw now that her tolerant silence must have seemed to him like deliberate cruelty. She had dragged him to Hayden, time and time again, although the sight of Georgie wearing Ellis's engagement ring must have hurt him dreadfully and Angela's own enjoyment of those squabblesome house parties, her refusal to be jealous of Georgie in any way, would have made him feel that his love for Georgie was of no account, not worth a moment's anxiety on the part of his beautiful popular wife.

She had never put herself in Davy's place, Angela thought miserably, never considered how, when he watched her sew the children's bridesmaids' dresses, he must have felt that she was driving the needle through his heart. And that would have been nothing compared to his agony when Georgie died. Angela was the only person who might have comforted him then, and she had not done so; she had not wanted it acknowledged between them that Georgie's death mattered to him. She had wanted Georgie to be yesterday's news, water under the bridge. She had wanted Georgie to be no more than a woman who, having had a certain difficulty in living, had died and would soon be forgotten. Angela flinched at her own lack of integrity. She had watched Davy fall apart and had done nothing because she knew that she was not the cause of his heartbreak, and, therefore, not at the centre of his being.

Davy was glad that the house was in darkness and hoped that his wife and children were all asleep. The effort of living with his family exhausted him; they seemed unbearably boisterous and demanding; planning holidays and outings, noisily pleasure-bent. He was living for show. His life was dead time. He was no more alive than Georgie; a loser de luxe.

Only when he was alone in his office, late at night, did he feel able to breathe normally, listening to the roar of the lions carried on a dusty summer wind, a sound that made the past grow bigger every minute. He had to force himself to go home, back to Angela who, in bed, offered him her warm peachy body sweetly and distractedly, making a gift of herself, which he accepted dutifully.

Later, when Angela slept placidly beside him, he dreamed of Georgie. It was always the same dream: they were in a deserted ballroom; she at one end, he at the other. 'I'm cold,' Georgie said, holding out her small hands to him so that he could see they were purple and stiff. He stretched himself towards her but, although the ballroom was empty of other people, he could not reach her. The gleaming wooden floor sucked at his feet as though it were deep mud; the air blocked his movements as

253

though it were made of stone. He would wake to feel tears dripping down his cheeks.

There was somebody sitting on the stairs, bunched and solid in the darkness and still as a statue. Davy snapped on the light and the bunched shape turned into Angela, an Angela that he hardly recognized, slack and vulnerable and subdued.

Still clinging to the banister, she said, 'Davy, I'm so sorry. I wanted Georgie not to matter. It was wrong of me; I should have helped you to grieve for her.'

There was a wondering expression in her eyes that were usually so clear and amiable. Davy realized that she hadn't the faintest idea what would happen to them now.

'Get up, angel,' he said, holding out his arms.

Her foot had gone to sleep and she stumbled over the hem of her blue dress. He was there before she fell, and she clung to him as though he were all that the world contained. He set her down gently on the ground.

'Happy landings,' he said.

IMPOSSIBLE THINGS

Penny Perrick

'WITTY, ZESTFUL AND BEAUTIFULLY OBSERVED ... A
GORGEOUS PIECE OF ESCAPISM'
Kate Saunders, *Independent*

Society Milliner Zanna Gringrich is so exotic and vividly
beautiful she seems to make the world spin faster. But
with her beauty comes irreverence and defiance. Lacking
any guilt, Zanna blithely cheats on Jewish family life for
the sake of her politician lover. It is this love affair that
forces her into a fatal connection with the stately pile of
Utley Manor.

Here, the same winds of change that dictate fashion are
destined to blow through the high windows and tall
chimneys of a house of outdated privilege, affecting each
and every one of Utley's inhabitants.

'IRRESISTIBLE'
She

'DECKED OUT WITH ZESTY DETAIL, SPIKY
CHARACTERS, A WHIFF OF BLACK FARCE AND BOLD,
INTELLIGENT WRITING, *IMPOSSIBLE THINGS* WHIRLS
WITH PANACHE'
Elizabeth Buchan, *The Times*

'I COULDN'T STOP READING IT ... I FELT AS IF I'D
BEEN THERE AND LIVED IT ALL. AND ZANNA: EVERY
TURN OF HER STORY PULLED ME FURTHER IN. IT'S SO
RARE TO READ A NOVEL ABOUT A TIME AND A PLACE
THAT MAKES *THEN* SEEM MORE REAL THAN *NOW*'
Rosie Thomas

0 552 99693 9

BLACK SWAN

A SELECTED LIST OF FINE WRITING
AVAILABLE FROM BLACK SWAN

99630 0	MUDDY WATERS	Judy Astley	£6.99
99618 1	BEHIND THE SCENES AT THE MUSEUM	Kate Atkinson	£6.99
99725 0	TALK BEFORE SLEEP	Elizabeth Berg	£6.99
99648 3	TOUCH AND GO	Elizabeth Berridge	£5.99
99687 4	THE PURVEYOR OF ENCHANTMENT	Marika Cobbold	£6.99
99622 X	THE GOLDEN YEAR	Elizabeth Falconer	£6.99
99589 4	RIVER OF HIDDEN DREAMS	Connie May Fowler	£5.99
99657 2	PERFECT MERINGUES	Laurie Graham	£5.99
99611 4	THE COURTYARD IN AUGUST	Janette Griffiths	£6.99
99685 8	THE BOOK OF RUTH	Jane Hamilton	£6.99
99724 2	STILL LIFE ON SAND	Karen Hayes	£6.99
99392 1	THE GREAT DIVORCE	Valerie Martin	£6.99
99688 2	HOLY ASPIC	Joan Marysmith	£6.99
99746 3	TUMBLING	Diane McKinney-Whetstone	£6.99
99449 9	DISAPPEARING ACTS	Terry McMillan	£5.99
99693 9	IMPOSSIBLE THINGS	Penny Perrick	£6.99
99696 3	THE VISITATION	Sue Reidy	£5.99
99608 4	LAURIE AND CLAIRE	Kathleen Rowntree	£6.99
99672 6	A WING AND A PRAYER	Mary Selby	£6.99
99650 5	A FRIEND OF THE FAMILY	Titia Sutherland	£6.99
99700 5	NEXT OF KIN	Joanna Trollope	£6.99
99655 6	GOLDENGROVE UNLEAVING	Jill Paton Walsh	£6.99
99673 4	DINA'S BOOK	Herbjørg Wassmo	£6.99
99592 4	AN IMAGINATIVE EXPERIENCE	Mary Wesley	£5.99
99642 4	SWIMMING POOL SUNDAY	Madeleine Wickham	£6.99
99591 6	A MISLAID MAGIC	Joyce Windsor	£6.99

All Transworld titles are available by post from:

Book Service By Post, P.O. Box 29, Douglas, Isle of Man IM99 1BQ

Credit cards accepted. Please telephone 01624 675137,
fax 01624 670923 or Internet http://www.bookpost.co.uk
or e-mail: bookshop@enterprise.net for details.

Free postage and packing in the UK. Overseas customers: allow
£1 per book (paperbacks) and £3 per book (hardbacks).